Danielle Jay lives in North West England with her two Chihuahuas, husband Jack and son Thomas.

Danielle Jay works as an English teacher and writes in her spare time. This is her first full-length novel. She is an avid reader and always shares her love of books on TikTok *@daniellejayauthor* and Instagram *@daniellejayauthor*.

To all the people brave enough to confront their past.

And to my mother, Jay, who was the greatest. I wish you could have read this.

Danielle Jay

MY SISTER'S SHADOW

AUSTIN MACAULEY PUBLISHERS®
LONDON · CAMBRIDGE · NEW YORK · SHARJAH

A CIP catalogue record for this title is available from the British Library.

ISBN 9781528999915 (Paperback)
ISBN 9781398420069 (Hardback)
ISBN 9781528999946 (ePub e-book)
ISBN 9781528999939 (Audiobook)

www.austinmacauley.com

First Published 2025
Austin Macauley Publishers Ltd®
1 Canada Square
Canary Wharf
London
E14 5AA

Thank you to Austin Macauley Publishers for giving me the platform to release my first novel. To my amazing friends and family who have supported me along the way. Also, to all the amazing writers and readers I've found on BookTok, you guys have been the best found family to talk about books to!

Thank you to my husband, Jack, for being so patient and believing in my writing the whole time. To my son for being my reason to breathe and giving me the push to finish this book. You are my shining light, darling boy.

To my work girlies, Jenna and Sarah, who I trusted to read my first draft. I love you both so much.

Prologue

The chapel was dark except for the flicker of candlelight, its shadows swaying on the stone walls like ghostly figures. Julia sat on the cold floor, her knees pulled to her chest, her arms wrapped tightly around herself. Her breath came in shallow gasps, her thoughts spinning so fast she couldn't catch hold of them. The air smelled of wax and damp wood, but beneath that, there was something sour—something rotten that she couldn't shake.

She pressed her forehead to her knees and rocked back and forth, her hair falling in greasy strands around her face. She couldn't get her mind to settle, couldn't focus, couldn't think straight. But one thought kept punching through the haze, sharp and bright as a needle: *I have to save her. I have to save the little mouse.*

She tilted her head back and stared at the wooden beams above her, her thoughts splintering again. She could still hear his voice, calm and low, the way he always sounded when he was trying to manipulate her. The one who held the strings, who pulled her into the dark and tied her there with knots she couldn't untangle. She hated him, hated the way his presence crawled under her skin and stayed there.

He was with her now. With *her*. A pounding heart against her ribcage, each beat loud and uneven. The walls of the chapel felt too close, pressing in on her, making it hard to breathe. She couldn't save the boy. She'd failed him in every way that mattered, and now he was gone—his small face still haunted her dreams, his cries echoing in her ears.

But maybe…maybe she could save the little mouse.

The thought gave her a brief moment of clarity, like a crack in a storm cloud letting the sunlight through. If she could get the girl out, far away from here, then maybe she could undo a small part of the damage she'd done. Maybe she could redeem herself.

She crawled forward, her palms scraping against the stone floor. Her head ached, her thoughts pounding in chaotic waves. She had to figure out how to get her out, how to sneak her away without him noticing. But where could they go? Who would help her?

Her hands shook as she reached for a candle on the altar, the flame flickering as if it, too, were afraid. She stared at it, willing it to give her strength, to burn away the fog in her mind.

She whispered to the flame, her voice trembling. "You're not taking her. Do you hear me? You can't have her. She's not yours."

But her voice sounded weak, pathetic. She didn't even believe herself.

The door to the chapel creaked open, and she froze, her breath catching in her throat. Her heart felt like it stopped entirely as she turned her head toward the sound.

Her stomach twisted as she heard a voice call out, calm and quiet, dripping with that same poisonous charm. "What are you doing in here?"

She didn't answer. She couldn't. Her body trembled as she clutched the candle tighter, her knuckles white. She had to do something. She had to save her little mouse.

But he was always one step ahead wasn't he? No matter what she did, he would find a way to pull her strings again.

The flame flickered in her hand, and Julia whispered to it one more time, desperate, pleading.

Help me. Please, someone help me.

But there was no answer. There never was.

Chapter 1

Lucy was seven the last time I saw her. In person, that is. I was twelve. She was my little sister, with mousy brown hair and the brightest blue eyes. Eyes that could make you crumble with a single glance. They weren't just piercing; they were unnerving, like she could see through every secret you ever had.

She gave me that look the first time Mum and Dad brought her home. She was four, and I was nine. I knew she was coming, but I wasn't ready. They had told me for weeks that I'd be getting a little sister. At first, I thought she'd be a baby, and I was confused when Mum never looked pregnant. It wasn't until things were set in stone that they explained how old she was and why.

"Her name's Lucy. She just turned four," my father said softly, trying to ease me into it.

"Jake, you'll be her big brother, just like you always wanted!" Mum added, her smile wide and hopeful.

"I wanted a brother," I muttered, not looking up.

"Well, you have a sister now," Mum replied, kissing my forehead. "And you'll love her just as much."

"Where is she coming from?" I asked, still not fully understanding.

"She's coming from another home, sweetie. But we're going to take care of her now. Hopefully for a long time," she said.

"Our family's growing," Dad added, placing his heavy hand on my shoulder. "We need you to step up and be a good big brother."

His tone wasn't just firm, it was a warning. Dad had a way of making you feel both calm and on edge. I knew that hand on my shoulder meant I should stop asking questions before his patience wore thin.

"Okay, Dad."

Nineteen years. That's how long it had been since she disappeared. Funny how you can go months, even years, without thinking about someone. Then, all at once, they're back in your mind, flooding your senses. I could hear her laugh, smell her strawberry shampoo, see her smile as she ran past me. Memories of her were so strong sometimes that they felt like dreams, but our childhood was never something to dream about. Not unless you wanted nightmares.

I hadn't been thinking about Lucy much recently. I was doing better. I lived in Manchester now with my wife, Jade. She had changed a lot for me. After years of therapy and medication to cope with Lucy's disappearance, I was finally in a good place.

"Okay, so I've got almost everything we need," Jade said, looking at the shopping list in her hand. "Just need to pick something up for your parents."

"You mean my mum," I corrected sharply.

"Well, yeah, your mum and Pete." She rolled her eyes.

"We don't need to get him anything. Just get Mum a bath set," I said.

"Jake, you can't be like this forever. I want them to like me," Jade pleaded.

"No, Jade. We don't need their approval or acceptance."

She didn't get it. I'd never explained the full extent of my family's issues to her. She didn't understand why I kept my distance, why I'd only seen my mum once in the past three years, and why we got married without her there.

"It's not about approval, Jake. It's about family. I want to be part of yours as much as you're part of mine," she said, raising her voice.

Family was important to Jade. I knew that. But my idea of family wasn't the same as hers. I didn't know how to be part of a loving, caring family like she did. My parents were strict and private. I didn't have cousins, aunts, uncles—none of that. It was just me, my parents, and, for a short time, Lucy.

"She likes crystals, right? And Pete's into whiskey," I finally said.

"Thank you," Jade replied, still annoyed.

"We'll arrange to see them over Christmas. I'll call Mum," I added, feeling the tension.

"Perfect." She sighed, not entirely pleased.

The next day at work felt like any other. It was December, and the students were more restless than usual, excited for the holidays. The rain outside made everything grey, but they didn't care. I let some of them come in early to decorate a Christmas tree in the corner of the classroom. It looked tacky, but they were proud of it.

I wasn't being a great teacher that day. I put on a Christmas film despite the head's warning to keep students productive until the last week. They deserved a break. We all did. The room fell quiet as the film played, the red and green lights from the screen dancing in their eyes.

That's when I felt it—the heavy weight pressing on my chest. It was like I couldn't breathe. I glanced around, but everything seemed normal. Except it wasn't. I was being watched. Not by the students, though. By someone else.

Standing next to the Christmas tree was a girl, too small to be in high school. Mousy brown hair. Big blue eyes. Lucy.

I froze. It couldn't be her. Lucy would be an adult now, if she were still alive. But there she stood, wearing the blue nightie with bees along the hem—the one she wore the night she disappeared. She had been seven then, but she still looked like that little girl in front of me now.

My mind raced. Lucy was gone. She'd been gone for nineteen years. I blinked, hoping she would vanish, but when I opened my eyes, she was still there. She looked different, though. Dirty, like she'd been rolling in mud. Her pale skin revealed blue veins, something I didn't remember from before. Lucy had always been obsessed with cleanliness. She wouldn't have let herself get so messy.

This wasn't Lucy. Not the Lucy I knew. Her eyes were hollow, void of that sharp, knowing look she'd always had. Her face started to change, dark veins creeping across her skin. Then her mouth began to open, slowly at first, then unnaturally wide. It didn't stop. Her jaw cracked as it dislocated, her tongue hanging limp. She stepped forward, and I gasped, my chair screeching against the wall as I pushed back.

Blinded by a sudden light, I heard Lexie, one of my students, call out. "Sir, are you okay?"

I looked around, disoriented. The lights were on, and everyone was staring at me—some worried, others laughing. I glanced back at the tree. Lucy was gone.

"I... I'm fine," I muttered. "Just startled myself."

"Sir, you screamed," Kyle said from the front row.

I cleared my throat. "It's fine. Let's get back to the film."

My heart raced as I tried to focus. I needed to call my mum.

Chapter 2

I hadn't told Jade about seeing Lucy. I couldn't put her through all that, not again. I needed to figure this out for myself. Maybe I should go back to therapy, though it clearly hadn't helped before. I worried I'd end up just like my father if I didn't get this under control. I'd become what I feared the most—him.

It had been far too long since I'd seen my father. That part of my life was something I'd gladly erase without a second thought. He had broken our family, and I would never forgive him for it. Just like Lucy, he was a mystery, and my mother was no help. She became a shell of herself after Lucy vanished. I had never accepted that she had simply disappeared without answers. They knew something about Lucy, and that knowledge had haunted my mind for nineteen years. Ever since that day, I had frequent flashbacks of the morning she went missing.

It was New Year's Day. The night before, we had celebrated at a party. My parents were well-known in Wirral, having built a life and legacy there, thanks to my great-grandfather. I'd had a privileged childhood, though my parents were often busy. My mother, however, had always been overly loving. She longed for a big family to fill our grand home, and when my father finally agreed to adopt Lucy, it felt like a dream come true.

I woke to the sound of shouting downstairs. This wasn't unusual, but on New Year's Day, it felt strange. They usually slept in late. I knew this because I was often the first to wake, making breakfast for myself and Lucy. I tiptoed to her room, hoping she hadn't heard the commotion. She hated it when they fought, always believing it was her fault. I would calm her down, promising that she wouldn't go back to foster care. That was her biggest fear, and it was heartbreaking to see how terrified she was.

But as I opened her door, I was taken aback. Her bed was made, her room tidy, and Christmas presents lay untouched in the corner. But her nightlight was still on. It was as if she hadn't even gone to bed. Confusion settled in my stomach. Lucy never woke before me, especially after a late night.

I headed downstairs, the argument growing louder. There was no way Lucy would be down there with this level of noise. I glanced at the clock in the hallway: 6:30 AM. Something felt wrong. Why had I woken so early? Had I heard my parents arguing? Or had something worse happened?

I strained to hear their words.

"Why would you not tell me this?" my mother's voice pierced through the chaos.

"You didn't need to know! Look at the state of you! You couldn't handle it!" my father shouted back.

"I would have protected her! This wouldn't have happened! We must call the police now!"

"No! We need a plan first. I need to make some calls. We have to handle this carefully, Annie, or it could turn out a lot worse for everyone."

"For everyone? Or just for you and your messed-up friends?"

I gasped. My mother had never sworn before, and the shock of it silenced me.

I stood frozen, the air thick in my lungs. I was about to be in so much trouble. I began to shake, tears welling in my eyes, yet I couldn't bring myself to move. Time seemed to stretch on forever.

"Jake, sweetie, is that you?" My mother's voice softened, a hint of panic breaking through.

I stayed silent, still too afraid to respond.

"Come here. I'll fix you some breakfast in just a minute." She knelt beside me, wiping my tears away and kissing my cheek.

I wanted to shout, to scream about how I hated my father and how he made us all feel. I wanted to tell her to do more to protect us from him, to demand to know what was happening to Lucy. But the words caught in my throat, and I kept my head down. Just like my mother, I was a coward.

"How about some bread dipped in egg today? If you go and get ready, it will be waiting for you when you come back," she offered, her smile faltering.

"Antonia let him go back to bed. It's too early for him to be up." My father's voice was low but firm.

I looked up at my mother, desperate for her to follow through with her promise of breakfast. But when I met her gaze, I noticed her eyes were bloodshot and puffy. She had been crying.

Something terrible had happened.

"Go back to bed, baby. Your dad is right; it's much too early. We're going back to bed too." She kissed my forehead and gestured for me to go upstairs.

I obeyed, retreating to my room. I somehow managed to fall back asleep, whether out of fear or exhaustion, I didn't know.

Hours later, I awoke to a hum of noise. The house was bustling with activity. Did we have company? It was still New Year's Day. I checked my alarm clock: 11 AM. Had I dreamt the earlier chaos?

Curiosity pulled me to Lucy's room again. But as I stepped out, I found my father standing outside my door. He shoved me back inside, his face tight with urgency.

"Hi, son. It's best if you stay in your room today, okay? Maybe have some more sleep. We were up late last night." He placed a hand on my shoulder, his grip too firm.

"But Dad, it's eleven! I can't sleep anymore. If I sleep much longer, I won't sleep tonight," I protested, echoing my mother's words.

"Fine. Just do me a favour and stay in here. Your mother and I will check on you if you need anything." His voice was calm, but there was an edge beneath it.

"Why do I need to stay in here?" I asked, surprised at my own boldness.

"Because…your sister…something has happened to her. We need you to cooperate." He spoke as if it were just another ordinary day.

"Is Lucy okay? She wasn't in bed this morning! I knew something was wrong—"

"Shut up!" he hissed, lowering his voice but amplifying the threat.

The silence that followed felt suffocating. I could see the terror in his eyes, a fear that matched my own.

"Just do as you're told and stay in here until I come to get you! And don't talk to anyone else. Not even your mother!" His finger jabbed my chest, and it hurt more than I expected.

"I'm sorry, Dad," I whispered, fighting back tears.

"Be quiet too. I don't want anyone to know you're awake. Just stay in here and keep to yourself."

"Yes, Dad."

"Lucy is missing. Someone took her in the night. We don't know who or what time. The police are here, working on it. You need to stay out of the way." His gaze remained focused on the door, avoiding my eyes.

The weight of his words crushed me. Lucy was gone. This morning's confusion began to crystallize into a horrifying reality. My parents had hidden it from me to shield me, but now it felt like betrayal. I was supposed to protect her.

"Okay, Dad." That was all I could manage. I had failed as her big brother.

As much as I had been reluctant to have a sister at first, she had transformed my life. We had learned to navigate our family together. Lucy, with her innocent smile, had taught me how to be a sibling. Now she was missing, and I felt utterly powerless.

"Just stay in your room," he repeated, a strange urgency in his tone. He knelt before me, searching my eyes as if weighing his next words.

"I love you, son."

The statement stunned me. My father, who had always been distant and stern, was now vulnerable. I felt a strange warmth from his embrace when he pulled me into a hug, but it was also suffocating. It was a rare moment of connection that I would never forget—our last hug. It was the only time I could recall him showing love, and it felt powerful yet heartbreaking.

I cried now, the floodgates opening as I remembered that day. It wasn't just about losing Lucy; it was about the disintegration of our family. It took something terrible for my father to acknowledge me in that way, but the damage was already done.

After years of turmoil, my parents had found different ways to cope, and their marriage crumbled under the weight of our grief. I had nearly gone past the point of no return, and I felt myself drifting there again. I didn't want this to impact my relationship with Jade like it had with my parents. I needed answers, or Lucy would forever haunt my mind.

I knew what I had to do, and even though I didn't want to, I had to go see my mother.

Chapter 3

Christmas was looming the following weekend. Jade had been thrilled when I asked her if we could visit my mum over the holiday period. Initially, she thought we would go for just one day, so a couple of nights' stay was more appealing to her. Family meant everything to Jade, and this trip would mean a lot to her. I worried, though, about how she would feel while I was trying to investigate my sister's disappearance. I hoped my mum might have more answers for me now that I was older and more stable. Having Jade there would also serve as a buffer between my mum and me.

Seeing Pete again was a necessary evil I dreaded. He was a parasite in my mother's life, having latched onto her at her most vulnerable. I wasn't around to protect her then, and neither was my father, so it felt like my fault. I wouldn't have let it happen if I had been there. Instead, she was stuck with someone who used her for her money and company. Pete was a loser in every sense—jobless, with the most ridiculous views on life, and a family that despised him. I never trusted him, and he would undoubtedly make it hard for me to get real answers from my mum. He was more controlling of her than my father ever had been, cutting in during conversations and amplifying her anxiety. If I wanted to speak with her alone, I would have to get creative.

I hadn't seen Lucy since that day in my classroom, but the nightmares had escalated, haunting me almost nightly. I could cope with her presence in my dreams, as long as she stayed there and didn't cross into my waking life. Jade had grown accustomed to my restlessness at night, but the frequency and intensity of the nightmares were wearing on both of us. I would wake in a sweat so thick I imagined it was like sleeping next to an ocean. Though Jade handled it well, her concern was growing, evident in the way she looked at me. I just had to make it to Christmas; hopefully, I could coax some answers from my mum. That was why I was seeing her again. It had to be linked to her appearance in my dreams as well as my reality.

"Goodnight," Jade said, kissing me softly.

"Night," I replied, my heart heavy with unspoken fears.

As I lay in bed, waiting for sleep to come, something felt different. I couldn't shake the odd feeling in my stomach. Jade's breathing grew deeper beside me; she had no trouble falling asleep. It was just my mind being too busy, too focused on Lucy. The mind is a powerful tool, capable of crafting personal hells, especially when left idle to contemplate past traumas.

Then I heard a voice.

"Jake."

It was unfamiliar at first, but it sent chills down my spine. It wasn't Jade. I could still hear her breathing. I decided to ignore it, chalking it up to my overactive imagination. It was my mind playing tricks on me.

"Jake."

This time, the voice was clearer, kinder, gentler.

I froze. My lips quivered, and tears threatened to spill. I was definitely awake. The jasmine candle Jade had lit earlier lingered in the air; I could never smell anything in my sleep. I glanced sideways at her, fast asleep, and still ignored the voice.

Minutes dragged on, and fear settled in. I mustered the courage to lift my head, but my body felt heavy, as if a weight was pressing down on me. I struggled to move, panic rising within me. I felt crushed, my breath becoming shallow. I looked at Jade, willing her to wake. I needed help; something was wrong.

"JAKE!"

The scream shattered the silence.

Lucy floated above me, face-to-face.

I screamed internally, unable to make a sound. Lucy's face was porcelain, fragile yet vicious. Her teeth were chipped, her skin pale, dark circles under her eyes that seeped into the creases of her face. The innocent girl I once knew was gone, replaced by a haunting spectre. Her hair, once a lovely mousy brown that my mother had brushed for hours, dripped with dark ink, staining my skin.

I lay there, unable to move, paralyzed by fear. Her eyes, once filled with innocence, were now void of humanity, a deep black that gripped my heart with terror. She blinked, fear flashing in her gaze for a brief moment before it hardened into anger and hatred.

Lucy's hands pressed against my chest, freezing and damp as if she had just emerged from a bath. Her expression dropped, and the pressure increased, crushing me as I felt a crack in my chest. Pain exploded through me, but I could do nothing—Not cry, not clutch the pain, not even throw her off. I endured the agony, my bones shattering one by one.

Then she opened her mouth, an abyss of darkness. A putrid stench engulfed me, rotting and foul. My stomach churned, threatening to betray me, but I couldn't move to escape it. I recalled the last time she had opened her mouth in my classroom, praying she wouldn't do the same so close to me now.

Her mouth hung open, the stench still overwhelming. I glimpsed something writhing within—at first, I couldn't discern what it was, but as it drew closer, I recognized it as her tongue. Damaged and grotesque, it bore scars and was dry, hardening as it neared. What had happened to her? Tears streamed down my face as I took in her transformation. My poor Lucy.

Suddenly, I could move again, and Lucy vanished. The stench lingered, her face burned into my mind. I sat up, desperate to calm myself before waking Jade. She had slept through the entire ordeal. Maybe I could convince her that I had slept soundly, if only to grant her some peace of mind for a day.

As dawn broke, I replayed the horrors of the night, pondering the ways Lucy could have sustained those injuries and who would want to do such a thing to her.

When Jade finally woke, she looked at me oddly, wrinkling her nose.

"What is that smell?"

That was all the confirmation I needed: I wasn't just imagining things. Lucy was trying to reach out to me.

Chapter 4

I had managed to get through the week with few dreams of Lucy and, luckily, no more sightings of her. She was always in my mind, of course, but I was grateful she had given me some time to breathe. However, I knew that wasn't enough. I had decided to see my old therapist again. Jackie had really helped me in the past, and after that horrific night, I knew I needed more than just answers.

Nervously, I waited outside her office for my appointment. As I sat there, memories flooded back—each previous visit a chapter in my story. I had been terrified at first, then comfortable, and finally, I had thought I was getting better. Now, shame washed over me for returning, as if I had let Jackie down. All the work we'd put in together felt lost. I was worse than I had ever been. The vivid images of Lucy lingered in my mind, hauntingly real. It felt like she had been there for a couple of days, not just a ridiculously vivid dream.

Lucy's sudden reappearance in my dreams had drained all life from me. The experience had forced me to take the last two days off work; there was no way I could face my students again—not when I risked seeing her in front of my class, not when the dreams had gotten worse. My body felt heavy, an anchor weighing me down, rendering me unable to deal with life. I had stayed in bed, trying to shut off my mind, but it fought back, each thought a battle I was losing.

Jade thought I was just ill; maybe she sensed I was feeling down. Christmas had always been a struggle because of how much I missed Lucy and the absence of a family to celebrate with. Jade probably believed I was just feeling sorry for myself.

"Jake, are you ready?" Jackie's voice cut through my thoughts, her office door open like a portal back to safety.

"Uh, yeah, yes," I stammered, startled. I was tuning out, too consumed in my personal hell to notice the world around me.

"Hi, Jake," Jackie said in her usual calm tone, her presence a balm to my frayed nerves.

"Hey, Jackie." I offered a sheepish smile, still weighed down by guilt.

Once we exchanged the usual disclaimers and she explained the therapy process again, we dove into the heart of the matter.

"So, Jake… What brings you back?" she asked, her gaze steady and inviting.

"Well, I've been having a hard time lately," I admitted, my heart racing.

Should I tell her the full truth? I hesitated, fear creeping in that she would send me to the hospital if I revealed the true extent of my struggles.

"Okay, so tell me about this hard time," she encouraged, her eyes unwavering.

Taking a deep breath, I began. "I've started to see Lucy again. In my dreams. They seem real, but I know they aren't. I get really scared of her, and it stops me in my tracks for days."

"Is there a reason you think you are dreaming about Lucy again?" Jackie asked, her tone gentle yet probing.

"I really don't know. I think I can't handle not knowing where she is or what happened to her. She was my only true friend as a child. I was the one she trusted, and I let her down. I was her big brother, and I didn't do what she needed me to. I could never find her, even after all these years. She's just gone. I don't know if she's still out there somewhere waiting for me, if she hates me for not coming to get her, or if she thinks I forgot about her. Maybe she isn't alive at all. Maybe she's just dead. Alone. Buried somewhere with no one to help her."

As I spoke, tears began to swell in my eyes, and I felt the pressure building in my chest.

"It sounds to me like you are taking on a lot of responsibility that isn't yours to bear, Jake. You were just a child when Lucy disappeared. The weight of that loss must have been incredibly hard to carry," Jackie reasoned, her empathy palpable.

I had heard this before, and it felt like she was repeating herself. "It was really hard when she was taken. I didn't have anybody left after she went. I was alone for years. But so was she. Maybe she still is, and I'm still here."

"Do you still have a support system? Do you still feel alone, Jake?" Her concern was evident, a stark contrast to the chaotic emotions swirling within me.

"I have Jade and friends at work, that sort of thing," I replied, my voice barely above a whisper.

"Good. Have you spoken to any of them about how you've been feeling?"

"No. I don't want to worry her, and I don't speak to my friends about Lucy." Not many people even knew I had a little sister. Talking about her felt like unearthing a wound that would never heal.

"Okay. Maybe if Jade knew what you were going through, you wouldn't feel so alone anymore. When you start to feel isolated, it seems to bring back those memories and feelings of loss. Those feelings remind you of your younger self— the loneliness, guilt, abandonment, and hurt. These emotions are valid, Jake. It's okay to feel them, but you also need to accept them."

She paused, giving me space to absorb her words. I took a deep breath, her insight slowly breaking through the walls I had built around my heart.

I knew she was right; I had learned this before. Yet, something felt different now. I was grappling with these feelings on a much higher level. Maybe I was just very ill. Maybe I needed to stay medicated and in therapy forever.

At the end of our session, Jackie referred me to my doctor to discuss my depression. She clearly thought I had exhausted the bounds of our cognitive behavioural therapy sessions.

The time came to go to my mother's house—back to the manor, as Jade would jokingly call it. My mother still lived there, clinging to our old home. I couldn't understand how she could stay there all the time. She had been just as broken as I was over Lucy, if not more so. I wasn't looking forward to seeing her. The house felt like a mausoleum of our shared grief.

Once, the manor had been a magical place. As a child, it was filled with laughter, friends, and countless games of hide and seek with Lucy. The sprawling grounds had felt limitless. Now, it loomed above me like a monument to our loss, an overwhelming expanse of memory that seemed to consume me.

We had played hide and seek so many times, my favourite game. I had always known the best spots to hide, but Lucy had quickly learned. I remembered a day when she discovered the old church on our property—a place I had always found eerie, but for her, it was special. The dusty pews, the towering statues, the scent of damp lingering in the air; I had thought it creepy, while she saw magic.

As I approached the church doors as my ten-year-old self, an unease settled in. The ancient handles felt foreboding, the weight of history pressing down on me. I pushed the door open, the loud creak echoing like a warning. If Lucy was inside, she would hear me now. My heart raced at the thought of being trapped in this dark, decaying space. But then I heard a giggle.

"Too scared?" Lucy's voice danced through the air, and I felt a rush of relief.

Fast forward to the present, the manor now felt overwhelmingly large, each room a shadow of its former self. My mother had tried to fill it with knick-knacks and collectibles from her travels, but the house had lost its warmth. The once vibrant colours faded into shades of grey and despair.

As I drove through the gates and up the drive, the porch came into view—where I had overheard one of the worst arguments between my parents. They had always fought, but after Lucy's disappearance, things had escalated. I remembered my mother in her rocking chair, lost in a book, when my father stormed in, fury radiating from him like heat from a flame.

"Antonia, what have you said to your friends now?" he barked.

"What do you mean? Me defending my son or me defending myself?" she shot back, her voice rising.

"Why do you have to open your stupid mouth?! You're making this whole thing harder than it needs to be."

"I'm making it harder than it needs to be? Me? I'm trying to protect our son!" My mother's voice was sharp, desperate.

"I'm trying my best to keep that at bay for all of our sakes! If you're telling people different stories, it only makes us look more suspicious!" He was shouting now, the tension palpable.

"I won't have them doing what they're doing to us, to Jake. I care about taking care of him now!"

"You need to be a grieving mother, Antonia. That's it."

"I am a grieving mother, which is more than what you've been doing!" Her voice cracked, breaking under the weight of her words.

"Then stop making it worse! If you slip up, you'll make us look more suspicious!"

A silence hung in the air, thick with unresolved anger.

"I'd rather him be safe at home," my father spat, "than tormented by those boys."

Tears stung my eyes as I remembered their hurtful words. My parents had blamed each other, and in turn, I felt the weight of their anger settle on my shoulders.

The reality of my visit loomed closer, an impending storm of memories and emotions. How would I face her? Would she even recognize my pain, or would it only be more of the same—her grief drowning out my own? The thought of stepping back into that world felt like stepping into the jaws of an ancient beast.

With a final sigh, I parked the car and braced myself for the confrontation that lay ahead. Would she still see me as her little boy, or had the years of silence turned me into a stranger? And would her pain mirror my own, or had time altered her grief into something else entirely?

Chapter 5

"Jake! Jade! Oh, welcome home!" My mother greeted us with a warm squeeze, her excitement almost overwhelming.

"Hi, Antonia. It's good to see you," Jade replied, managing a polite smile. This was only the second time Jade had met my mother—the first had been before we were even married. Jade had insisted on meeting my family before the wedding. She had never been to this house before, though; her only glimpse of it had been through old photos from my childhood. Now, the house looked different—worn, tired.

I glanced at the porch, at the spot where my mother used to sit and read. I used to overhear my parents' arguments from that very place. The chair was gone now, and the porch felt deserted, as if she no longer spent time here. It didn't surprise me. Since I left, Mum had become more of a recluse. The porch had once been where she'd read to Lucy and me, watching us play outside. She'd always wanted children, and Lucy's disappearance had devastated her. My grandmother had often told me how lucky we were to have such a loving mother, how Mum had dreamed of being one since she was a little girl. I used to feel lucky too, but everything had gotten so complicated. Now, the porch looked like it hadn't been painted in years, creaking underfoot as if it could collapse at any moment.

"Come on in. Was the drive alright?" Mum asked, ushering us through the door. I could feel the small talk building—so much time had passed since we last saw each other that jumping straight into anything meaningful felt impossible.

"Hey, guys," Pete called from the staircase, sighing as if about to deliver bad news. Instead, he just stood there, not moving.

"Hello. How are you both?" Jade asked, her voice polite. I stayed silent, knowing Jade would have words for me later about it.

The moment stretched awkwardly. Pete didn't seem to acknowledge Jade's greeting, and my mother surely noticed my lack of response. Jade's words hovered in the air for a second longer.

"We're doing great, Jade. We're so happy to have you both here for Christmas. I couldn't believe it when Jake called!" Mum's smile was directed more at Jade than me.

"Of course it's overdue. They're married now," Pete chimed in from his spot on the stairs, still not approaching. His words hit the nerve they were meant to— the mention of our wedding brought a chill.

Another silence followed. The wedding had been a sore point between me and my mother. She hadn't been invited, and we still hadn't resolved the reasons why. I hated Pete for a lot of reasons, but mostly because he'd swooped in when my mum was vulnerable, keeping the wedge between us firmly in place. I expected this comment from him.

"Yes, it's been too long. At least we have plenty of time to catch up now," Jade smoothly deflected, her voice calm. She had only met Pete once before, but she knew exactly who he was through my stories.

We unpacked in silence, and I gave Jade a tour of the house. She looked around in awe—our worlds were so different, and this house, with its grand size and fading elegance, fascinated her. But I had grown to despise it. Its grandeur only reminded me of how out of touch my family had been, especially after Lucy's disappearance. Moving away to university had opened my eyes to just how sheltered my life had been, locked in the bubble of the King family.

"Oh my God, you guys have a music room?" Jade exclaimed.

"It's more of a ballroom, really. We used to host parties here," I said, feeling the weight of my own indifference. Jade was curious about every detail, but the room wasn't what it used to be. The once-opulent gold and emerald walls had faded, and the entire place was covered in dust. My mum had clearly shut it off, one of many rooms no longer cared for.

"How many people fit in here?" Jade asked, wide-eyed.

"About two hundred, maybe."

The piano sat untouched in the corner, a relic from another time. I used to polish it with Lynne, our maid. Lucy was sometimes allowed to handle the violin, though Lynne was strangely stricter with her than with me. Staring at the piano, a memory from my childhood flashed in my mind.

It was a Saturday morning. I was playing the piano after polishing it while Lynne cleaned nearby. My parents were out, as they often were, leaving us in Lynne's care. Lucy sat on the floor, watching me play.

"Lucy, get up off the floor. You'll get dirty," Lynne scolded her, but Lucy just rolled her eyes, making faces at me when Lynne's back was turned. Lucy didn't seem to mind Lynne's firm hand with her, but it always bothered me how differently she was treated.

"I'm just lying here," Lucy said with a shrug. "You wouldn't mind if Jake was lying down."

"Don't you dare speak to me like that. Go outside. You're distracting your brother," Lynne snapped.

"No, she's not," I said, defending Lucy, not meaning to sound rude. I liked having her around while I played.

"You need to learn your place," Lynne said sharply, grabbing Lucy by the arm. "You're lucky to be here, and you need to act like it."

"Ow, you're hurting me!" Lucy cried, struggling against her grip.

"Lynne, she was just listening to me," I pleaded, but Lynne ignored me and forced Lucy out of the room, slamming the door behind her.

"You see that behaviour, Jake? That's not how a King should act. You were always a good boy because this is your family's legacy. Lucy will never have that. Your parents are too lenient with her," Lynne said, her voice cold.

I didn't like how Lynne spoke about Lucy. She wasn't just adopted; she was my sister. She belonged to our family as much as I did.

The memory tugged at me as I stared at the dust-covered piano. I hadn't played much after Lucy disappeared. I wiped a finger across the keys, and the sound of the single note cut through the silence of the room.

"Are you okay, babe?" Jade's hand on my arm brought me back to the present. I had forgotten she was there, lost in the memory.

"I'm fine," I lied, my voice distant. "Just thinking."

"If you need to talk, I'm here. I love you, Jake. But you have to let me in. I know how much this place hurts you. Maybe being here will help us find some answers about Lucy," Jade said softly.

"I'm trying, Jade. It's just…impossible sometimes," I admitted, the weight of it all pressing down on me.

"What do you need to know? Is it about Lucy, or about your dad too?" she asked, surprising me. My dad wasn't a topic we usually touched on.

"I just need to know why she won't leave me—why she haunts me. Why am I the only one who still cares about her?"

"We need to talk to your mum, but you need to be gentle with her. She's anxious around you, Jake. You have to find a way to start the conversation without attacking her."

"I don't know if I can. She's lied to me my whole life."

Jade's face hardened. "Jake, I've been patient, but I won't let you drag me into this darkness too. You need to face it, for us. I won't start a family with you until you're at peace with this."

Her words hit me hard. I knew she was right, even though they hurt.

"I'm sorry," I said weakly.

"I love you, Jake, but this has to end. Talk to your mother. Find the answers. Let this be over," she urged, taking my hand.

"I'll try," I promised, knowing it was time to face the truth.

Chapter 6

Jade

The moment the words left my mouth earlier, I regretted them. Jake didn't deserve that, not with everything he's been going through. I've seen him slipping again, retreating into that dark place where the world becomes too much. This time, it feels worse, more consuming. When we first met, he was in a bad way—hallucinations, paranoia, distance. I'd hear him talking to himself, drenched in guilt, apologizing over and over to Lucy. His sleep was haunted, soaked in sweat, as if he couldn't escape whatever nightmare held him captive.

It had taken so long to get to a place where we could breathe. Therapy, medication, the support of our friends, and my constant care had brought him back, but when he slipped, I felt the weight of it crushing down on both of us. When Jake was good, he was brilliant. He had this way of lighting up a room, of making me feel like the world was a little less heavy. But when the darkness set in, it drained me. His paranoia left him frozen, and I had to keep everything afloat—housework, bills, meals, appointments, even reminding him to take care of himself. Sometimes he wouldn't speak to me for days, as though he was lost inside himself, and I was just a shadow on the edges of his life.

I don't think Jake knew how close I came to walking away last time. Our friends had urged me to leave, to take care of myself. "You can't save someone from themselves," they said. But I saw so much potential in Jake, a future that could be brilliant if only he could escape his past. So, I stayed. I told him flat out I wouldn't live like that forever. I'm not his mother, even though sometimes it feels like he sees me that way. When I met Antonia, I understood why.

Antonia…she's something else. At first glance, she's warm, inviting even. But the more time I spent around her, the more I realized how cold she was. Vacant. I tried to picture her as a mother, as someone who raised two children, but the image wouldn't stick. The stories Jake told me about his childhood never quite added up either.

About a year ago, we argued about his family. I thought if he spent more time with them, it might help him move on. I'd read somewhere that reconnecting with your past could be healing, but Jake resisted. His family was off-limits, a wound too deep to touch.

"Babe, you can't ice them out forever," I'd said.

His face twisted with anger. "You wouldn't understand. You had a perfect childhood. A normal life."

I laughed, stung. "It wasn't perfect. But thanks. Yeah, it was just normal. I didn't have a servant and my own private church."

His shock was palpable. I'd never brought up his privileged upbringing before because, to me, it didn't matter. But in that moment, I realized it did to him. He saw me as an escape, as someone who could take him away from that life, and maybe as a way to spite his parents.

"I never asked for that," he'd said quietly. "None of it mattered. Not when our life was hell. My dad hated me, and my mum...she never wanted me. Not like she wanted Lucy. They chose Lucy. She was perfect. I was just...what they got stuck with."

The bitterness in his voice chilled me. I knew his father had spiralled into madness after Lucy's disappearance, and that he'd tried to kill himself and Jake in a car because, in his deranged mind, Lucy told him to. His mother? She was worse. She hit Jake, left marks on him, and isolated him after Lucy disappeared. Lynne, the housekeeper, seemed to be the only one who cared for him, but even she kept the family's secrets. Jake was practically a prisoner in that house until he turned eighteen.

Despite everything, I couldn't shake the feeling that Jake's mother wasn't a complete monster. Losing a child does unimaginable things to a person. It doesn't excuse what she did, but I could empathize with her pain. Jake, though, could never forgive her.

"My mum put out a cigarette on me once for asking about Lucy's room," he told me one night. "When she found me in there, she threw an ornament at me. I don't remember much after that. I woke up in my bed days later. Lynne told me not to say anything, and I didn't. Not until now."

Hearing that made me feel so small for pushing him to reconnect. How could I ever understand what that did to him? Maybe it wasn't something that could ever be fixed.

The memories swirled in my mind as I filled the bath in the en-suite. This house…it was so grand once, but now it was just a shadow of what it had been. The bath was golden, freestanding, with these strange little cherubs on either end, their faces contorted in pain. I stared at them, unsettled by their twisted expressions.

As I reached for a towel, I saw her. Lucy.

She was standing behind me, her hair matted, her ivory dress stained, and those blue eyes—Jake always talked about her eyes. Mesmerizing. Beautiful. But the Lucy I saw wasn't the girl from the photos. She smiled at me, and in an instant, she was gone. I screamed, stumbling backward. My elbow caught the hot tap, burning me, and I cursed as I shoved my arm under the cold water, trying to steady my breathing. This was all in my head. It had to be. Jake had shown me pictures, and I'd read things online about Lucy's disappearance. It wasn't real. It couldn't be.

I undressed and stepped into the bath, trying to relax, but the tension wouldn't leave me. The room smelled stale, like something rotting. And then I saw her again.

Floating above me. Her face was twisted, dirty, bloodied. Her dress, once ivory, was now smeared with rust and red stains. I froze. My breath caught in my throat as I whispered to myself, "This isn't real. This isn't real."

But Lucy's breath was cold on my skin, and then I felt it—something crawling. I jerked my head and came face to face with her. Her eyes were black now, her mouth dripping with blood and pus. Her teeth were broken, decaying, and from her lips, something crawled—a bug. Then another. And another. I gasped, but they poured into my mouth, choking me. I tried to scream, but I couldn't. My body went limp as the weight of them pressed down, filling my throat, making it impossible to breathe.

"Jade!"

Jake's voice cut through the darkness, and suddenly, I was out of the water, coughing, gasping for air. Jake's arms were around me, his face pale with fear.

"What happened?" he asked, his voice trembling.

I couldn't tell him the truth. I couldn't let him think I was seeing the same things he saw. "I… I slipped," I lied.

He didn't believe me. I could see it in his eyes. But he didn't push. He just held me, and I wondered if he'd seen her too.

As he wrapped me in a towel, my heart raced. Was I losing my mind? Was this what Jake had been going through all these years? I felt anger bubbling up inside me—anger at Jake for letting this haunt us both. I couldn't let this destroy me too. This was where I had to draw the line.

Chapter 7

Jade

After the incident in the bath, I had gotten ready for dinner, but the weight of what happened still hung heavy on my mind. We were having a sit-down meal with Antonia and Pete, something Jake had dreaded. Honestly, I was nervous too, but I didn't want to add to Jake's anxiety—not after the near-drowning incident. Antonia and Pete had unsettled me when we arrived that morning, though outwardly warm, I could sense Antonia's resentment simmering beneath her forced smiles. She resented not being part of Jake's life, missing our wedding, never being invited to our home, or included in family holidays. It wasn't my fault they had a strained relationship—it had been fractured long before I came into the picture—but her bitterness felt directed at me anyway. I was the one who convinced Jake to come for Christmas, something that had never happened before.

Pete made me uncomfortable too, but he was part of the package. His shaggy white beard, stained with coffee, and his habit of wearing sandals and Hawaiian shirts—even in the dead of winter—clashed with the cold, polished atmosphere of Jake's family. Jake often remarked that his mother had settled for Pete because she had no one else left from her old life. That life had disintegrated, and Pete was all she had now. It was hard to fathom how someone who'd endured so much trauma could lose all her friends, but that was Antonia's reality.

As we sat down for dinner at the grand, brown table, the air felt stifling. It was just the four of us, but Lynne was serving, which struck me as bizarre. I had assumed she'd eat with us, but Jake had told me that wasn't how things were done here. Before Lucy disappeared, they had a chef and several other staff, but those days were long gone. Lynne, the only one who remained, now juggled the cooking and other household duties. The whole setup felt like a sad attempt at clinging to a past life Antonia couldn't let go of. She looked almost regal in her red dress, her hair styled in a loose bun, her makeup heavier than usual, as if she were trying to preserve an image of herself that had long since faded.

"The soup is lovely," I said, attempting to ease the tension.

"Thank you," Antonia replied with a smile, though she hadn't cooked it.

"Yes, Mum, Lynne's gotten really good at making Martha's old recipes," Jake added. He'd mentioned earlier that Martha had been their cook for years.

I saw Antonia's jaw clench slightly at the mention of Martha.

"Exactly," Pete interjected. "That's why we no longer needed Martha. Lynne works just as hard, and it costs us less." He squeezed Antonia's hand.

Jake leaned back in his chair, his expression darkening. "I don't know, Pete. You weren't around much when Martha was here. Her food was something else. Remember how much Lucy and Dad loved her apple crumble, Mum? We had it every Sunday night."

Jake's voice softened as he recalled the memory, and for a moment, I could see the child he had once been, happy in this house before everything fell apart. Antonia's eyes brightened too, if only briefly.

"Yes, Lucy did love that," she said softly, but the warmth in her voice vanished when Pete shot her a warning glance.

"Let's talk about the present instead of dragging up the past," Pete said, slurping his soup loudly. "So, what are you both up to now? Still teaching?"

"Yes, Jake's still at the high school," I answered quickly, eager for neutral ground. "I've just started lecturing at the university."

"Oh, a university lecturer, huh?" Pete said, eyebrows raised. "What's your subject?"

"History and culture. I'm teaching first and second years while I finish my PhD."

Pete blinked, clearly caught off guard. "Oh wow, a girl doing history. Good for you. I'd have pegged you for medicine or something science-related, you know, with your background – a lot of you Chinese go into that field, right?"

His tone was casual, but his words hung in the air like a slap. The whole table fell silent.

Jake's jaw tightened, his fist clenching on the table. "Her background?" he hissed.

"Jake," Antonia cut in, her voice strained, "Pete didn't mean anything by it. It's just a misunderstanding."

"No," I said calmly, though my heart was pounding. "I know exactly what he meant. Not everyone can handle successful women."

Pete opened his mouth, but I wasn't done. "It's not about me being a 'girl'. And for the record, I'm not Chinese, you ignorant idiot."

Pete's face flushed with anger. "Ignorant idiot?" he shouted, pointing a finger at me. "You come into my house and insult me?"

"This isn't your house," Jake spat. "It belongs to my father's family, and you're only here because they let you be. You were nothing before you met my mother, and you're still nothing. You've latched onto her like a parasite because you have no family, no friends. You're a nobody."

Pete's face turned crimson, his hands shaking with rage. For a moment, I thought he might snap, and then he did. With a guttural scream, he lunged across the table, grabbing Jake by the throat.

Everything blurred as I stood up, my heart racing, Jake's eyes wide with fear.

"Get off him!" Lynne roared, seemingly appearing out of nowhere, slamming a silver tray down on Pete's head with a loud thud. Pete let out a cry of pain as he staggered back.

"Sweetie, are you okay?" Lynne asked, rushing to Jake's side. He was gasping for air, trying to calm his breathing. She wrapped her arms around him, kissing his forehead like he was a child. It felt odd to witness, but it was clear she still saw him as one, having helped raise him for most of his life.

Antonia silently left the room, dragging Pete with her, not offering a word to anyone. The whole scene felt surreal. We hadn't even finished the starter, and this was already the strangest dinner I'd ever attended.

"I'm so sorry he's such a dickhead, sweetheart," Lynne said, turning to me after making sure Jake was okay.

"It's alright, I was just caught off guard," I said, still trying to shake off the tension.

"I heard what he said to you. He's like that all the time, no matter how much Antonia tries to defend him. It's not right. I know you're half Thai and half British, and I told them that before you came. I remember you explaining it when we met…the last time," Lynne said, her expression apologetic.

"We can just leave," Jake muttered, shaking his head.

"No, please don't," Lynne pleaded, her voice breaking. "It's been so long since I've seen you. I don't know when you'll come back again. It'll blow over. Pete will probably stay out of the way. He's gone all day tomorrow anyway."

Her face, lined with deep wrinkles, seemed to carry the weight of the life she'd lived. Lynne looked like she was in her sixties, and it struck me how odd it was that she'd spent her whole life here. Jake had told me once that Lynne's husband had worked at the house too, but he left when Jake was a newborn, so Jake had never met him. Apparently, Lynne had been so heartbroken that she stayed with the Kings, pouring herself into caring for Jake. He was her distraction and, it seemed, the person she loved most. She was the only one from this place he stayed in touch with, and that said a lot.

"We're not going home yet. We just got here, and I'm sure we can sort this out. Every family has its problems," I reassured her. Plus, I wasn't keen on driving two hours back home in the dark.

"Lynne, I need to stay for myself," Jake said, his tone shifting. "I have to figure some things out."

"What things?" she asked, her voice soft with concern.

Jake's family didn't know the full extent of his struggles. They knew he had a hard time as a teenager, but after he turned eighteen, he had kept his mother out of it. If they understood how deep his pain went, would they give him the answers he was seeking? If those answers even existed. What if there were no answers? Lucy had just disappeared, and that was it. No explanations. Just an unsolved mystery.

"I need to understand what really happened to Lucy," Jake said, his voice thick with emotion. "It never leaves me. That night…it's always there. I need to move on, Lynne. I'm hoping Mum and maybe some old friends can help. I was shut down as a kid…maybe now I can finally get some closure."

"No, Jake, that doesn't sound like a good idea," Lynne said, shaking her head. "Your mother doesn't like talking about Lucy or your father. It took her a long time to even start to recover. Those wounds…they never heal. You just learn to cope. And people in this town? They won't want to discuss Lucy either. The whole thing was too much for everyone. The reporters, the TV shows— they've stopped coming, and we're grateful for that. You might not remember, but this town went through hell. So many people were accused, families torn apart. It wasn't just your family. There's a reason your mother keeps to herself, and it's not just about grief."

Jake's jaw clenched, his frustration simmering beneath the surface. "Lynne, you don't get it. You don't understand what it's like for me. I see her. In my dreams, in flashes during the day—it's like she's haunting me. And it's getting worse. I'm losing my mind. I can't keep living like this. Do you know what it feels like to be haunted by your own brain? To look into the dark every day, wishing it would just end so I could have some peace?" His voice broke, the raw emotion cutting through the room.

Silence fell. The weight of his words hung heavy. I'd never heard Jake speak like that before. The darkness had crept back into his life, and it was suffocating him.

"Oh, Jake," Lynne whispered, her face softening. "Sweetheart, none of this was your fault. You know that, don't you? You were just a child. There's nothing else to know. Everything that could've been found out has already been uncovered. You've seen the documentaries, read the articles, heard the speculation. That's all there is, Jake. Nothing more." Her voice trailed off, laden with exhaustion.

Jake stared at her, the tension between them palpable. I felt like an outsider in the room, watching something I wasn't supposed to witness.

"You were here, Lynne," he said, his tone sharp. "You knew the family, the people coming and going. What do *you* think happened?"

Lynne's expression hardened. She wasn't used to being challenged like this, and the shift in her demeanour was telling. Clearly, talking about Lucy was a subject no one wanted to touch, and it was starting to feel like Lucy had been forgotten—not just by the town, but by her own family. It was heartbreaking. She had only been seven years old, and no one seemed to be fighting for her anymore. Why was Jake the only one who still cared? The weight of that responsibility was crushing him, and maybe that's why everyone else had distanced themselves from Lucy's memory—it was too painful. But it didn't feel right, as if she was being erased on purpose.

"I don't know, Jake," Lynne replied, her voice clipped. "Lucy was a troubled girl. She used to talk about wanting to go back to her old family all the time. Said she saw people she thought she knew hiding in the garden, watching her. But she was a kid, and kids make things up. She had a wild imagination and didn't care who she upset. She drove your mother mad, constantly talking about her real family. Honestly, I don't think she ever really liked it here. Never showed any gratitude, never said thank you unless someone told her to. So, no, it wouldn't surprise me if someone from her old life came back for her, and she just went with them, no struggle. That would explain why there was no evidence. She probably left willingly."

Her words hit like a punch to the gut. Lucy had just walked away? But then why had there been no trace of her, no sign of her anywhere after all these years? The way Lynne spoke about Lucy made my skin crawl. She clearly didn't care for her, which was disturbing. How could someone harbour such resentment toward a little girl who'd already been through so much? Even if Lucy had been difficult, she was a child—an innocent in all of this.

Jake's eyes flared with anger. "No. Lucy liked it here. I know Mum and Dad weren't easy, but they loved her. They adored her, Lynne. And Lucy loved being with us. She wasn't planning to run away. She was *seven.* No seven-year-old can just plan an escape like that. And what—you think someone just walked in, past the gates, past all the people here that night, past the alarms, and no one noticed a thing?" His voice was laced with disbelief.

Jake wasn't buying Lynne's theory, and neither was I.

"Jake, you were a kid. You don't know what it was actually like for Lucy. I think she always knew why she was here, and it upset her. She didn't belong with us. If your mother hadn't been so selfish in taking Lucy, she would probably still be alive."

Lynne froze, her own words hitting her with the weight of their truth. It was the first time someone in Jake's family had acknowledged what everyone feared—that Lucy was likely dead. But no one had ever said it out loud.

"What do you mean 'still be alive'?" I asked, my voice quick and sharp.

Lynne's face paled. "No, I didn't mean it like that… I just meant—"

"No!" Jake interrupted, his voice cracking. "You said it. You think she's dead! Why? What makes you think that?" His voice had risen, panic flooding his words.

Lynne began to tremble, her face crumpling as if she'd suddenly become much smaller. "I just think she's not with us anymore. That's all. If she were alive, they would have found her by now, Jake. I still think she went willingly, but I don't believe she lasted long." Tears streamed down Lynne's face now, her words coming out between sobs.

"Why do you think that?" Jake's voice was quieter now, but no less intense. There was a desperate need for answers that he was barely holding back.

Lynne covered her face with her hands. "There are things you don't know…about Lucy, and how she came here. Where she really came from."

Jake's breath hitched. "I know she was in care," he said. "I figured out she was abused, just from things I picked up on."

Lynne nodded, her hands shaking as they dropped to her lap. "She was abused, Jake. Horribly. When she arrived here, she looked like a rag doll—bruised, filthy, barely spoke. We had to keep her in a separate part of the house at first. We couldn't let anyone see her like that, not even you. Her hair was matted, her teeth were rotten, and her skin was so pale…almost like she'd never seen sunlight. She liked the dark, always kept her curtains closed. I spent hours just cleaning her, brushing the dirt from under her nails, trying to make her look like a child again. She was so fragile, so…broken."

I could see the shock in Jake's face as he absorbed this new image of Lucy. The weight of it was clear—how had he not known?

"I never knew any of this," Jake said, his voice barely a whisper.

"You couldn't have known. You were just nine, and we couldn't explain it all to you at that age. And then, when she disappeared, no one talked about her anymore. If she did go back to the people who had her before, I doubt she survived. I believe she would have died from neglect, if nothing else."

Lynne's head dropped as she spoke, her voice breaking again.

"Who had her before she lived here?" I asked, cutting through the silence that had settled like a heavy blanket.

"I don't know," Lynne admitted. "I wasn't told much. All I know is that it was kept very secretive. Your parents didn't even tell me about her until minutes before she arrived. I always thought something was off, like maybe they got her under strange circumstances. Your mother wouldn't have wanted anyone to see her in that condition. It was like she was hiding Lucy until she could make her presentable."

Jake was pacing now, his mind racing. "What if Mum and Dad *did* get Lucy illegally?" he asked, his eyes wild with the possibilities. "Maybe she wasn't adopted properly at all. That's why it was such a secret. They might have even *bought* her. If it was through an agency, they would've cleaned her up before she came to us, right? But when I met her, she was already in the house—already living there, and no one ever explained why. It was all a lie."

Jake's thoughts were spinning out of control, but I couldn't blame him. Everything he thought he knew about Lucy, about his family, was unravelling.

"It was just to help her adjust to the house and recover. That's what your mother said, at least. But I really don't think it's wise for you to dig into this, Jake. You might uncover things about your family that you'd rather not know. There's so much history there, but maybe it's worth visiting your father. He could have some answers for you. Your mother will probably be too upset to talk tomorrow," Lynne suggested.

I felt a wave of relief wash over me that Lynne had mentioned seeing his father; that way, I didn't have to bring it up. I had yet to meet him and had no idea what to expect. All I knew was that he was mentally unwell and unable to care for himself, confined to a hospital, and according to Jake, rarely received visitors. I couldn't help but wonder if Jake thought this treatment of family was normal; he didn't seem particularly troubled by his father's situation. There was so much about Jim, Jake's dad, that remained shrouded in mystery, another topic Jake avoided discussing.

"I can't see him, Lynne. You know I can't do that. I won't let him mess with my head," Jake replied firmly.

"Well, he's your best shot at finding answers, Jake. You won't get far with your mum. Trust me, I haven't," she sighed, placing a comforting hand on his shoulder.

"You need to let go of your mother, Jake. This isn't your fault. The sooner you accept that, the better. If you let the past consume you, it will—just look at your father! Please, don't let your mind win this battle. I don't think I could bear it if something happened to you," Lynne said, kissing his head gently before rising to leave the room.

"I'll make you some tea to take to bed," she smiled, stepping out into the hallway.

"Looks like we have to go see my dad," Jake said, his tone heavy with resignation.

Chapter 8

Jake

I had been resolute about not making the trip to see my father. It had been years since I'd last seen or heard from him—since I was seventeen, I think. Those later years living with him had been a nightmare. I'd read somewhere that mental health problems can be hereditary, but my father had brought this upon himself. He drank himself into madness, refusing any help my mother desperately tried to offer. After everything we had endured with Lucy's disappearance and the subsequent ostracism from our community, he somehow managed to make our lives even more unbearable.

Home felt like our personal hell, with him playing the role of a tormentor. I realize now he was battling his own demons, but it didn't excuse the pain he inflicted on my mother and me. It hadn't been an immediate decline after Lucy went missing; his drinking started about two years later, when I was fourteen and feeling incredibly isolated after being pulled out of school.

"ANTONIA!" my father bellowed.

I jolted upright in bed, having just drifted off while reading a comic. The sound shocked me awake, and it took a moment to comprehend what was happening.

"ANTONIA!" he shouted again, his voice distorted and unrecognizable. There was a primal growl underlying his words. Was he hurt?

I stood up, creeping toward the door, but before I could open it, he roared again, "GET HERE NOW, YOU BITCH!"

The force of his scream made me jump. I had witnessed my parents argue before, heard them shout, and even seen them strike each other on a few occasions, but this felt different. Their fights had been escalating lately, each disagreement flaring into a heated exchange. I noticed my mother hadn't been sleeping in their bedroom for quite some time. I didn't inquire about it; I knew the reason.

My hand trembled on the doorknob. Should I step outside? I glanced at the clock—it was just after midnight. My mother was likely asleep unless my father had woken her. I weighed my options: confront him or pretend to be asleep. His rage felt more intense than usual, having started drinking whiskey around seven after an awkward, silent dinner.

Thud. Thud. Thud.

He was climbing the stairs, dragging his feet behind him. If I didn't know it was my father approaching, I might have thought a bear was lumbering down the hall. He grunted with each movement, his heavy hands thumping against the walls for support.

My room was the first in the hallway, and I knew he would see me if I opened the door now. Terrified of the monster drawing near, I quietly turned the lock on my door, backing away as the loose floorboards began to tremble beneath his weight.

"Ugh, ANTONIA! COME HERE!" He thundered at the top of the stairs.

My mother had to have heard that, even from the guest bedroom.

"Jim, go to bed. You'll wake Jake up," my mother reasoned, her voice steady yet strained, just outside my door.

"Oh, there she is. My WHORE of a wife! You finally decided to show your face. Remember when you used to sit with me and drink?" His words slurred together, thick with alcohol.

"Jim, you're drunk. Just go to bed and sleep it off," my mother replied in a hushed tone, but her calmness felt like a thin veneer over her anxiety.

"NO! YOU DO AS I SAY NOW! NOT THE OTHER WAY AROUND." My father's voice echoed, and I could hear movement in the hallway as something heavy thudded against the wall opposite my room.

"Jim! Stop! Please don't do this to yourself," my mother pleaded, her voice trembling.

"IT's NOT MY FAULT. She was my baby too! I miss her." His voice cracked, and I could hear the sob in his throat.

"It is your fault, Jim. We all know it. You need to learn to live with yourself. But I will never forgive you, so keep on drinking," my mother replied, her breath coming in ragged gasps.

Thud.

Thud.

Silence enveloped the house, stretching on indefinitely as I stood frozen in place, dread pooling in my stomach.

"Oh my God! Antonia! Wake up. Are you okay?" Lynne's panicked voice cut through the stillness.

"Oh no. Oh no! Jim, what have you done?!" Lynne's tone shifted, sounding almost animalistic in her distress.

Snapping out of my stupor, I unlocked the door.

My mother lay on the floor, unmoving, unresponsive. Blood trickled from her head, and dark purple marks bloomed on her neck where he had gripped her. It had all happened while I stood on the other side of my door, listening. I had done nothing to stop it.

"Jake, quick! Call an ambulance. Tell them your mother has fallen," Lynne instructed, urgency lacing her words.

It took a moment to comprehend what she wanted me to do. Lie.

"Jake, now! Quick! Jim, go drink some water and then get into bed. You were out tonight," she urged.

I hadn't even noticed my father slumped on the floor, head in his hands. When he looked up at me, bloodshot eyes glistening with tears, the stench of alcohol burned my nose. Did he even know it was me standing there? Probably not.

I dashed downstairs to the phone and remained there until the ambulance arrived, while Lynne sent me back to bed, insisting that I wouldn't be seen. She promised I could visit my mother tomorrow.

The following day, I did visit her, with my father by my side. We hadn't exchanged a word during the car ride. That silence made me acutely aware of how frightened I was of him. He was sober now, and Lynne had returned early to ensure he was presentable.

"He was out all night at his parents'. You and I woke up when we heard a bang and your mother shouting before she lost consciousness. We didn't see how she fell, and she doesn't remember," Lynne explained before we left.

I played along with the story because that's what I had been instructed to do. I knew my mother would prefer it this way. It was usually her who concocted these narratives. Lynne had grown so accustomed to listening to them that she could take over seamlessly. Part of me felt disappointed in Lynne, but I understood: we were her life. If she didn't adhere to the peculiar status quo set by my parents, she would be let go. I could forgive Lynne; she was just as trapped as I was.

That marked the beginning of our trips to the hospital with my mother. Sometimes, it was I who ended up in the hospital. Even those experiences didn't prompt her to take a stand against him. Eventually, when he began to harm himself, that's when we could finally get rid of him. It was still a huge embarrassment for my mother to have my father sectioned, but it was a necessary step. I visited him a couple of times during his hospital stay, but each time he seemed to decline further.

Now, fourteen years had passed since I last saw him in person. I had been just a teenager back then. At thirty-one, I was still as anxious as I had been during those visits. Each time I prepared to see my father, I would feel sick—my head would spin, my hands would shake, and I'd struggle to breathe evenly. This was all before I even stepped foot in front of him. Once my mother stopped forcing me to visit, I never went back. While he couldn't hurt me anymore, that wasn't my main concern. I feared becoming like him—manic, unpredictable, unhinged, violent, and broken. His illness hadn't developed overnight; it had been a slow, gradual decline fuelled by alcohol. Doctors had told us that the stress and trauma of Lucy's disappearance had been too much for him to bear, and his mind had sought to create a way to cope.

"He's just fucking weak. This is all his own fault," my mother would say, taking a drag from her cigarette, a habit she oscillated between. She had no sympathy for him. The love between them had vanished the moment we lost Lucy.

I kept all my voices and hallucinations to myself while growing up. I didn't want my mother to see me as weak, too. She managed to remain strong and composed while grappling with the loss of her daughter and the instability of her husband. If I succumbed to madness, I feared she might crumble under the weight of it all. The shame of not being strong for her was unbearable. In some ways, I think my mind had tried too hard to meet her expectations, and now I was suffering the consequences. If I didn't find a way to manage my visions soon, I'd end up like my father. Visiting him felt like a necessary evil; I had to confront my fears to find the answers I sought.

As Jade and I pulled up in front of Ashmoor Hospital, I swallowed hard. The forty-five-minute drive felt far too brief. Jade attempted to make small talk, but I was too absorbed in thoughts of how terrible my last visit had been. What if he was the same this time? And what if Jade witnessed my unravelling? I could almost see images of my father, giggling maniacally to himself, his laughter echoing in my ears. I remembered how the spit had splattered silently onto the table where we'd sat.

"She's there! She's there! She's there! She's there!" My father sang, his gaze fixed on a corner of the room as he clapped his hands together.

During my last visit, I had stopped trying to communicate. It felt pointless—he never really understood me or listened. Sometimes, I wondered if he even recognized my presence. His intense stare bore into me, wide-eyed, as if he were trying to determine whether I was real or just a figment of his imagination.

"Can you feel that? Her breath on you? I feel it all the time. She never leaves me. Never leaves her dad," he murmured, lost in his own world.

"Oh, there she is, my big girlie. Isn't she pretty? We take such good care of her. She's in better hands with me and her mummy and her brother."

I sighed, five minutes into our visit, wishing I could leave. The nurses had smiled reassuringly when I checked in, likely aware I was the only seventeen-year-old visiting a parent alone. They knew my mum had stopped coming but seemed to understand. My dad was a handful; there were times we'd been turned away because he had caused too much of a scene and had to be sedated.

In moments like these, parts of him reminded me of Charles Manson—his speech patterns, the erratic movements, the way his spine hunched unnaturally as he tapped his feet and teeth in an unsettling rhythm that became the backdrop of our visits.

Clack. Clack. Clack.

An eye twitching involuntarily, I clenched my fists, my nails digging into my skin, a welcome distraction from the noise of his incessant clacking.

"Oh, don't say that. No, no, no, no!" His hands shot to his ears as tears streamed down his face.

"I never meant to, Lucy! I thought it was the right thing to do. No! No, no, no! I wanted to protect you! I didn't want them to have you! I'm sorry. I love you. Please!"

He sank to the floor, drawing his knees up to his chest, resembling a small child caught in a moment of guilt rather than my fully-grown father. I wasn't surprised; this was his new normal. His outbursts had escalated with each visit, and I'd come to expect this version of him.

"AHHHHH! NOOOOO! PLEASE STOP!" He slammed his head against his knees, continuing to scream.

His breathing quickened, harsh and ragged, his face contorted with pain and glazed over with raw fear. As his arms trembled and his body stiffened, I felt as if I were witnessing a seizure unfold before me. Yet, I remained seated at the table, a silent observer. Did he realize I was there? Did he understand that I was just watching him suffer, devoid of concern? Was this his new torment—haunted by the memory of me sitting there, doing nothing?

That memory was the last I held of my father, the one I had always believed would remain etched in my mind. When I walked out of the hospital at seventeen, I never expected to return. Now, as I stared at the grey building before me, I inhaled deeply, steeling myself to enter the place that housed him.

We stepped through the door into the main reception, greeted by the stale scent that seems to cling to most hospitals. The squeak of shoes echoed on the shiny floors, and the overhead lights flickered slightly, their harsh brightness illuminating the sterile halls. Everything looked just as I remembered: the beige walls, the beige ceiling, the beige floors, all bordered by a scarlet outline. The place was in desperate need of an update.

"Hi, we're here to see James King," Jade announced at the reception desk.

I glanced at the woman behind the desk. Her name tag read "Sue," and I recognized her instantly. She had aged during the fifteen years my father had spent here; there were new lines etched into her face, and her once long hair was now cut short. Still blonde, it framed her face, which had matured into the features of a woman in her forties. The beauty mark under her left eye remained unchanged. The last time I had seen her was the day I last saw my father, when she was just starting out in her nursing career.

"James King?" Sue's expression shifted from confusion to surprise.

Her eyes widened, and she pulled her glasses down from her forehead, almost as if to ensure she was seeing correctly.

"Oh, my goodness! Jakey! It's been ages! Come here!" She smiled, rising from behind the desk.

Jade's brows furrowed, and she tilted her head, clearly perplexed by the warmth of Sue's greeting.

"Hey, Sue. I know it's been a while. How have you been?" I asked, stepping forward to hug her.

"I'm good, kid! Well, you're not a kid anymore, are you? I'm still here," she said, glancing toward Jade.

"Uh, Sue, this is my wife, Jade. Jade, this is one of my father's nurses, Sue, she also used to babysit me when I was young. She takes care of my dad here," I introduced them, gesturing between them.

"Oh wow, what a small world! It's nice to meet you," Sue said warmly.

"It's been quite some time since you last visited. What's been going on?" she inquired, her confidence shining through. Sue clearly felt at ease with me.

"I just came to visit while I'm in town. I'm seeing my mum for Christmas," I replied, deflecting the question. There was no way I was going to share the true reason for my visit.

"Oh right, so you haven't been here in over a decade. I would have noticed if you'd signed in to see your dad," she remarked, her tone bordering on accusatory.

"No, I haven't been since I was a teenager," I admitted, heat rising to my cheeks as embarrassment washed over me. I hadn't come here to be judged for being a terrible son.

"Oh…well, I suppose life just goes on," she said, offering a smile that didn't quite reach her eyes. The judgment lingered in the air as she returned to her side of the desk to retrieve the sign-in sheet and our visitor passes.

"ID, please. Your father will be thrilled to have some company; he hasn't had many visitors over the years. There was a time when he had none, you know. I think that isolation made things worse for him," she sighed.

"Hasn't had many? Did any of his family come to see him?" I asked, relieved at the thought that he hadn't been entirely alone this whole time.

"I'm not sure they were family. They seemed more like old friends. They didn't say much, and they hardly spoke to him during their visits. It was more like they were just checking in. I remember a few men coming from your house; they would visit your dad and head straight to his office. But it was always brief—never more than ten minutes. I found that strange, especially considering they didn't engage with Jim at all," Sue explained.

"Do you know any of their names?" I inquired.

"Uh, no, not right off the top of my head. It's been quite a while since one of them visited. I'm not really supposed to do this, but I can check while you're visiting and see if I can find anything," Sue said with a smile as she took the sign-in sheet from us.

"Thank you, Sue. You really don't have to, but I'd appreciate it if you could. It might help me ask them some questions."

"Not a problem, Jake. Enjoy your visit."

"Has Dad…gotten any better?" I asked hesitantly.

"He has more good days than bad now. But there are still times when he struggles for extended periods. It really depends on how he's feeling. He still talks about Lucy, so just be prepared for that. There's still a lot of guilt he carries. I'm truly sorry about your sister, Jake," Sue said, giving me a sympathetic glance as she buzzed us in.

Chapter 9

Dad had his own room, but today he was in the communal area, sitting by the large bay window, absorbed in a book. A nurse told us he favoured that spot for reading. I immediately understood why—the window was almost identical to the one in Lucy's room. She used to sit there for hours, lost in her books. We still had shelves overflowing with them at home, all because of Lucy. Books had been the only thing she ever really asked for. Before Lucy, my Dad never read to me, but once she arrived, he started to. It wasn't for me, though. It was because Lucy was there. There was something about her that brought out a different side of him, something fatherly. I guess I just wasn't enough to inspire that kind of attention on my own. But if I got some of it, I didn't care.

"There he is. He might not be too talkative at first. He's not long had his meds, but he should be glad to see you. He talks about you sometimes," the nurse said, nodding toward the armchair by the window where Dad sat, engrossed in *To Kill a Mockingbird*.

I took in his appearance. He'd aged more than I expected. He was in his early sixties now but looked closer to seventy. Deep lines etched his pale, hollow face. His once dark hair had turned grey, greasy, and unkempt. I wondered if they even bothered washing it here. But then again, why would they? It's not like he ever left the building. His hands, once strong and capable, now trembled slightly as he turned the pages, fragile and withered. Seeing him like this—my once larger-than-life father reduced to such a frail state—hit me harder than I thought it would.

As I walked closer, passing the other patients, I noticed the variety of their conditions. Some looked entirely ordinary, while others blended seamlessly with the drab, beige surroundings, rocking, muttering, or humming to themselves. But my Dad—he just sat quietly, absorbed in his book. It was such a stark contrast to the erratic, volatile man I remembered from my last visit. A surge of anxiety shot through me. I hadn't planned what to say. What if he didn't recognize me?

What if I triggered something, made him worse? Or what if, after all these years, he still couldn't give me the answers I needed?

I stood in front of him, feeling like a kid again, unsure and awkward. Jade, standing behind me, gave my arm a gentle squeeze of reassurance.

"Dad…it's me," I managed to say, my voice cracking slightly under the weight of the moment.

He didn't respond immediately, but I saw the subtle tension in his body as he gripped the book tighter. At least he had heard me.

"Dad, it's Jake," I repeated, softer this time, trying to sound reassuring, though my insides were a mess of nerves. Did he even recognize me after all this time?

Slowly, deliberately, my dad closed the book, his movements painstakingly careful. He adjusted his posture but still didn't turn toward me. I sat down in the chair opposite him, studying his face up close. His yellowed teeth, the heavy bags under his eyes—he looked as though he hadn't slept in days, maybe even weeks. In that moment, looking into his tired face, I realized that in some ways, we were still alike. We were both haunted by Lucy, both unable to move on.

"I, uh… I've come to see you, Dad. It's been a long time," I added, desperate to break the suffocating silence.

Finally, he moved. His head lifted at a glacial pace, and for a fleeting moment, his eyes flicked up toward Jade, then back down again. He still didn't acknowledge me directly. Instead, he began rubbing his head, his hand moving more and more forcefully as if he were trying to erase something that was stuck in his mind.

"Dad… This is Jade, my wife. Don't worry that you don't know her. She's family." I forced a smile, trying to hide the tension boiling inside me.

It was harder than I thought it would be, sitting in front of him after all these years. I hadn't realized just how much anger I'd built up, how deeply it had settled into me until this moment. Every part of me still felt like that little boy craving his attention, while he acted distant, as though I wasn't worth acknowledging. His silence now felt no different from the years of emotional neglect when I was younger—only this time, I wasn't sure if it was a deliberate act or if his illness had swallowed up the man I once knew.

"Dad, I'm only here for a couple of days, to see Mum for Christmas. I wanted Jade to meet you," I lied, the words feeling heavier than I expected.

Still nothing. The silence lingered awkwardly, and I started to wonder if it would look bad if we left. Then, finally, his voice cut through the quiet, hoarse and loud as if it had been unused for a long time.

"Where have you been?" he asked.

The question hit harder than I expected. "I…uh, I've been…living away for a while. I went to university and then stayed there, I guess. I just needed to come back for some answers, actually, Dad," I admitted.

"I didn't know where you went. Antonia wouldn't tell me," he said, his voice low as he looked down.

The realization struck me. By not visiting him, I'd left him without either of his children. He had no idea where I was, what I'd been doing. For all he knew, I could've been dead. That must've pushed his mind even further into its spiral.

"Has Mum been to see you?" I asked, even though she always claimed she hadn't visited since the day he was admitted.

"Yes. Not in a long time now. But she used to, before she remarried." He shrugged like it was nothing, but the bitterness was clear.

"Oh, right. Are you doing, okay?" I ventured cautiously.

"Ha. Haha. HA!" He laughed, clapping his hands together, startling me with the sudden shift.

"That's funny, real funny, Jake. Look at where I am. With all my friends in the loony bin, and I'll die here. That way I'm of no trouble, no trouble at all." His words were sharp, cutting through me with each syllable as he shook his head.

"I just meant…how are you feeling, in general?" I asked, feeling foolish for asking.

"Just great. I'm still crazy, if that's what you're wondering." His hands trembled as he spoke. "I see your sister everywhere. In my dreams, when I'm awake, at night, in the middle of the day. She never leaves me. But that's my fault. I deserve it. The meds keep her at bay most of the time, but when she comes back…she's more terrifying than ever." His voice broke as he shook harder, visibly haunted.

"Dad, I think I'm sick like you too," I confessed, the weight of the words pulling at my chest. "I see her too. It's been going on for years now, and I think I'm going to end up…"

"Like me? In here?" he interrupted, his eyes locking onto mine for the first time. "And you don't want that, huh?" He let out a bitter chuckle. "Maybe it's guilt, son, eating you alive. Don't be so hard on yourself, kid. You aren't at fault…it was me that should've died."

His last words echoed between us, a raw, painful truth hanging in the air, too heavy to escape.

"Died? Is that what you think happened to Lucy?" I asked, my voice shaking with tension.

My father's face contorted with horror. His body froze, and I could see him struggling with his thoughts, trying to decide what to say. Had I caught him out?

"Dad! Do you know what happened to her?" My voice was louder this time, my heart pounding in my chest.

He turned away from me, staring at the window as he rocked back and forth in his chair. His face twisted into painful expressions, but he remained silent.

"Jim, it would be really great if you could talk to us," Jade said gently, trying a different approach. "I never got to meet Lucy, and I'd love to know more about her. I've only heard bits from Jake."

She sat down across from him, her voice soft but steady. She waited patiently.

"Lucy was an angel. An absolute sweetheart," my dad finally muttered, his voice thick with emotion. "I could never have imagined having a daughter as beautiful as her. We had this…bond, a great bond. I miss her so much." His eyes filled with tears as he spoke, and I felt a tight knot in my stomach.

For the first time, he turned to look directly at Jade. I hadn't talked to him about Lucy much after she disappeared, so I didn't really know how he felt about her. I knew my parents adored her—she was the one they'd chosen, after all.

"I'm sorry for asking this, Jim, but…why did you adopt Lucy?" Jade asked softly. "Did you meet her earlier? Was there something special about her?"

My dad's eyes darted to mine and then immediately looked away. He stared at the floor, his lips pressed tightly together.

"We wanted another child," he said after a long pause. "Your mother…she didn't carry well, and she was getting older. I heard about a girl, Lucy, from one of my friends. I… I loved her. I wanted to save her from the life she had, so we arranged the adoption."

Jade's brow furrowed. "Her life? What was wrong with it? Was she your friend's daughter?"

"No," he replied, his body tensing up again. His lips quivered. "She wasn't. She came from a bad background. I knew people in the local council—they told me about her situation. It was…really bad. Antonia wasn't sure about it at first. She thought it was too risky, that Lucy wouldn't trust us. But I told her Lucy would be good for us. That we could help her…that your mother needed another child."

"She had a child," I muttered, the anger bubbling up inside me. His words felt like a slap in the face. I was standing right there, yet he spoke as if I didn't exist.

He glanced at me again, then quickly turned his attention back to Jade, avoiding my gaze. His breath quickened, his head shaking slightly. I saw the veins in his neck bulging as he clenched his jaw. He raised his trembling hands to his head, gripping his scalp tightly, dragging his nails down his skin. Blood began to seep through his fingers as he clawed at himself.

"Dad! Stop! Don't do that!" I shouted, rushing to his side and grabbing his hands, trying to pull them away from his head.

"It's my fault! It's my fault!" he screamed, kicking me away. "It started with me!"

"Dad, please! Stop this!" I pleaded, wrapping my arms around him in an attempt to calm him down. For a brief moment, he stilled. His body sagged against mine as he sobbed uncontrollably.

"I'm so sorry, son. It's my fault she needed Lucy," he whispered, his voice trembling. "It's my fault Lucy was taken. I deserve to be locked up forever. I should've died instead."

"Excuse me," a nurse interrupted, gently but firmly taking my father's arms and guiding him away from me. "Come on, Jim, you need to calm down. Let's go back to your room. You've done really well with your visit today." She smiled reassuringly at him as she led him toward the hallway.

"I'm sorry," she said, turning to us. "I think you'll have to leave for now. He's too stressed. But please come again—he did better this time than during other visits."

I stood there, frozen, unsure of what to say or do.

"Jake, it's okay," Jade said softly, wiping a tear from my cheek. I hadn't even realized I was crying. "We can come back."

"No…yeah, I know. It's fine," I muttered, swallowing the lump in my throat. "I don't need to see him again. He doesn't know anything anyway."

"That's not true, Jake," Jade insisted, her eyes wide with conviction. "He knows something. He was hiding things from us. The way he talked about Lucy's adoption—there's something off. He's thought about what he needs to say, and that's not what someone who's mentally unstable does. Your dad knows something. And if he does, then maybe those people who still visit him do too."

"What could be off about the adoption? She was just adopted—what are you getting at?" I asked, feeling an unexpected surge of defensiveness toward my family.

"Nothing definite yet," Jade replied, her voice calm but serious. "But we really need to ask your mum more questions, especially about those friends who visited your dad. And I've been thinking, it might be useful to find out who Lucy's birth parents are. We don't even know if they're still alive, if they were the ones responsible for her rough past, or if they even know what happened to her. Wouldn't they have been informed when she went missing?"

Her concern was clear, and it unsettled me.

"I never thought to ask," I admitted, feeling foolish for not considering this sooner. "I just assumed they knew, or maybe they didn't care. I always thought she was in a foster home before we adopted her...but now I'm not sure about anything."

As we made our way out of the hospital, Sue stopped us at the reception desk. She handed me a slip of paper with several names written on it—names of the men and one woman who had visited my dad over the years. I recognized a few immediately: our reverend, my old headmaster, the police commissioner, and even the mayor. All had been close friends of my father.

"Good luck, Jake," Sue said, her voice soft but sincere. "I hope you find some answers. Nobody here has forgotten Lucy. Your dad's mentioned some odd things over the years, so I know there's more to this story. If you need anything, just reach out." She offered a reassuring smile before turning to answer the ringing phone on her desk.

Jade, who had been reading the list over my shoulder, smiled as we stepped outside. "What did I tell you? People around here know more than they let on. We're going to get you some answers, Jake. Maybe we'll even find her."

She gave me a quick kiss, her optimism lifting me slightly. We got into the car, but my mind was still racing. Overwhelmed yet strangely relieved to have Jade by my side, I started the engine.

As we drove away, I glanced in the rear-view mirror at the hospital. A chill ran down my spine as I saw something—or someone—on the roof. Lucy. She was standing there, holding my dad's hand. My entire body froze, paralyzed by the familiar wave of fear.

I went numb.

Chapter 10

The funeral was set for the Friday after Christmas, extending our intended stay from a few days to nearly two weeks.

We sat in silence in the hallway after telling Mum what happened. She had been standing by the stairs, but as soon as I finished, she crumpled, collapsing onto the mahogany steps. Her body shook the staircase as her scream ripped through the air, sharp and agonizing. It was a sound I had heard before—when Lucy disappeared. The wind outside howled in eerie sync with my mother, as if the entire world was grieving my father. Pete wrapped his arm around her, his eyes drilling into me with a scowl.

"Why did you have to go and see him?" she had screamed that same day, when Jade and I returned from visiting Dad.

Her eyes, red from crying, held not just sorrow but something else—anger. A deep, burning resentment. Hatred. And it was aimed at me. In her mind, I had pushed him. My visit had driven Dad to jump. At the police station, I had to answer endless questions about his behaviour during our visit. The nurses had reported that he had been making progress, that his sudden death had shocked them. There was no explanation for how he'd reached the roof. No cameras had caught him, no one had seen him leave his room, and he'd been sedated after our visit to help him calm down.

I hadn't told anyone about seeing Lucy on that rooftop, standing next to him. She remained motionless as we raced towards his body, crimson pooling on the ground below. Her eyes, hollow and dark, locked onto mine, never once shifting, as if she were watching everything unfold for me. And she stayed. Even now, in my mind, she never moved away.

"You knew how ill he was. We stopped seeing him years ago! Why would you think it was a good idea to visit?" Mum cried, the desperation in her voice rising as she tried to make sense of it. "You knew how fragile he was!"

I sat there, frozen in guilt. Jade gently rubbed my hand, her touch a lifeline in the sea of my mother's fury. "He wasn't to know, Antonia. Jim was sick," she said softly, trying to calm things down.

"We know that, Jake," Lynne, standing by the banister, added. She hadn't looked at Mum once. In fact, her face remained unnervingly calm, almost detached. She had known my father for thirty years, yet her expression showed no emotion. If anything, she seemed indifferent to the news of his suicide.

Mum, on the other hand, was unravelling before us. "No!" she screamed, tears streaming down her face as her hands covered her head. "You knew! You knew he wasn't strong enough, but you just had to push. You always push, Jake! Until there's nowhere left to go! Nothing is ever good enough for you. You've always been difficult, from the moment we got you. This wasn't how it was supposed to be." Her voice broke as she wept into her hands.

I could hear her anger and resentment in every word. Since Lucy's disappearance, my mother had become more honest—brutally so. Any softness she had when I was younger had disappeared, replaced by a bitter edge that seemed to cut deeper with each passing year.

"We stopped seeing him to protect him, Jake. It was for his own good," she whimpered. "Why did you have to bring up Lucy? It's too painful. We can't keep reliving this. You need to learn to live with it. The pain will consume you." Her eyes didn't meet mine anymore, as if I was already a lost cause.

"You're going to end up just like your father, Jake," she said, lighting a cigarette with shaking hands. Her voice was laced with exhaustion and finality. "And maybe that's for the best. What's the alternative? You become like me? Not a chance. No matter how hard I tried to raise you to be better, you're still the same—smug, entitled, just like him."

The flame from her lighter flickered in the dim hallway, casting an orange glow across her tear-streaked face. For a brief moment, everything seemed suspended in that dim light—her pain, my guilt, the suffocating atmosphere of the house.

I noticed Lynne's expression shift ever so slightly, a faint, almost imperceptible smile. It caught me off guard—her subtle enjoyment of my mother's anguish. But before I could process it, I was overwhelmed by my own feelings. The weight of the day had drained me, the hallway seemed to close in, and I felt like I was suffocating under the tension.

"I'm sorry, Mum," I finally spluttered, my voice cracking as tears welled up. "I shouldn't have gone to see him. I thought it would help, but I only made it worse." The words tumbled out, and before I knew it, I was crying.

Jade pulled me into a hug, and I could feel Lynne's hand gently patting my back, offering a cold, almost detached form of comfort. I felt embarrassed, breaking down in front of them. My father would have never cried like this. His pain was hidden behind his drinking, behind his silence. Maybe Mum was right—if I wasn't careful, I'd turn out just like him. I had to stop this endless search for answers. It was driving me mad, and I was getting dangerously close to the edge.

After what felt like an hour of shared tears in the hallway, Pete helped my mother to bed and started making some phone calls. Lynne went to prepare dinner, though I doubted anyone would have an appetite. Jade guided me to our room and tucked me into bed before heading for a shower.

"I'm so sorry," she whispered, pressing a gentle kiss to my forehead.

I closed my eyes, wishing to drift into sleep until the next day.

Jade smiled at me warmly, placing her hand over mine as I started the car. The colours of the morning felt light and calming, mirroring the weight that had lifted from my chest. The anxiety of meeting my father was finally behind me; it hadn't been as horrific as I had feared. While it hadn't yielded the answers we desperately needed, it marked the beginning of something. Maybe this was the first step toward healing for my family and the road to my own recovery.

As much as I resented my family for everything that had transpired after Lucy's disappearance, a part of me yearned for reconciliation. I needed us to come back together; Lucy wouldn't have wanted us to remain apart like this. My father still had time to be saved—he had spent too long haunted by our past, just as I had. Perhaps we could rebuild our relationship as father and son. Surely, it had to be better than how we were currently coping with the shadows of Lucy's absence, even after all this time.

As I checked the driveway ahead, eager to leave the hospital behind, a knot of worry tightened in my chest about my father. The car rolled forward, and the building shrank in my rear-view mirror until only the roof was visible. Its flat black surface appeared worn and in need of repair, much like the rest of the structure.

Suddenly, a foot and leg emerged onto the rooftop, dirty-white and devoid of laces. It clearly belonged to a patient. The foot was followed by a white leg and then a white top, until the entire figure rose to overlook the grounds of the hospital. The person's hand was pulled slightly back, holding something. The longer I stared, the more became visible.

A small crimson shoe, fastened tightly with Velcro, appeared beside the man. Bare, pale legs followed, marked with scratches and bruises, purple blotches dotting the skin. An ivory dress billowed gently in the wind. One shoe had a red bow attached, while the other was missing. A chill ran through me.

I looked back at the man, and my breath caught in my throat. His rugged features, which had only recently occupied my thoughts, were now shockingly clear. He was shaking, and his expression was one of torment. Bloodshot red eyes locked onto mine through the rear-view mirror, as if he knew I was watching him.

"Goodbye," he mouthed, his face looming closer in the mirror despite his body being far away on the roof.

I gasped as I saw him release Lucy's hand. Her mousy brown hair flowed behind her, a radiant smile illuminating her face—one I hadn't seen in years.

"Jake, are you okay?" Jade asked, her voice filled with concern.

In that moment, one foot slipped off the roof, and my father leaned forward.

I slammed my foot on the brake. Jade, who hadn't yet fastened her seatbelt, was thrown forward, her head and hands colliding with the dashboard with a loud thud.

"Jake, what the hell?!" she exclaimed, panic rising in her voice.

I watched in horror as my father took another step off the ledge, plummeting toward the concrete headfirst, leaving my sister behind.

As I watched him plummet toward the ground, a paralyzing helplessness enveloped me. I was forced to witness the tragic destruction of his own body. With each window he passed, he gained more momentum, and I could see Lucy peering over the edge, her expression a mixture of curiosity and despair.

The sound was beyond comprehension. It was reminiscent of a car crash, but the sickening crunch of bones seemed to stretch on forever. The heavy thud of his body hitting the pavement was followed by the nauseating splatter of flesh, a visceral assault on my senses. A splatter of blood trickled down the back window, marring the glass with its stark red hue. Then, an eerie silence descended, as if the world itself held its breath. Was I the only one to witness this horror? Jade had heard the sound, but she sat frozen, clutching her head in shock.

I flung open the car door, yet the world remained eerily quiet. I should have been aware of the door creaking open, or of Jade's frantic words trying to reach me as I stepped out. Her panicked expression flashed through my mind, but my feet moved of their own accord, guiding me back toward the hospital. Out of the corner of my eye, I noticed the entrance doors burst open, figures spilling out. I was certain Sue was among the onlookers.

My feet carried me to the spot where my father lay. His head was a grotesque mess, like the mushy peas served alongside fish and chips. Blood was everywhere, but it was the other matter—grey, pink, and even hints of green and blue—that made my stomach churn. Chunks of flesh and brain had splattered across the pavement, reaching far beyond where I had parked just moments before.

In a horrifying realization, I saw that his neck was twisted in my direction, one eye still open, reflecting a mix of confusion and pain. His chest rose and fell slowly; he was still alive but dying. Did he see me standing there, paralyzed by the sight? Did he understand the choice he had just made?

I looked up, and there she was, still watching us. Lucy's smile had vanished, replaced by dark, hateful eyes. Her hands were clenched into tight fists. What had she done?

Dragging my gaze away from her, I was forced to focus on my father. He had stopped twitching; his breaths had ceased altogether. That was it—he was gone. Any hope I had of mending our relationship vanished in an instant. Just ten minutes ago, I had been speaking to him, and now he lay dead before me. Lucy had taken him.

Suddenly, hands were around me, pulling me away. A sheet was draped over my father's body, but it couldn't conceal the scattered remnants around the ground. Tears streamed down my face, and the haunting image of his crushed eye and splattered brain replayed in my mind, burning itself into my memory. I had never seen a dead body before, let alone my own father's, laid out in such a grotesque manner.

Shaking uncontrollably, I searched for Lucy's gaze again, but she had vanished from the rooftop. It was then that I felt her presence to my right. Out of the corner of my eye, I caught a glimpse of her dress fluttering in the breeze. She was staring intently at my father.

Her icy hand slipped into mine, her tiny fingers wrapping around tightly. Lucy had always been cold, but this was different—this chill coursed through my entire body, intensifying my tremors.

"Please stop," I whispered, desperate not to be overheard. This was the last place I wanted to be deemed insane.

"Find me. Don't be like them," Lucy urged, her sweet, soft voice resonating in the chaos around us.

"Is that why you killed Dad? Because he didn't find you?" I asked, my heart racing.

She turned to me, her face returning to its innocent form. No bruises, no cuts—just the warm glow of the little girl I once knew. Her eyes sparkled as they caught the sun, and she let out a soft giggle.

"Daddy is the one who put me here, silly," she said, her smile fading as she glanced toward Jade, who was pushing through the crowd, trying to reach us.

"Jake!" Jade shouted, her voice laced with panic. Lucy pointed at her and burst into hysterical laughter.

"I'll play with her!" Lucy cried, her grip on my wrist tightening to the point where I worried it might dislocate. I needed to get to Jade—to warn her, to protect her.

"No, leave her!" I pleaded, struggling against Lucy's hold, but she wouldn't let me go.

I jolted upright, my heart pounding loudly in my ears, reverberating through my entire body.

"Jake, it's OK. Don't worry; I think it was just a bad dream," Jade said, her voice soothing.

The room was cloaked in darkness, with only a sliver of moonlight spilling through the curtains. I glanced at the clock.

4:45 AM. I had slept for hours, yet it felt like mere minutes. I inhaled deeply, then exhaled slowly, attempting to calm my racing heart.

"She was there. With Dad," I admitted, my voice trembling.

"Who was?" Jade asked, her brow furrowing.

"Lucy."

There was a moment of silence before she replied.

"Sweetie, Lucy wasn't there. She couldn't have been," she said, placing her hand gently on my forearm.

"No, she was there! She stood next to him before he jumped. It was her," I cried, tears spilling down my cheeks.

"Jake, it's been a long day and an even longer night. You're under a lot of stress, and dreams like that can feel real," she reassured me.

"You're not listening to me! She did this because of my dad! He did something to her! Don't you get it? That's why we're haunted by her! She blames us!" I shouted, frustration boiling over.

"Jake, please calm down. I know it's hard, especially after everything that's happened. But—"

"NO! Stop lying to me! Lucy is here; she's always been here! With me, with Dad, probably even with Mum! You have to leave before she comes for you!" I gripped her shoulders tightly, my voice rising in urgency.

Jade's eyes shimmered with fear, and her body quivered beneath my hands. She looked terrified.

"I'm sorry," I said.

"Let go of me," she whispered.

I released my grip, feeling the weight of my actions.

"She's already visited me once. But maybe I was just imagining it, Jake. Lucy has been on my mind constantly since we got here. I think my mind is just playing tricks on me. The mind is a powerful and scary place, but it's not real. You have to remember that. Think of all the years you spent in therapy, on medication, dealing with your emotions—when you didn't see her. It's not a coincidence. Please, Jake, don't get lost in this," she pleaded.

"You saw her?" I asked, dread creeping into my voice. Was it already too late for Jade?

She sighed. "Yes, I saw her. In the bath. It was her, but it wasn't really her. I've been thinking about her so much that my mind is scaring itself with something I'm imagining."

"She's going to try to get to you. I think she's really upset with our family. Something happened to her, I know it. I don't think she's alive. My dad knew what happened to her and never said anything. Now he's gone. I should never have gone to see him."

"You can't blame yourself, Jake. I think we need to get you to see someone. We have to leave here. This house and these people are not good for you. It's no wonder you've gotten worse. In the morning, I'll call the doctor, and we'll go home," she insisted.

I couldn't let her take me home. I needed to stay to find Lucy. If I left now, she might only get worse, and Lucy could try to take Jade away from me too. I had to convince her not to leave.

"No, it's OK. You're right. I'll call the doctor in the morning. She needs to hear what I've been experiencing. But I can't leave my mum right now, not before the funeral. I think you should go home for Christmas to be with your family. I don't want to keep dragging you into all of this," I said, stroking her arm gently.

"OK, if you promise to get help. I'll come back for the funeral. You can't go through that alone," she replied, relief washing over her as she hugged me tightly.

Chapter 11

Jade left the following morning. It wasn't a long or tearful goodbye. She slipped out before my mother even stirred, taking our car and leaving me here, stranded. The house was part of a community, but it felt more isolated, surrounded by sprawling land and woods. As a child, I had loved the vastness, especially with Lucy or my friends around. We used to play hide and seek for hours, exploring every nook and cranny. But now, it felt empty, almost suffocating, far too large for the few of us left. If you could even call us a family anymore.

It was Christmas Eve, and instead of being on the road with Jade, heading to her family's for the holidays, I was here, alone. Jade was driving the two hours back on her own, probably feeling awful. She had seen my father die—had seen Lucy too. I dragged her into this mess, my tragic spiral, and now she was part of it. She didn't deserve that. What if she ended up like me? Would she ever be able to escape the darkness that surrounded me, or would it consume her too?

I thought I'd found happiness, even if it was fleeting. But with Lucy resurfacing so vividly, the past had broken through like never before. It wasn't just memories or nightmares; she was real to me now—tangible. I could feel her presence, smell the damp earth clinging to her. Lucy was there, but I didn't know how. It wasn't like before. I couldn't dismiss this as my mind playing tricks or grief manifesting into something ghostly. She was different now, more solid, more...angry.

I'd read about spirits trapped between worlds, stuck in time. That could explain Lucy, but if that were true, it meant she was dead. And as much as I hated admitting it, I had always known that was the likeliest explanation for her disappearance. But I could never accept it. Dad had drilled into me the importance of hope, the need to believe she was still alive, somewhere. My grandmother had been even more convinced. She was adamant Lucy would return, unharmed, someday. Her certainty always nagged at me—how could she be so sure?

Grandmother Constance. I hadn't seen her in years. After Dad was sent away, she vanished from our lives too. No birthday cards, no Christmas visits. I assumed she blamed us, blamed me, for what happened to him. I never had the courage to reach out.

Constance was terrifying. I could see where my father got his temper from, except she didn't need alcohol to fuel her rage. Our family's wealth came from her side, and she never let anyone forget it—especially not my mother. She was obsessed with our position in society, with maintaining her iron grip on the town. People respected her, but it was a respect born out of fear. She owned large chunks of the town and crossing her was a mistake few dared to make.

What always struck me as odd, though, was how happy she seemed when Lucy arrived. I don't recall seeing her smile much, but the day Lucy was adopted, Constance was…pleased, almost eager.

"Oh, I can't wait to be a grandmother again," she had said, her rare smile softening her sharp features. "I was so hoping you two would have another child."

She turned to me, her gaze piercing. "Jake, aren't you excited? You're finally going to be a big brother. It's always better to have siblings than to be an only child. Strengthens the family. And now we have one of each—a boy and a girl. It's perfect."

Her voice had a strange edge to it, like she wasn't just talking about our family but something bigger. "We're doing such a good thing for the community," she added, "and we'll have to make an announcement in the paper once Lucy's settled in. It'll make us look…charitable."

I remember feeling uneasy then, but I was too young to fully understand why. Something about the way she spoke of Lucy, of the adoption, as if it was more about maintaining appearances than about love. Was there more to this than I had realized?

"No, I don't think that's appropriate, Connie. She's a child, not some prize or charity case. We aren't doing this for you or your image," my mother said coldly.

My grandmother's smile faltered, but she shrugged. "No, of course not. You're doing it for yourself. As usual. And no judgment—I'd want one of my own if I were you. A little girl… There's nothing like it. Maybe now you'll finally know what it's like, though it's still not quite the same," she added with a sigh.

I was too young to understand what she meant, but I knew enough to sense the tension. Fighting wasn't unusual in my house, and this felt like just another one of those moments.

"Okay, Mum. That's enough," my father said, his voice weary.

My mother stood up and left the room in silence, her footsteps brisk. I watched her go, wanting to follow, but I stayed where I was, caught between the two.

"Sorry, I suppose. I was only stating facts," my grandmother said, turning her attention to me. "I was talking to you anyway, Jake."

She leaned in slightly, lighting a cigarette with a deliberate, slow motion. "So, I hope you're ready for your little sister. I wouldn't expect much attention from your mother once Lucy gets here."

"Mum," my dad said again, his voice sharper now. I could feel the shift in the room, the change in his tone sending a shiver down my spine. My stomach churned, though I didn't know why.

"Jake, go to your room. We'll introduce you to Lucy when she's ready. No point in waiting around," my dad said, his eyes on me but his mind clearly elsewhere.

"Okay, Dad." I stood up quickly, eager to escape the thick tension hanging in the air. I headed to my room, but as soon as the door clicked shut, I pressed my ear to it, hoping to catch something of the conversation.

The voices were too low, just a muffled exchange between my dad and grandmother. But one sound came through clearly: the heartbreaking sobs from my mother's room. Her crying echoed down the hall, loud and raw. It was a sound I didn't hear often, and I wished I hadn't heard it then.

I stopped listening after that, curling up on my bed, confused and uncomfortable. I didn't understand why my mother had gotten so upset. She was usually so good at ignoring Grandmother's cutting remarks, but this time…this time, something was different.

I stood in my old room, leaning against the door like I had so many times before, listening to my mother's sobs. But now, her cries were for my father's death. I never expected her to react this way. They hadn't spoken in years, and it seemed like she hated him. I didn't blame her for that; in the end, my father had been an unbearable person to be around. I expected some grief, but nothing like this.

After Jade left, I had stayed in my room all day, drifting in and out of sleep, disconnected from the world. Sometimes, I could hear footsteps in the hall, my mother's muffled crying, doors closing—just faint echoes of life around me. But I ignored it all.

"Jake," a voice whispered, almost inaudible, like a breath. Then, a soft tapping at the door. I stayed still, pretending I hadn't heard it. The tapping continued, steady and insistent. I figured it must be Lynne, trying to coax me out of my isolation, but I wasn't in the mood to deal with her. After a while, the tapping stopped, and I closed my eyes again.

Suddenly, a loud thud jolted me awake. I sat up in bed, gasping, my heart racing. The room felt darker than before, and my curtains, which had been closed earlier, were now drawn open. Lynne must've come in and tried to wake me up at some point. But something didn't feel right—there was a strange tension in the air, a pressure in my chest. The usual sounds of the house had gone; no footsteps, no closing doors. Just silence.

What was that thud?

I threw off the covers and stood, the cold air of the house biting at my skin. A shiver ran down my spine as I walked to the bay window. The draft coming through the open curtains was freezing. I reached to pull them shut when I noticed someone outside, walking away from the house, heading toward the woods. Squinting, I realized who it was. My mother. She was barefoot, wearing nothing but a nightdress, stomping across the uneven ground with an eerie determination.

What the hell was she doing?

Panic surged through me. I hurried to shove my feet into shoes and bolted through the house, racing to the back door. The entire house was plunged into darkness, and no one else seemed to be around.

"Pete?! Lynne?!" I shouted into the emptiness. "Mum's gone outside!"

There was no response. I burst through the back door and into the cold night air, yelling for her. "Mum!" My voice echoed through the quiet, but she was nowhere to be seen. I ran toward the woods, my heart pounding. Twigs snapped beneath my feet as I sprinted.

The woods—so familiar yet so haunting now. I hadn't run through them like this since I was a kid, chasing Lucy in games of tag. The scent of damp earth and rotting leaves hit me, the same as it had always been. The trees loomed over me, thick and towering, blocking out the sky and the last slivers of light from the house.

"Mum!" I called again, desperation creeping into my voice.

Nothing. No response. Just the same eerie silence as before.

I stopped, trying to listen for anything—footsteps, movement, anything at all. But there was only the sound of my own ragged breathing.

"MUM!" I shouted, louder this time. But still nothing.

I pushed forward, trying to figure out where she could've gone. The only things this way was the town, if you went far enough, a treehouse Lucy and I used to play in, and the lake. But it had been years, and I wasn't sure if I could even remember the way. As kids, Lucy and I had marked some of the trees to keep from getting lost, but now, in the darkness, I couldn't make out any of the marks.

Why would my mother come here, of all places? She had always hated the woods, hated getting dirty. What could have possibly drawn her out here now?

Then I saw it. A flash of white in the distance—her nightdress.

"MUM!?" I lunged forward, urgency propelling me.

"MUM, please stop! Just wait!"

As I drew closer, I could make out her figure. She wasn't running, just jogging slowly.

"Mum! Stop! What are you doing?" I knew she heard me; I could hear her heavy breathing, the sound of her feet crunching against the soil, marked with tiny cuts that didn't seem to bother her.

I was close enough to reach out and touch her when we emerged into a clearing. The lake lay still and round, smaller than I remembered. We both paused, allowing me to catch my breath.

"Mum, why are you here?" I panted.

"Because this is where she is," my mother replied, her voice calm as she approached the lake.

"Who?" I asked, bewildered.

"Lucy, who else?" A small laugh escaped her lips.

"Mum, Lucy can't be here. She hasn't been in a long time. Do you know where you are?" I was beginning to worry she might be sleepwalking. This wasn't the same woman who had been sobbing just hours before; she seemed almost serene now.

"Of course I do. I've come here many times to see her."

A chill ran down my spine, and my heart sank.

"What do you mean, Mum? Do you see Lucy?"

"Yes, sometimes when I'm here. Or when I miss her. None of her clothes smell like her anymore. It's been too long. So I come here. Sometimes, one of her teddy bears still carries her scent, as if she's just played with it."

We had swum in this lake, racing from one side to the other. Dad had bought us a small paddleboat to enjoy together, or with Lynne. Our summers were filled with laughter here, even on chilly days when we would brave the cold to go out on the water. Mum hadn't shared many of those moments; she always hated the walk through the woods. Perhaps she regretted missing out on those times.

It struck me then: my mother was suffering from Lucy's absence just as much as Dad had been. A wave of worry washed over me.

"Mum, let's just go back. It's freezing, and we need to warm up. We can come out here for a walk tomorrow," I suggested gently.

My mother gazed at me, her expression vacant. It was as if her mind had drifted away, lost in another time or place. Her breath came in shallow, raspy gasps, and her wide eyes appeared almost blank. Her lips were pale, and her cheeks looked thin and rough, giving her a haunting, familiar appearance. It reminded me unsettlingly of the look my father wore the last time I saw him, just before he was sent away to the hospital.

"You need to say goodbye to him. I don't know how long he'll be gone," she had told me then.

"Do I have to? He scares me," I had pleaded.

"Yes, Jake. It's the last time for a long time, I promise. He's deranged, and if he doesn't get fixed, it'll affect us too."

"Can't I just wait until he gets back?" I asked.

"No, Jake. I don't know how long he'll be there. You need to do this for me, okay? I'll warn you—he doesn't look good, and he's gotten worse since you last saw him. Just go in and out as quickly as you can. Don't listen to a word he says. He's just spouting nonsense at this point. Don't let it upset you." She rubbed my shoulders and guided me toward the front room, where my father sat in a wheelchair, waiting to be taken away.

His wrists were strapped to the sides of the chair. I knew he was in bad shape, but this felt excessive. A male nurse named Daniel, who had been caring for him, stood behind the chair, ready to transfer him to what would be his final home. He offered me a reassuring smile, but the judgment in his eyes was unmistakable.

It was clear how he felt about our decision to place Dad in care. I didn't care, to be honest; he didn't know my father like we did. It was his job to be compassionate and understanding, but that look likely stemmed from his perception of me as a neglectful son. He would be right from his perspective, but he hadn't lived through the years of turmoil we had.

My father stared vacantly past me, his gaze fixed on the bay window behind me. I wasn't sure he even recognized that I was standing there.

"Hey, Dad. I just wanted to say goodbye for now. I'll come to see you when you're settled in. Hopefully, you'll have a room with a view like that one," I said, attempting to catch his attention.

There was no response; he continued to look right through me.

Sighing, I pondered my next words. "Okay, Dad. I hope you start feeling better soon. I want you to know I'm going to miss you, and maybe when you come back, we can hang out more like we used to. I've missed…you. The you I remember."

For a moment, his eyes flicked toward me, then returned to the window. He had heard me, but not enough to respond.

"I love you, Dad." The words slipped out, heavy with a sense of finality, as if I feared I might never see him again. A small part of me sensed that visiting him frequently would be a struggle.

"I love you too, son." His voice was raspy, and he leaned forward, hands outstretched in a gesture that seemed unfamiliar yet familiar. It felt strange to see him like this, but I didn't want to disturb his calm. Perhaps going to the hospital was indeed the right choice for him.

I leaned in for the embrace. He still felt like my father and even carried the familiar scent I remembered. It had been ages since I hugged either of my parents. In that moment, I felt smaller, almost safe. My eyes welled with tears. Since Lucy's disappearance, I had lived in a state of anxiety and fear. For a brief moment, I felt the comfort of being loved again. Maybe I had pushed my father away too quickly, not allowing him the chance to show me he could still be there for me.

Suddenly, a sharp, piercing pain shot through my ear, jolting me back to reality as I tried to pull away.

"Ahhhh!" I screamed as I recoiled in shock.

My dad pulled back, revealing scarlet blood dripping from his lips and teeth. "No, Jim! Don't do that!" Daniel exclaimed, gripping his shoulders firmly.

"That's from Lucy! She said to tell you hi from Hell! That's where this whole family is headed! All the way down for what we've done!" He screamed, his voice a mixture of rage and anguish.

"Calm down! Please, Jim! Not today," Daniel urged, trying to hold him steady.

"She hates us all, especially her! Even you and me! What did we ever do to help her? Nothing! She's gone because of us!" His face turned a deep shade of red, eyes bulging wide, as if he were about to explode.

"Jake, we need to get you out of here now!" my mother said urgently, pulling me away just as she had when we first entered the room.

Dad's voice grew more frantic, screaming erratically at my mother as she ushered me away.

"Oh my God, Jake! Your ear! Did he do that to you? Oh Jesus… At least he's going now… Take him away, please, Daniel!" she commanded, her voice laced with panic.

A few moments later, as my father was wheeled past us, he wore that same vacant expression that had become all too familiar. It was chilling how swiftly he could shift from one extreme to another. I finally understood my mother's decision; it was far too dangerous to keep him at home.

"Mum, we need to go home," I urged, taking her arm and guiding her back toward the house. But then, a chill swept through me, freezing my body in place as if I'd plunged into icy water. There she was—my beautiful little sister—smiling at us, radiating warmth and innocence.

A knot tightened in my stomach, and my head spun. My eyes must be deceiving me; they had done so before. I felt too fragile to shoulder the responsibility for both my mother and myself.

"Lucy! Sweetheart! Come here! See? I told you Jake was here! We're all together again, baby!" My mother cooed, her voice filled with an unnatural joy.

"You can see her too?" I asked, my voice trembling.

My mother looked at me, her expression a mix of confusion and delight. "Of course, I can, Jake. I can always see my baby. She's in a great mood today after feeling sad. I'm so glad you're back to your normal self, sweetheart. Come on, let's all play together!" She extended her arms to both Lucy and me.

"Mom…this isn't real." I glanced at Lucy, her presence almost tangible. But it couldn't be. She couldn't still be seven years old.

"Some things can't be explained. I used to think like you and your father, and it drove me mad. I refused to acknowledge her, but once I allowed myself to accept her again, everything made sense. You just need to trust her, Jake. She's still your little sister." With that, my mother intertwined her fingers with mine and pulled me closer.

Lucy stood quietly, her radiant smile lighting up her face, her eyes sparkling with a youthful innocence.

"Hi, baby." My mother squeezed Lucy's small hand. "Shall we go to the lake or the treehouse? Somewhere we can all have fun together?"

Lucy beamed and nodded shyly. This was how she had been when she first joined our family—soft-spoken, bashful, and adorably cute. I felt an overwhelming urge to speak to her. If my mother could see her too, then maybe I wasn't like my father after all. Perhaps I had been driving myself mad with my doubts. Ghosts weren't something I had ever believed in, but if this was Lucy, then I would gladly accept it, no matter the cost.

Yet, accepting that she was a ghost meant acknowledging that she wasn't alive anymore. It meant confronting the terrible truth that something horrific had likely happened to her after her disappearance. Was my mother not curious about that? Did she not care about finding answers regarding Lucy? Perhaps that was why we could see her now—so we could discover what happened and bring her home…or what was left of her. It had been so long—nineteen years. I was thirty-one now, and Lucy should be twenty-six. We should be adults celebrating Christmas together with our parents and partners. Instead, it was just me and Mum, the remnants of a family torn apart.

I wondered what Lucy would have done with her life. She had always loved flowers, helping my mother plant them with the gardener, Bill. Afterward, she would gather them into arrangements and decorate the house. Maybe she would have become a florist. Not that any of my family would have approved of such a choice unless it turned into a multimillion-dollar enterprise. I had already been a disappointment for moving away to become a teacher.

"Jake, would you like some tea?" my mother asked playfully, her laughter bubbling as she nudged Lucy. In her hand, she held a dusty pink plastic teacup from Lucy's old tea set, the grime and dirt clinging to it like a long-forgotten memory. I hadn't returned to this place much since Lucy disappeared, and I regretted not saving some of her things for myself.

As I took in my surroundings, I felt a rush of surprise. How had I ended up here? The scent of pine filled the air, and the rough wood scraped against my legs as I shifted. We were in the treehouse, which now felt small and cramped compared to how grand it had seemed during my childhood. Our names and drawings were still carved into the wooden walls, a testament to the countless hours we had spent making this our secret hideaway. Once Dad built it for us, we would often retreat here, even in winter, bringing a heater and blankets, waiting for Lynne to come and find us. Being away from the house was a relief for Lucy; it spared her from Lynne's strictness and kept us from our parents' constant admonitions about noise. I think my parents enjoyed having us out of the house as much as we did. When they adopted Lucy, they probably didn't realize that bringing a new child into our home meant sacrificing the peace they had known with just one.

Lucy was the best thing that ever happened to me. Without her, I felt hollow; her disappearance left a void that I didn't think I could ever fill.

"What are you doing?!" Lucy exclaimed; her eyes wide as she watched me carve 'Jake K' into the wood on my side of the treehouse.

"I'm marking my territory, so everyone knows this is my space. Here, use this," I said, handing her a sharp rock. It wasn't the wisest idea to give it to her; she was only five, and I was just ten—hardly an expert on safety.

"Are we allowed to do this? What if we get in trouble?" Lucy's voice trembled with worry. She had always been so fearful of getting into trouble.

"Don't worry, Lucy. This is our treehouse; we make the rules here." I winked at her to reassure her.

"Are you sure?" she asked, still hesitant.

"Yes! Mum won't come out here; it's too dirty, and Dad doesn't care. He probably won't come up here either." I reassured her.

"Okay, Jake." A smile lit up her face as she pressed the rock against the wood.

On her side, she wrote: Lucy and Jake's place. Her spelling had improved since she joined our family. My parents had chosen to homeschool her, claiming she was too far behind for regular school. At the time, I accepted it, but now it seemed odd—most kids start school around four. It was just another sign of my family's impossibly high standards.

Lucy was always so considerate, never thinking only of herself. She had a kind heart, unlike many children who, through no fault of their own, acted out of ignorance.

I gazed at the engraving in the dusty treehouse, where the once-white letters had faded to a muddy brown. The words were barely visible in the dim light of the night, and a chill crept up my spine at the sound of a creaking branch outside.

Then, a giggle echoed through the room—unmistakably Lucy's laugh. It resonated with a strange mix of serenity and haunting nostalgia.

My mother was still playing with her, her attention solely on Lucy. I had always felt loved by her, yet there was a lingering absence I couldn't quite comprehend, even before Lucy came into our lives. I had almost forgotten what it was like to be with my mother and Lucy when it was just the three of us. It felt like I was the third wheel, an uninvited guest in their bond.

Lucy didn't mean to, but she captured my parents' focus in a way that left little for me. Lynne was the only one who treated me consistently, even when Lucy's needs became overwhelming. I had been such an easy child to care for, but Lucy required constant attention. Her night terrors often filled our home with piercing screams, typically dealt with by my mother or Lynne. Sometimes, in her fear, Lucy would withdraw into silence for days, and it didn't take much to frighten her. I remembered the time my father playfully shook her shoulder, just as he had done with me, only for her to burst into tears. My mother had explained that it was due to her past, saying it would take time for her to adjust, but those struggles persisted throughout the three years she spent with us.

"Jake, what are you doing?" Lynne asked, her brow furrowing with concern.

"W-What's happening?" I looked around, disoriented, finding myself near the house at the edge of the woods.

Barefoot and chilled to the bone, I stared at Lynne, confusion washing over me.

"Jake, oh my God! Get inside! You look so pale!" She hurried towards me, urging me to move back toward the warmth of the house.

"How did I get here? Have you seen my Mum?" I stammered.

"Yes, Jake, she's in bed. I just brought her breakfast. When I went to wake you up, I noticed you weren't there. What were you doing out here?"

"I… I was with Mum. She must have left me at the treehouse."

"What? That's impossible," Lynne replied, annoyance creeping into her voice.

"No, I followed her last night! When I caught up to her, she took me to the old treehouse. The one Lucy and I used to play in." I insisted.

"Jake, you must have been sleepwalking." She patted my back, offering a sympathetic smile.

"No, Lynne, I wasn't! I swear, Mum took me there last night. We were in the treehouse together." I longed to mention Lucy, but I feared I'd sound crazy. I wasn't ready to end up like my dad.

"Jake, that treehouse was torn down ten years ago. It was old and rotting, so your mum had Bill take it down. You haven't used it since you were, what, twelve or thirteen? They couldn't keep it standing forever. You must have just imagined it while you were sleepwalking," she explained.

My head spun, and my vision began to blur. She had to be mistaken.

"No, Lynne! My mum and I were there last night! I swear! I felt the wood against my legs, I could smell the pine. It was there, Lynne, I promise! Come look with me!" I grabbed her arm and took off running.

"Jake, stop! You're hurting me! Please, just stop!" she pleaded, struggling to keep up. I barely registered her discomfort; she was fit for her age—she could manage. It wasn't far, anyway.

As we neared the towering tree that once held our sanctuary, disbelief washed over me. My legs gave way, and I struggled to catch my breath. The tree stood bare, its former presence reduced to mere scars on the ground where the treehouse had been. It couldn't be true; I had just seen it! The memories of being there were fading, leaving me to question if it had all been a dream. Or worse, could I be hallucinating again? If I couldn't separate reality from illusion, how could I ever trust my own mind?

"See, Jake? I told you it was just a dream. This place can play tricks on you—believe me, I've seen my fair share of oddities here. You're not the first one to sleepwalk," Lynne said gently. "Let's head back. Once I catch my breath, I'll whip up something for you to eat. You and your mum will need to regain your strength to face Christmas and the funeral. It's going to be tough, but I'll be right here for you." She pulled me into a comforting embrace.

Chapter 12

"I had too much to drink, Jake. I don't remember anything," my mother said when I asked if she recalled last night.

Her tone was dismissive, shutting down the conversation as quickly as it started. I didn't believe her, but after what Lynne had said about me sleepwalking, doubt crept in. Could it really have been a dream? No, I knew it wasn't possible. I saw the treehouse—or what was left of it—with my own eyes. Still, the day passed with my mother avoiding me, staying holed up in her room. Now, she was downstairs, setting the table for Christmas Eve dinner. That was something she used to love—painstakingly arranging everything, down to the tiniest detail. It had been years since I'd seen her do it.

She worked in silence, making place cards adorned with little drawings of robins and candy canes, lighting candles that smelled of cinnamon and pine, smoothing out the tablecloth until it was perfect. Lucy had always helped her with this part, those four Christmases she was with us. I didn't realize at the time that the last one, nineteen years ago, would be our final Christmas together. Just one week later, she was gone.

"Like this, Mummy?" Lucy had asked as she placed the cutlery, waiting for my mother's approval.

"Yes, sweetie, that's perfect!" Mum had smiled at her, gently straightening the silverware Lucy had just arranged.

I watched them from the living room, as I always did. Mum never asked me to help set the table. She knew she wouldn't be patient with me if I made a mistake, like she was with Lucy. Maybe it was because I was older or because I was a boy, but the standards were always different for us. Lucy never noticed. She seemed so happy that day, and why wouldn't she be? It was Christmas Eve. I was off from school, so we could spend the entire day together, and there were no tutors interrupting us. We both knew tomorrow would be filled with presents, a day of spoiling after Santa's visit.

Lucy still believed in Santa. I kept up the act for her. I had figured it out pretty young, probably when I realized it was always Mum asking what I wanted for Christmas, never Santa. But Mum never asked Lucy what she wanted—she just knew. It hurt, knowing that Lucy, in only a few short years, had somehow become closer to my parents than I ever had. She fit into their lives so seamlessly. And while I had drifted away from them, I had clung to Lucy. She was easy to love.

"Hey Jake, why don't you go help your mother and sister?" Lynne suggested, giving my shoulder a gentle squeeze.

I glanced toward my mother. Her expression was unmistakable—she didn't want me involved. She shot Lynne a sharp look, and for a moment, it felt like they were having one of their silent arguments. It wasn't the first time I'd seen them communicate like this, as if words were unnecessary.

"It's fine, I don't need to," I muttered, trying to avoid making things awkward.

Lynne's expression shifted to frustration. For someone employed by my family, she never hesitated to speak her mind. It always surprised me how she got away with it—disagreeing with my parents, even leaving abruptly when she was upset. I sometimes wondered how she still had a job. Perhaps it was because she'd been with us for so long.

"Jake, go help set the table. I'm sure your mother would love to make memories with both of her children. You know, some people aren't lucky enough to have even one child, let alone two. One day, when you're older, you'll realize just how important it is to cherish these moments—not just for yourself, but for the ones who love you," Lynne said, her tone soft but firm, a heavy sigh escaping her.

I knew she was speaking from experience. My dad had told me she'd once been married and tried to have kids of her own, but none of her pregnancies had lasted. He also warned me never to ask her about it, to avoid reopening old wounds. Lynne had known me since birth and had practically raised me, so I understood her protectiveness. From what I'd gathered, she had been my primary caregiver in my early years. I hadn't asked why, but I suspected my mum had struggled with postpartum depression. It would explain the distance between us, the lack of connection she seemed to share with Lucy instead. And I had made peace with that—it wasn't her fault.

"Yes, Lynne, you're right. Making memories with your family is important," my mother suddenly chimed in, her voice unnaturally sweet. "Come join us, Jake. Everyone should be with their family at Christmas." She smiled, a forced smile, before turning to Lynne. "Feel free to leave early today, Lynne. I'm sure you're eager to spend time with your niece."

Her sudden generosity threw me off. Normally, she expected Lynne to stay for dinner, help clean up, and even put Lucy and me to bed while she and my father went to Midnight Mass. I hugged Lynne goodbye, feeling uneasy as she left sooner than usual. Something about it felt...wrong.

"Merry Christmas, Lynne," I said, giving her a hug.

"Merry Christmas, Jake. I love you so much." She squeezed me tightly, her arms warm around me.

"Merry Christmas, Lynne!" Lucy's voice rang out with excitement, her joy purely about the holiday, not Lynne's departure. But I knew Lynne wouldn't take it that way. For some reason, she was less patient with Lucy.

"Have a nice Christmas. I'll see you all on Boxing Day." Lynne flashed a quick smile before heading towards the hall to grab her coat and bag. She stayed overnight once or twice a week and still had her own room here from when she looked after me more frequently. She'd even spent Christmas with us a few times—before Lucy joined the family. I missed the attention from her on those holidays.

"Mum, does Lynne have to go? Can't she stay for dinner, at least? Or even for Christmas, like she used to? Please, Mum." I pleaded.

"No, sweetie. Lynne's niece is staying with her, remember? She has to go home." Mum's tone was clipped, her back turned to me as she arranged the table.

"But this is her home. It'd be nice to have everyone here for once. Maybe Julia could come too?" I suggested. Julia, Lynne's niece, had come on outings with us and even stayed here a few times to help Lynne when Mum was away.

The sharp sound of clashing silverware filled the dining room.

"No, Jake! Julia can NOT come here for Christmas! Christmas is for family, and Lynne and Julia aren't part of ours! Are we not good enough for you? Me, your father, Lucy? Why do you need Lynne and Julia? They don't want to spend time with you. Lynne is *paid* to be here, that's all! It's nothing to do with you!" Mum's voice rose as she angrily fumbled with the cutlery.

Lucy whimpered quietly on the other side of the table. She hated shouting, any loud noise, really. Mum always scolded me if I raised my voice in front of her.

"Now look what you've done! Go to your room, Jake, and don't come down until your father's back." Mum turned away, continuing to set the table, ignoring Lucy too.

I left the room, doing as I was told. Lynne was waiting just outside the door, her coat and bag in hand. She put a finger to her lips, gesturing for silence, and took my hand.

"Where are we going?" I whispered as we slipped out of the front door.

"I think you're due some time with your second family. You can come and see Julia with me for a bit, and then I'll ask your dad to collect you."

"Shouldn't we tell my mum?" I hesitated, a knot of worry tightening in my chest.

"No," Lynne said firmly. "She's in a mood today, and I doubt she'll even notice you're gone, not if I'm not around to remind her."

I knew Lynne was right. My mum rarely bothered to check on me when Dad and Lynne weren't around. She was always with Lucy. If I wasn't with her, it was like I didn't exist. That was my normal. After Lucy disappeared, Mum started to pay more attention to me, but it wasn't out of love. It was more out of obligation.

Lynne took me to see Julia, and I was excited. Julia was always warm and kind, giving me all her attention. She had this way of making me feel special, and I hadn't seen her since that day Lynne took me away. After Lucy disappeared, our family became isolated, keeping everyone out except Lynne. Julia just...disappeared from our lives too. I never understood why, especially since she was such a big part of Lynne's life.

"How are you, honey?" Julia greeted me with her usual glowing smile, pulling me into a hug. Her wavy golden hair brushed against my face, and that familiar coconut scent washed over me. It was comforting, a smell I'd always associated with her, something that made me feel safe as a child. I hadn't answered her because I didn't want to admit what had happened with Mum.

"He's a bit upset, I think," Lynne explained, giving Julia a look. "His mum wouldn't let him help with the table, and when he suggested I stay longer, maybe even invite you, she went off on him."

Julia's face fell. "Oh...is that right?" She looked at me with concern.

I nodded slowly. "I'm sorry. I just thought it would be nice to have you both there. I didn't want to feel so alone."

Julia ran her fingers through my hair. "Why do you feel alone, sweetie?"

I sighed. "Mum's always with Lucy. She takes her everywhere and leaves me behind. Sometimes I just want things to be different, you know?"

Julia frowned. "Oh, baby, that can't be true. I know how much your mum loves you. I remember when you were a baby—she adored you. Maybe she's just spending more time with Lucy because she's younger."

"I hope so," I said quietly. "But sometimes she's just…mean. She treats Lucy the way she used to treat me, and now I feel left out."

Julia's expression darkened as she looked over at Lynne.

"She's horrible to him, Julia," Lynne interjected, her voice tight with frustration. "She shouts at him for no reason, ignores him, and leaves him out of everything she and Lucy do. It's cruel. I'm the only one who checks on him when his father's not around."

Julia's grip on my hand tightened. "Is that true, honey?"

I hesitated, then nodded. "Yeah… I haven't done anything to upset her."

Julia looked heartbroken, her thumb gently stroking the back of my hand. "Oh, sweetheart… I'm so sorry."

"Of course you haven't done anything to upset her, love. You're such a sweet boy… Come here. I'm going to sort this out; don't worry. She just needs to understand how her actions are affecting you," Julia said, pulling me into a warm embrace. I could feel her heartbeat against me.

"It all comes down to Lucy. They're so focused on her, making sure she gets all the attention possible. I understand that she needs it, but it's been years now—it's ridiculous! Little Lucy knows exactly what she's doing, I swear. She can put on her cute act for everyone else, but I see it. I see everything; she knows she's got it made," Lynne said, lighting a cigarette.

I didn't understand why Lynne was being so harsh towards my sister. She had always been strict with Lucy, but this felt different. Even at twelve, I recognised that Lynne was being unfair. Lucy had come from foster care and had clearly been through a lot; I remembered how feral she'd been when she first arrived. My parents had literally kept her hidden for three weeks while she adjusted to our home and started to talk.

"Well, perhaps we just need to remind Antonia and Jim of a few things," Julia suggested, her frustration evident.

"You can do that. I'm done getting involved," Lynne replied tersely.

That marked the end of their discussion about my sadness, but I overheard more hushed conversations as I waited at the end of the drive for my dad to arrive. When he pulled up, he didn't get out of the car.

The drive home was quiet. I assumed my dad was aware of everything, and I braced myself for the trouble I expected to face from both my parents. But to my surprise, as we pulled up outside the house, my father turned to me.

"I haven't told your mum that you went to see Julia. It would upset her too much to know. If she asks where you've been, just say you were out playing and I picked you up by the gate," he advised, his face looking worn.

I thought about the lie for a moment. I could picture myself saying it in front of her—and probably Lucy too. Lucy would definitely know it was a lie. I wasn't brave enough to venture outside after my mother had sent me to my room. She wouldn't say anything to our mum, but she would likely ask me when we were alone. I just had to hope Lucy wouldn't tell anyone.

"Okay, Dad, I won't," I promised as we got out of the car.

I watched my Mum set the table alone, aware she was lying to me about seeing Lucy the night before. It struck me that she probably knew I was lying about where my Dad had picked me up, but she chose to believe me—likely for her own peace of mind rather than mine. I couldn't accept her lie, though. This was different. She knew Lucy was trying to reach out to us, and there had to be a reason we were both experiencing it. My father had likely kept his own thoughts to himself, and the outcome of that was not something I wanted for myself.

"Jake, you can help if you want. Do the cutlery," she commanded while writing out the place cards.

"Uh… Sure," I replied, confusion swirling in my mind. I hadn't offered my help, assuming it wasn't wanted.

A wave of anxiety coursed through me as I struggled to remember the proper way to arrange everything. After watching my Mum do it for so long, I suddenly felt lost. She noticed my hesitation.

"Jake, if you don't know how to do it, just ask. That's why I stopped asking you to help when you were a child. You'd just stand there pretending to look busy until I dismissed you. I knew you didn't enjoy it, so I eventually stopped asking. Just do what you know, and I'll take care of the rest," she said softly.

I hadn't considered that her decision might have been aimed at making me more comfortable, rather than a lack of trust in my abilities. I had assumed, based on Lynne's reaction, that it stemmed from malice. Lynne had always felt like another mother to me when I was a child, but I needed to remind myself that she wasn't actually my family, and there was clearly something deeper going on between my Mum and Lynne.

Suddenly, my phone buzzed in my pocket. I hadn't really been on it much—this had turned into an unintentional electronic break. The signal here wasn't great, but I also realised I had been too lost in my own thoughts to keep up with the world outside. It felt like ages since I had arrived, even though it had only been a few days.

"Sorry, Mum, it's Jade. I'll be right back," I said, stepping into the next room.

"Hey," I greeted, waiting to hear her voice. It felt like an age since I'd last seen her.

"Hey, honey. Are you alright?" she asked.

"Yeah, I'm fine, but I miss you. Things just don't feel right here," I admitted.

"I know; I felt the same way when I was there. But that's what I wanted to talk to you about. I feel awful for leaving you there, and now that I'm home, it just doesn't feel right being without you on Christmas. I shouldn't have gone; I think it all just got too overwhelming, and I needed a breather. But I should be with you. You're going through so much, and now you're doing it all alone." Her voice trembled, thick with unshed tears.

"No, really, I'm fine. You stay with your family and enjoy your time. It's pretty miserable here, and I can't see that changing anytime soon. If I didn't have to be here, I wouldn't be," I reassured her.

"Jake, the only reason you're even there is because I pushed for it so much! I didn't realise how it would feel; I had no idea. I shouldn't have done this. I'm going to come back and be with you; it all feels wrong. I've been thinking about you and your family, even Lucy, ever since I left. I don't know why, but I just know I won't feel better until I'm with you, even if it's there. I'll stay until the funeral, but then I think we need to leave."

"I might have to stay longer than that, but you can go. I don't want you driving yourself crazy about my family, because it'll always affect you. I'm trying to deal with it while I'm here. After speaking to my mum and Lynne, I can think of some other people I could try to track down for answers," I told her.

"Jake, I just have this horrible feeling. If there were answers, surely they would have surfaced by now? It's been nineteen years! For all we know, Lucy could have been taken in by a family who couldn't have children and lived a happy life with them, not even realising she was missing. I've heard of that happening."

"Jade, that isn't what happened. Lucy was seven; she'd remember us. Whatever happened to her wasn't good. If she's still alive, she isn't living a good life. But I don't think she is alive. I can feel it. It's as if she's in another world. Her presence feels like how my dad does now. I just know he isn't here, and that's how it feels with Lucy too," I explained.

"If you can accept that, maybe your father's funeral will provide the closure you need for them both," she suggested.

We said our goodbyes, and she promised she would be back that night after dinner, so at least she'd miss that family affair. I only wished I could do the same.

We had dinner earlier than usual, around four o'clock, which suited me fine since I hadn't been eating much since I arrived. My Mum wanted to rest before going to Midnight Mass, which I planned to skip. I wasn't religious, and as far as I could tell, neither was she; perhaps it was just something that offered her some comfort. I felt like Jonathan Harker in *Dracula*, trapped in a labyrinthine house with a lurking monster as dusk fell. I felt decayed, not quite to the point of losing fingernails, but definitely weaker than when I first got here. I understood why Jade didn't want to return for long; she could probably sense the life being drained from her too.

I was struggling with fatigue, bloodshot eyes, battered feet from sleepless nights, and dry skin. My slender frame made me anxious about seeing Jade again; I looked utterly repulsive. The least I could do was shower, though I felt so exhausted from sleep deprivation that I could have used a rest before she arrived. This wasn't the cheerful Christmas Eve that most of the world was experiencing. People were busy enjoying time with their families, watching films, and wearing matching pyjamas. There was none of that here.

Bill, the handyman and gardener, was still around after having dinner with us, working on some odd jobs. I wondered why he didn't have a family to rush home to; it felt as if this place just absorbed people and kept them here. Lynne was also lingering after dinner, cleaning up what seemed like the entire house. It was a stark contrast to the last Christmas we spent with Lucy right before she went missing.

Nineteen years ago

After Lynne left following her argument with my mother, my dad brought me home, and my mother accepted my lie about playing outside alone in the freezing cold. It was time for our family dinner. There was an underlying tension between my parents; they both knew the truth about my outing with Lynne and Julia, even if they didn't acknowledge it openly. If I had still believed in Santa at twelve, I would have been afraid of waking up to find nothing but coal in my stocking. But Lucy was blissfully happy, revelling in the Christmas spirit and all its traditions. That year marked a new one for us: instead of heading to bed for an early night under Lynne's watchful eye, we were going to Midnight Mass for the first time with our parents.

The chapel was on our family's land, situated on the far east side of the property. This arrangement allowed my dad's friends to drive straight to the gates without having to navigate the dark grounds late at night. With no streetlights, only those familiar with the property could make the journey from the house to the chapel after dark.

After dinner, we settled in to watch a Christmas film and sip hot chocolate. I felt too old to enjoy family time so thoroughly; I remembered my friends at school complaining about having to spend time with their parents. But for me, such moments were a rarity. It felt special to be together, just the four of us, engaging in normal family activities. Dad was relaxed and not caught up in work, and Mum had enjoyed a glass of wine, easing into the evening. Lucy was happily drawing a picture for Santa Claus while we gathered around the fire for warmth.

Looking back now, that was probably the safest I had ever felt in my life. On other Christmas Eves, we would be tucked away in bed early, giving my parents time to prepare for the night. But I preferred this togetherness. We often felt like disjointed individuals sharing a house rather than a cohesive family enjoying each other's company. That Christmas Eve changed everything for me, and I was glad Lucy experienced it too. It was a glimpse of how a real family should connect. I had hoped it would be the start of a new tradition and that my parents enjoyed it as much as I did. My mother even played with my hair as we watched the film—not Lucy's, but mine. In that moment, she chose me, and I felt special. This was the kind of attention Lucy had grown accustomed to, but I didn't take it for granted. I wished we could have stayed like that forever.

It was just past eleven at night when we set off for the chapel, needing to arrive early to greet our guests. The cozy warmth of the car was no match for the biting cold that awaited us outside. I shivered as we made our way to the chapel, Lucy and I bundled up in our matching scarlet coats. As we drove, I sensed a shift in my mother's mood. The light-heartedness that had filled the car moments before gave way to an air of nervousness that seemed to wrap around us.

"It'll be fine, Antonia," my father reassured her, squeezing her hand in an effort to ease her tension.

"Lucy, stay close to me the whole time, okay? Don't speak to anyone—just wave. And keep your eyes on the hymn sheet if you get lost," she instructed, her voice firm.

"What about me?" I chimed in, suddenly feeling left out. Was I not supposed to look at anyone either?

"No, Jake, you're fine. You know some of the people who'll be there. Your headmaster will be attending with his family," my father replied.

I doubted any child enjoyed having their headmaster mingling with their parents, but it seemed inevitable in our family. My parents had connections with everyone in positions of power. After all, Kingston School was named after our family, and we owned most of it. My grandmother never missed a chance to remind everyone of that fact.

"Do I have to talk to Mr Andrews?" I asked, hoping for an out.

"No, son, you don't have to. But the polite thing to do would be to say 'Merry Christmas' when you see him. You've been raised properly; you're not rude," my father said sternly.

"Why can't I talk to anyone?" Lucy asked, her voice unusually loud, reverberating in the confined space of the car.

My mother sighed. "Lucy, I just need you to be a good girl and not draw attention to yourself, okay? This is the first time some of our friends will see you, and I want to make sure they leave with a good impression of you as a quiet girl in church. Midnight Mass is really important to them, so let's be respectful."

She smiled at Lucy, gently stroking her cheek, but the tension hung in the air, thick and palpable.

It had never struck me as odd that Lucy hadn't met some of my parents' friends since they adopted her three years ago. At twelve, I accepted everything my parents did without question. But now, as we headed to Midnight Mass, I sensed an underlying tension that puzzled me. Other kids attended church services, and I had gone before Lucy joined our family. Yet my parents were excessively protective of her, and I couldn't help but feel envious. They seemed to invest so much care into a child who wasn't biologically theirs, while I often felt overlooked.

When we arrived at the chapel, my parents greeted the minister who was officiating the service. It was Reverend Thomas, the same man who visited my school and took care of the local church.

"Reverend Thomas, good to see you," my father said, shaking his hand warmly.

"Good to see you too, all of you. Antonia, Jake…and is this little Lucy?" Reverend Thomas responded, his surprise evident as a smile spread across his face.

"Yes, it is. She's a little shy," my mother explained when Lucy didn't answer.

"Ah, I can see that. She won't even look up, the poor thing! But I can still tell she's a very pretty young girl. You'll have to get used to the attention, sweetie, especially as you get older."

I was baffled that my father didn't find that remark rude. Yet I was expected to engage with people. I felt a wave of frustration, but I couldn't even blame Lucy; she was so friendly and eager to connect. She likely wanted to chat with Reverend Thomas, while I would have preferred to be left alone. Once Lucy had emerged from her shell, she thrived on meeting new people, whereas I would have happily embraced the idea of being home-schooled.

Reverend Thomas, an older man probably in his sixties, seemed ancient to me, reminiscent of my grandmother. His wispy silver hair fluttered in the breeze as he gestured for us to enter the chapel. While my father and the reverend exchanged pleasantries about the details of the mass, my mother led us to our seats.

As we settled into the wooden pews, the chapel felt both familiar and foreign. The flickering candlelight cast dancing shadows on the walls, and the scent of pine from the decorations hung in the air. I couldn't shake the feeling that this was an occasion steeped in expectations that felt heavy on my shoulders.

Lucy seemed mesmerized by her surroundings, her wide eyes taking in the stained glass windows and the ornate decorations that adorned the chapel. I glanced at her, wishing I could share in her innocence and excitement. Instead, I felt like an outsider in my own family, acutely aware of the weight of unspoken rules hovering over us.

"Remember, Lucy, just be good," my mother whispered as she smoothed her dress. "Stay close to me, and don't make a fuss."

Lucy nodded, her small hands gripping the hymn sheet tightly. I felt a pang of sympathy for her; it was as if she was being set up for an audition in front of an audience she didn't even know.

As the service began, Reverend Thomas stepped up to the pulpit, his voice booming with warmth and authority. He spoke of joy, love, and the importance of family, but I couldn't shake the gnawing feeling that our family was far from the ideal he painted.

I caught my father's eye, and for a fleeting moment, I saw the tension in his brow, the way he clenched his jaw as he listened to the reverend's words. It was a subtle reminder that beneath the surface of this gathering, there were unresolved issues lurking in the shadows, casting a pall over the festivities.

When the congregation began to sing, Lucy's voice joined the others, sweet and unrestrained. I couldn't help but admire her bravery. She seemed so at ease, while I sat in silence, feeling more disconnected than ever.

As the night wore on, I kept glancing at my parents, hoping to catch a glimpse of the joy I longed for, but all I saw were the strained smiles and forced laughter that felt so far removed from the warmth of our previous Christmas. I couldn't shake the feeling that this was a night that would linger in my memory—not as a cherished moment, but as a reminder of how fragile our family ties truly were.

I observed my parents as they mingled with a mix of familiar and unfamiliar faces—men in suits with their wives. Lucy and I were the only children there. The chapel quickly filled up, with around fifty guests in total. These were the people my mother referred to as their 'closest friends': my father's business associates, councilmen, contractors, police superintendents, and even the Mayor himself.

Jude Collins, the Mayor, approached us while our parents were busy greeting others. I knew it would fall to me to interact with him, as Lucy wasn't allowed to speak. My heart raced; I despised talking to strangers, and facing someone as important as the Mayor felt daunting.

"Hi, kids. Your dad asked me to keep an eye on you both. It's Jake and Lucy, right?" he said with a friendly smile.

"Yeah," I replied, though it felt like a weak response. He knew our names, having visited our house many times.

Jude crouched down to meet Lucy's gaze, studying her for a moment before speaking again. "Lucy, aren't you lovely?" He brushed his hand gently against her cheek, but Lucy remained silent, her eyes downcast. "Let me see those eyes, sweetheart. I'm a friend of your father's."

Lucy glanced up, clearly uncomfortable. How could I communicate this to the Mayor without sounding rude? I wanted to avoid causing any trouble today. I shifted my gaze back to my parents, who were watching us with concern. My father's face was etched with anxiety, as if he wanted to intervene but felt compelled to stay back. His foot took a tentative step closer before halting abruptly.

"Mr Mayor, I think we're supposed to be taking our seats for Reverend Thomas," I blurted out, eager for him to leave. There was something about my father's 'friends' that unsettled me. They didn't behave like regular people, they carried an unnerving aura with them.

"I can assure you, young man, that I will take my seat when I'm ready. I'm the mayor, after all. Your dad asked me to keep an eye on you. It's important to show respect to adults; you shouldn't question us," he said sternly. "You'd do well to take a lesson from your sister and learn to be quiet and obedient. Lucy is excellent at doing what she's told. That's why we like her so much." He continued to fixate on Lucy, and I was confused by his words—he hadn't spent enough time with her to know that.

With nothing else to say, I stayed silent. He was right; I was just a child. My parents continued to glance over at us, increasingly worried as Jude Collins admired my sister's features.

"You can come sit with me and my wife for the service, sweetheart. I'll let your dad know," he said, taking Lucy's hand and leading her to the other side, where his wife awaited. She was a young woman with bright red lipstick and a matching handbag. She smiled warmly at Lucy and patted the seat beside her. Lucy, still looking down, obediently took her place next to the woman. I couldn't fathom why Lucy was so compliant, always doing what she was told without question.

My mother quickly sat beside me, her face flushed and her body tense. "What did he say to you?" she asked sharply.

"He said Lucy was good and that I should be more like her. I tried to get him to leave us alone—"

"Never talk to him again. Unless I'm there. You should have told your sister to stay here. I asked you to watch her, and you couldn't even do that," she hissed quietly.

Her anger radiated off her in waves. I glanced across the aisle to see my father chatting and laughing with Jude. He leaned down, said something to Lucy, and patted her on the head before turning back to us.

"I'm sorry, Mum," I said, feeling pathetic. I didn't fully understand what I'd done wrong, but I could sense it was serious.

"Just be quiet, Jake," she snapped, her words laced with venom. They stung deeply, making me feel like a failure, even in the simplest tasks. My father took his seat beside us just as Reverend Thomas approached the front of the chapel, ushering in a quieter atmosphere.

"She's just sitting with them," my father whispered to my mother.

"She's sitting with him," Mum corrected, her voice barely above a whisper.

"Not now, Antonia. She'll be fine."

"You disgust me," she replied slowly, a tear rolling down her cheek. I was bewildered by her distress over Lucy sitting with the Mayor and his wife. Christmas was important to her, and she was very attached to Lucy, but I didn't think she would have reacted this way if I had been taken to sit with someone else. I wished she could love me with the same intensity, that she'd want me by her side as much as she did Lucy. But I knew she never would.

As the mass continued, I noticed my mother remained completely still, barely breathing and staring straight ahead. She didn't join in any hymns or prayers, keeping her mouth firmly shut. Normally, she would be smiling and singing the loudest, encouraging both me and Lucy to join in if we paused for even a moment. This year, however, she was too consumed by anger to participate, even in pretence.

My stomach twisted at the thought; when my parents fought, it could last for days. My dad would be furious that she wasn't playing her part, calling her embarrassing and raging at her for acting this way in front of their friends. This Christmas was shaping up to be anything but joyful.

After the mass, as most guests filtered out, my father stood at the doors bidding farewell to our friends. My mother took my hand and led me to the car, telling my father that she wasn't feeling well and to bring Lucy to the car as soon as he was finished with Jude Collins. They lingered at the front, chatting with Reverend Thomas and his wife. Lucy appeared more relaxed now, smiling as she conversed with the mayor's wife, seemingly settling in better than she had when she was first taken away.

In the back of the car, I was freezing cold. My mother sat in the front, lighting a cigarette. "The next time I ask you to watch your sister, you need to pay attention. Don't ever let a man take her away, Jake. You must look after her, even if it's someone you know," she reminded me, her voice sharp.

I figured she didn't want a reply, so I stayed silent. Then I heard her gasp and jump in her seat. Suddenly, she flew out of the car, screaming. My father shouted at me from the entrance to the chapel, "JAKE! STAY THERE!" I froze, my body half out of the car.

It was dark, but I could make out Lucy's small figure being helped into a white car—by the mayor. My mother reached them, practically crashing into the car. "NOOOOOO!" Her voice was a wild mixture of desperation and fury. "No! You can't have her! How dare you! Give me my baby!" She screamed, lunging toward the car like a wild animal. My father was behind her, trying to pull her away. A loud thud rang out, and my mother collapsed to the ground.

"Jude, you can't…" my father started, but their voices lowered, becoming indistinct. Moments stretched as I tried to process what had just happened. My mother rolled over, looking at me helplessly, her wails echoing through the night as tears streamed down her face.

"Come on, sweetie," my father said gently to Lucy as he lifted her from the car. They walked past my mother, and the mayor's car sped away. I managed to scoot back into the car as Lucy settled in next to me, as if nothing had happened. "Are you okay?" I asked, concern creeping into my voice. She stared at me; her expression blank.

"Yes. I was just spending time with Mr Collins," she replied flatly, her gaze fixed ahead. I followed her line of sight and saw my father lifting my mother by her arm, his face a mask of anger as he shouted at her.

Reverend Thomas waved at me from the doorway of the chapel, a distant figure in the growing darkness.

Chapter 13

Jade

My mind raced the entire drive home, circling back to thoughts of Jake and his sister, Lucy. I had tried to immerse myself in family time, but it all felt hollow now. Jake was in pain, and I had left him alone to bear it. His father had died right in front of us, and I had turned my back. My family's concerned glances lingered on me, but I could feel their judgment too—how could she abandon Jake when he needed her most? Guilt and shame gnawed at me until I finally picked up the phone and told Jake I was coming back to his childhood home.

I had set off just after seven, hoping to share dinner with my family. I couldn't face another evening at his mother's table. I had tried so hard to love her, to fit into the role of the dutiful daughter she seemed to crave, but now I understood why Jake had kept me away all those years. There was something unsettling about her—she felt unhinged. I suspected she knew more about Lucy's disappearance than she let on. Trusting her seemed impossible, but maybe if I could get close, she might inadvertently reveal something.

Years ago, when Jake first mentioned his missing sister, I had found it strange. I'd googled the case, but there was hardly any information—just a handful of newspaper articles and the occasional anniversary piece. Where were the public appeals? The faces of missing children on milk cartons and billboards? Jake's family was wealthy; why hadn't they hired a private investigator? It seemed as if they had all resigned themselves to the idea that Lucy would remain lost forever.

The trees lining the road were becoming increasingly indistinct as the snow fell thicker and faster, transforming the landscape into a swirling white blur. It felt almost blizzard-like; I had never experienced such weather in England. The sound of the snow against the car roof resembled a dozen birds flapping their wings, and my visibility continued to dwindle.

Then, in a heartbeat, my headlights caught the fleeting figure of a small girl. Panic surged through me as I screamed and jerked the wheel to the left, but my car skidded, and I lost control. The impact struck me like a bullet, propelling me forward. My face collided with the steering wheel, pain shooting through me as warmth trickled down my forehead, soaking my cheek before dripping onto my hand.

Through the snow-covered window, I caught a glimpse of the girl still standing there, dressed in a blue nightdress and barefoot. I could barely make out the delicate pattern along the hem of her dress, but I could see the small brown teddy bear clutched in her pale hand. Her mousey-brown hair cascaded down past her shoulders, partially obscuring her face. As she approached the car, her blue eyes locked onto mine. It was only then that I noticed the large wound on her forehead, framed by dried blood and dirt. Strangely, instead of fear, I felt a sense of comfort wash over me.

My vision blurred, everything fading into an indistinct haze. I reached my hand toward my stomach, instinctively hoping to soothe the baby growing inside me. I hadn't even told Jake yet; I wanted to share the news in person after taking a test on my way home.

As I succumbed to the cold and the fatigue, a blast of frigid air hit my face, and I drifted into an unsettling sleep.

Chapter 14

Jake

The thud echoed through my room, jolting me upright. I had been expecting Jade any moment, and a surge of panic gripped me. I dashed down the stairs, catching a glimpse of my mother emerging from the kitchen.

"What was that noise?" she asked, but I barely heard her. I burst through the front door, the icy wind slapping my face as I stepped outside. My breath caught in my throat; the snow was thicker than before, and as I squinted against the blizzard, a faint light flickered in the distance.

As I drew closer, dread settled in my stomach, revealing the source of the light. Jade's red Ford was crumpled against one of the trees lining our long driveway. Gasping, I fought my way through the snow, each step sending a biting chill through my toes. I had no time for shoes.

"Jade!" I called, panic lacing my voice.

The snow obscured the window where she should be. I yanked the door open, my heart racing as I peered inside. There she was, slumped over the steering wheel, her eyes closed, blood trickling from her forehead.

"Jade!" I shouted, panic rising in my chest. I unbuckled her seatbelt and struggled to lift her out of the car. My arms felt weak, and I fought against the surge of dread. With a final burst of determination, I heaved her up, willing every ounce of strength to flow through me. Slowly, Jade's eyes fluttered open, and she locked onto mine.

"You left her," she murmured, her voice barely above a whisper. I understood the weight of her words instantly. It was a coldness that seeped deeper than the frigid air outside—a chilling anxiety that settled in my bones, reminiscent of those late-night moments when you realize you're not alone. Lucy was here, somehow sending me a message.

"Jake, I've called the hospital! We need to get her inside—it's freezing! And you're barefoot!" my mother urged, her voice laced with urgency.

"Let me help," Pete said, gently taking Jade's arm and draping it over his shoulder. Together, we struggled to carry her into the house and laid her on the couch.

"Oh, Jake! Your poor feet! What have you done?" my mother exclaimed, her voice rising in alarm.

I glanced down to see my feet, now a mottled blue and purple, staring back at me like frozen stumps. It had been a foolish decision to venture outside without shoes. I sank to the floor, overwhelmed by exhaustion, unsure how I had managed to stay upright for so long. My mother hurried to wrap blankets around my feet and shoulders, while Pete did the same for Jade.

I should have been the one helping her. I felt utterly useless.

"Oh, Jake. I'm sure the paramedics will check on you too when they arrive," my mother reassured me, her voice trembling slightly. "They said it might be a while because of the snow, so I called Dr Orton as well. He'll come as quickly as he can—luckily, he was at the Monroe's Christmas Eve party, so he should be here soon."

I hadn't seen Dr Orton in years. The last time was when he tried to diagnose me with schizophrenia, which sent me fleeing to another doctor in a different city—someone who didn't know my history or the traumas I'd faced. The last thing I wanted was for him to see me like this, especially with Jade in the mix. Jade already thought my upbringing was excessive; if she found out we had our own on-call doctor, I'd never hear the end of it. It could very well be the last straw for her. I felt so out of place in her world, despite my best efforts to fit into her life after I left home.

Pete was gently patting Jade's forehead with a damp cloth as she groaned softly. But if Dr Orton was the closest option, then that was for the best. I wanted Jade to receive care as quickly as possible, but I couldn't bring myself to leave her side, not with them discussing me behind my back. I couldn't let them poison her thoughts about me the way they had poisoned my own.

My mother had lit a fire, adding logs to ward off the chill that clung to the room. An uneasy sense of déjà vu washed over me. I was transported back to that Christmas Eve, after Midnight Mass, just before Lucy vanished. We had come home to this very room, where my father had lit the fire while my mother lay on the couch, cradling her head in her hands. Lucy and I had sat quietly, watching her slowly recover. Lynne had made us hot drinks, while my father sipped whiskey, engaged in a hushed conversation with her. I couldn't recall the details, but I remembered Lynne's anger simmering beneath the surface, after being called back so late on Christmas eve. Once my mother regained her composure, she sent us off to bed with a merry Christmas wish. But the excitement I usually felt for the holiday had vanished; I sensed that when my mother was cross with Dad, it meant turbulent days lay ahead, and I would bear the brunt of her anger.

There was a sharp knock at the door.

"Thank God, Doctor Orton is here!" my mother exclaimed, rushing down the hallway to answer it.

"Here we go," Pete sighed, clearly sharing my disdain for the so-called medical genius.

"Marcus! Thank you so much for coming so quickly on Christmas Eve!" my mother greeted him with an enthusiastic hug and a kiss on the cheek.

Her face lit up with a brightness that seemed almost unnatural. I always found it strange how she could flip the switch for guests. But that was my mother— trained by her wealthy upbringing and her relationship with my father to put on a show. It was something my dad never had to think about as long as he remained polite enough.

"It's no bother at all, Antonia. I was just a few minutes away, though the roads were treacherous," Doctor Orton replied, shaking his head with a hint of frustration. "I'm truly sorry to hear about Jim. It's just horrible. I wish I could have done more for him, but once you go to Ashmoor…well, you know what I said when we admitted him. It's hard to come back from that."

He had been the last doctor to have significant contact with my dad before they took him to the hospital, where he had languished. It felt fitting that he had tried to have me declared insane shortly after, as if he held a personal vendetta against our family.

"No, it's alright. I always knew something like this would happen…he was just too fragile after Lucy," my mother's voice trailed off as they approached the doorway to the living room.

"Here she is… Jade, sweetheart, are you awake?" My mother gently guided Doctor Orton toward the couch where Jade lay. A small groan escaped Jade's lips as her eyes fluttered open.

"Oh dear, that's quite a nasty cut," Doctor Orton said, leaning closer. "Jade, I'm Doctor Orton. I've been treating the King family for thirty years, so you're in good hands." He flashed a smug smile, and I couldn't help but feel a twinge of annoyance. Now Jade would know we had a personal doctor instead of relying on the usual clinic like everyone else.

"Hi," Jade replied, her voice barely above a whisper.

"How are you feeling?" he asked, his tone professional yet reassuring.

"Dizzy and a little sick," she admitted.

"That's understandable; hitting that tree must have been quite a shock. How many fingers am I holding up?"

"Two," she answered correctly, a flicker of confidence emerging.

"Good. Now, follow my finger."

He continued with a series of tests, his demeaner calm and reassuring. After a few minutes, he turned his attention to the cut on her forehead. Thankfully, it wasn't deep enough to require stitches and looked worse than it was. By the time he finished cleaning and applying a bandage, Jade appeared much better, her confidence returning as she began to engage in conversation more freely.

"Thank you, Doctor Orton. I can't believe I made such a fuss over nothing. I'm really sorry you had to come out here on Christmas Eve," Jade said, her voice a mix of embarrassment and relief.

"It's no trouble at all. That's what I'm here for. Besides, I was eager to meet the newest member of the family," he replied, casting a quick glance at my pale feet. "Jake, maybe next time you should wear some shoes to keep your feet from freezing!"

Jade's expression shifted as she hesitated. "Oh, before you go…could you check something else?" Her voice wavered, her eyes darting anxiously around the room.

"Of course, what do you need?" Doctor Orton leaned in, sensing her unease.

Shakily, she stammered, "I…uh… Can you check for a baby's heartbeat?"

"Are you pregnant? If so, how far along?" he asked, his tone shifting to professional concern.

"Yes, I am, but not very far at all—maybe just a couple of weeks."

Silence fell over the room, and I struggled to process her words.

"Well, congratulations to both of you! Antonia, it looks like you're finally going to be a grandmother!" Doctor Orton announced, a smile brightening his face.

I felt breathless, trying to find the words, but my vision blurred with emotion.

"I can't believe you two didn't tell us! This is wonderful news," Pete chimed in, giving me an encouraging pat on the back.

Jade smiled at me, her eyes shimmering with joy. "I only found out today, and that's one of the reasons I was so eager to come back."

Finally, I regained my composure and embraced her tightly. This wasn't part of our official plan, but now that it was happening, I realized I wanted it. We had watched friends start families of their own, but I hadn't given it much thought for myself. Jade would make a wonderful mother, but I worried I didn't have the right guidance after the nightmares of my own upbringing.

"Are you okay?" she asked, pulling back slightly to look at me.

"Yes, I'm glad. Are you?"

"Yes." I felt warm tears fall from her cheeks onto my neck.

"This is a marvellous Christmas present," my mother joined in the embrace. Instinctively, I recoiled from her touch, a wave of discomfort washing over me. Six years of abuse after Lucy's disappearance had made me wary of her sudden closeness.

We broke the hug to allow Doctor Orton to check on the baby, though he couldn't do much without the proper equipment. He advised that we head to the hospital as soon as the ambulance arrived.

"Jake, your mother mentioned your recent struggles. If the dreams are returning, you really need to see someone," Dr Orton said, lingering in the doorway as if hesitant to leave. "It's more than just depression when it comes to your family history. Don't let it consume you the way it did your father. You don't deserve that fate."

He paused, giving me a steady look before continuing. "Call me the day after Boxing Day, and we'll sort something out. I'll see you on Friday for the funeral, and congratulations on the baby." With that, he offered a polite smile and headed outside with Pete, who had volunteered to help clear some of the snow.

I should probably help too, but I couldn't bear the thought of being around him any longer than necessary, especially after he'd just diagnosed me with various disorders.

After what felt like an eternity, the ambulance finally arrived an hour later. By the time we were seen and discharged from the hospital, it was nearly five in the morning. Thankfully, both Jade and the baby were okay, which brought me immense relief. The nurse had informed us that Jade was six weeks pregnant, a reality that felt surreal. I had imagined the day we'd discuss starting a family, but now it was thrust upon us under such chaotic circumstances. I wished we could keep this news from my mother and Pete for a while longer, but there was no escaping it now.

"You didn't mention you thought you might be pregnant," I said as we drove home. This conversation had been on my mind since I found out, but with everything that had happened, the hospital had hardly been the right setting for it.

"I didn't really know. I just noticed I was late and felt nauseous. I ended up taking the test at a service station during our drive back. I wish I could have told you in a better way," she said, her gaze fixed on the road ahead.

"It's okay. I'm just relieved you're alright. Is this what you really want?" I asked, immediately regretting my question.

"Yes, of course. I… I wasn't really thinking about it before, but it feels like the next step."

"So, you want to become parents?" I probed again, trying to wrap my head around the news. While I knew Jade was ready and would be a wonderful mother, the reality of it left me feeling uncertain. I hadn't been well lately, and I couldn't bear the thought of repeating my father's mistakes.

Jade took a deep breath and met my gaze for a brief moment. I kept my eyes on the road; patches of snow still clung to the sides, and the icy surface made driving treacherous.

"Jake, I don't really know. A couple of months ago, I think I would have been thrilled. But right now, I'm not so sure. We need to figure things out, especially with your family. You have to mend things with your mum and find the closure you need. You may not get the answers you seek—honestly, I'm not sure you will. I want that for you so badly, but you need to understand that it's possible you won't find closure. And if we're going to have a family, we need you to be strong."

Her concerns mirrored my own. I was the problem.

"I know. I'm going to try, I really am. We'll stay for the funeral and help my mom with a few things, but then we're leaving—and we're not coming back. Being here has only made everything worse; I was fine for years. We just need to go home and forget all of this. I'll go back to therapy… I'll arrange it as soon as possible." I gripped the wheel tighter, my knuckles turning pale.

Jade placed her hand gently on my thigh. "Jake, I think that's exactly what you need to do. I believe in you. You've been here before, and you can find your way back to normal again."

Her encouragement was well-intentioned, but I hated the implication that I wasn't normal. The support felt great, yet it rang hollow. She didn't truly understand what I was facing. This was so much worse than before. I was seeing my little sister more vividly than ever, and she was dead. I didn't want to admit it, but I wasn't envisioning her as the twenty-six-year-old woman she should be now; Lucy was still seven in my mind, and the conviction that she was haunting me was growing stronger. Ever since her disappearance, I'd tried to forget her and the tragedy that surrounded it, and I had done a commendable job—until now. My memories and guilt had resurfaced a couple of times, but never this intensely. I hadn't returned home while grappling with these feelings, and it was exacerbating my dreams and my mental state. I wasn't sure if I was spiralling or if Lucy was truly trying to reach out to me. Even saying it aloud sounded insane, yet I could differentiate between my mind playing tricks and experiencing something inexplicable.

"Jake, I will help you through this. No matter what. We just need to get through the next few days. Are you okay?"

I wasn't okay.

"Yeah… I'm just really tired. Tired of everything. I miss her. I don't understand why it seems like I'm the only one who cares about what happened to her, and why it only seems to affect me!" I burst out.

"You know, when we were young, my mum and dad adored her. They bent over backward to make sure she was happy and safe. She was completely loved. But once she disappeared, it was like they just stopped caring. Nobody talked about her much, unless it was just the three of us at home. I don't think she was just kidnapped, Jade. Something isn't right. I've never felt the same after she vanished." I confessed, feeling more vulnerable than I had with anyone other than my therapist. Talking about Lucy had always been a taboo, something I had learned to avoid.

"Maybe it was too hard for them to talk about her? They might have just wanted to stay strong for you," Jade suggested gently.

"No, you don't understand. She wasn't allowed to be spoken about. When she was, it felt like I'd brought up an awful topic. When family or friends came over, nobody mentioned her. It was almost as if she didn't exist. The police came when she first went missing, but then never again. I didn't realize it at the time, but that's not normal. When a seven-year-old goes missing, there should be a massive investigation, right? They should want to find a little girl. It should have

100

made headlines…but there was nothing." I looked at Jade, my heart heavy with helplessness.

"I've always thought that was strange. Your family has money too, so why wouldn't they put all those resources into finding her?" she said, her voice quickening as if her mind was racing with theories of its own.

"I think we need to reach out to more people besides your mum because you haven't gotten answers from her in years. The funeral might not be the best place to bring up Lucy, but you'll have a chance to see a lot of people you wouldn't usually encounter…they might have information that could help," Jade suggested.

"You're right. Derek Hall will be there; he was a close friend of my dad's. He was a chief superintendent and worked on the case at the time…he should have some information. He's still pretty high up; he's the commissioner for the region now," I replied, recalling him. It was strange how someone could slip from memory for years, only to resurface when they were needed.

"That's exactly who we should talk to! You're not a child anymore; you have every right to know what happened in the case. If your mom won't tell you, I'm sure he will," Jade said, sounding hopeful.

"I'll try to speak with him, but it's a matter of whether he even shows up… I'm not sure if he and my mum were on good terms when he left. I don't even know if he visited my dad while he was in Ashmoor…" My stomach twisted at the memory of the hospital and my father's final moments. Tears welled in my eyes as I blinked furiously, trying to keep them at bay. It still didn't feel real that he was gone; I hadn't fully processed it yet.

Here I was on Christmas Day, driving back from the hospital with my pregnant wife, lost in thoughts of my deceased father and my missing sister. This wasn't how I had envisioned spending the day just weeks ago, when I was in my classroom, gripped by terror at the sight of Lucy for the first time.

"Jake, you're going to be a great dad," Jade said, her voice steady and reassuring. "I know you're worried about your mind and what happened to your dad, but you aren't him. You're going to be amazing. I love you." She smiled as I took her hand and kissed it, slowing the car as we approached the gates.

I waited for them to open, my heart racing as we drove down the long drive. We couldn't see the house yet, but I could sense it looming ahead. My blood ran cold, and tension coiled in my muscles as I held my breath. This place felt anything but welcoming; an unsettling energy hung in the air. Jade shifted in her seat, crossing her arms and tapping her fingertips nervously against her nails.

The atmosphere was thick with anxiety and fear, suffocating in its intensity. Home should be a sanctuary, but this one felt like the opposite as it finally came into view. No lights shone from the windows yet—it was still early. At least I could avoid my mother for a few hours.

Chapter 15

Jade and I slept through most of Christmas Day, utterly drained from everything that had happened. I wasn't exactly eager to face my mum and Pete downstairs. Classical jazz floated through the house, mingling with the clinking of glasses and bursts of laughter. Somehow, despite everything, they'd managed to find some holiday cheer.

Jade was still resting, so I decided to go looking for answers on my own. Most of my dad's things had been cleared out, but he'd handled all of Lucy's adoption paperwork back then. If I wanted any hope of finding something about her past—about how she came to us—I'd have to search through whatever was left of his old records. Asking my mother was pointless; she'd just lie or shut me down.

The attic seemed like the best place to start. It stretched across the entire house, packed full of years' worth of family belongings, like a crypt for old memories. I hadn't been up there since I was sixteen, back when I'd helped mum store some of dad's things after he was admitted to the hospital. I remembered seeing a few boxes with old notepads inside, some still with pens tucked between the pages. I never knew him to keep a journal, but it didn't mean he hadn't. If one of those notebooks held anything useful—anything that could shed light on Lucy's disappearance—I had to find it.

I moved quietly, climbing the narrow, creaking stairs up to the attic. Each step felt colder, as if the chill here had seeped in from years past, preserved alongside everything left behind. When I reached the old brass doorknob, it was icy, tarnished from years of neglect—definitely not a place my mother visited anymore. Turning the handle, I braced myself, hoping the door wouldn't betray me with a loud groan. It only creaked softly, and I let out a breath I didn't realize I'd been holding.

The attic was exactly as I'd remembered but even more cluttered, almost frozen in time. Boxes were stacked haphazardly, their labels faded, and white sheets cloaked long-abandoned furniture and forgotten toys. Dust coated everything, turning the place into a gray, untouched archive. My father's belongings must be here somewhere; I was certain some of them had ended up here when he was admitted. I scanned for any clue among the piles—anything that might hold answers about Lucy, or about us.

As I sifted through, I saw fragments of my own life packed away, things I had long forgotten or never bothered to collect. But there was nothing marked with Lucy's name. Her belongings had been preserved in her room, like a haunting tribute, untouched and cherished, while my old room had simply become a guest room—nice, neutral, forgotten. I guess that's what happened in this family: if you disappeared, you became a relic. But if you stayed, you became a burden.

I spotted it—a box I had carried up all those years ago—sitting at the back near a tiny window with the thinnest pane of glass. This corner had become a haven for dust, and a thick layer covered the box where my father's notebooks were stored. I grabbed an old sheet draped over a dusty mirror and used it to wipe away some of the grime, exposing half of the mirror in the process. I promised myself I would put it back later.

Inside the box, there were at least fifteen to twenty notebooks. I began to flip through them carefully, noting the varied contents—some pages filled with business meeting notes, reminders, games of noughts and crosses, and doodles. Then, I stumbled upon a thick leather-bound book. The first page caught my attention with the words:

"Sunlight Society of Black Bears" Jim King – Keeper of the Books.

What the hell was this? I had never heard my dad mention being part of a society, let alone that he held the title of "Keeper of the Books." While I knew he had a tight-knit group of friends, I never thought they would form an organization. I flipped through the pages, desperate to make sense of it all. There were numerous entries, dates, times, and notes about transactions, mostly from the 1990s. My heart raced as I reached the year 2001—the year Lucy entered our lives.

I leaned in closer to scrutinize the details. The entries were bizarre, filled with peculiar names, many of which were animal references. For example, 'Dog' was 'loaned' to Ted Andrews on March 9, 2001, for one month. What did that even mean? Then I saw 'Tiger', which was 'gifted' to Jude Collins on April 5, 2001, permanently. But it was the next entry that made my breath catch: 'Mouse' was 'leased' to Jim King on October 31, 2001, for £2,000 per month for three years, facilitated by Derek Hall.

I dropped the book, its thud reverberating in the silence of the attic. My stomach churned as the implications settled in. My father had always affectionately called Lucy his little "mouse," and I had thought it was a simple term of endearment. Now, it felt like a coded reference to something far more sinister—the purchase of a child. I had never known the specifics surrounding Lucy's adoption or the circumstances leading up to it. I was only nine when she came to live with us, and I had assumed that the adults had discussed matters I wasn't privy to. Yet, her arrival felt so abrupt; I remembered my mother scrambling to prepare her room, sending Lynne out to buy clothes in a hurry, as if she had just materialized in our lives one day.

It was glaringly obvious now: my father had effectively bought her from a friend for three years. That was how long she had been with us—just over three years. But why only three years? What happened once that time was up?

I felt a wave of nausea wash over me as I tried to piece it all together. The implications were too heavy to bear. Did my parents even know the full story behind Lucy's adoption, or had they been kept in the dark just like me? My mind raced with questions I couldn't answer. What kind of life had she led before coming to us? Had she been a victim of something far more sinister than I ever imagined?

I leaned back, trying to process the weight of what I had just uncovered. Suddenly, a dark shadow flickered in the corner of my vision. I glanced around, but nothing was there. A chill crept up my spine, and I sprang to my feet, clutching the notebook tightly as I rummaged through the rest of the box. Other books contained similar transactions, but there was no further mention of Lucy. Surely there had to be some documents related to her? Did my mother know about all this? It was hard to believe she would let my father engage in such actions. There had to be another explanation. My parents were wealthy; they didn't need to resort to illegally acquiring a child.

As I lifted another book, a loose photograph slipped from its pages and fluttered to the ground. My heart stopped when I recognized the figures in the image. I knelt down, my breath hitching as I picked it up. My dad's familiar grin stared back at me, his arm draped protectively around Julia's waist. A small bump protruded from her white long-sleeved T-shirt, indicating that she was pregnant. She looked younger than I remembered, almost like a teenager, and though her hazel eyes were filled with a hint of pain, she wore a smile.

I studied the photograph, taking in the sight of my dad and Lynne's niece together. His hand gripped her tightly, and a strange sense of intimacy radiated from the image. I hadn't realized he and Julia had been this close. They knew each other, of course, but not to the point of sharing photographs and holding each other like this.

That bump on Julia's stomach made my knees buckle; fortunately, I was already crouched down. I had never known Julia to have a child, and that was something Lynne would have definitely told me about. She often spoke of Julia—like a mother would to her daughter—sharing countless stories of their time together. I had met Julia many times, especially after Lucy moved in, when I found myself alone while my mother took Lucy out to 'bond'. Julia was always wonderful with me, almost like the big sister I never had. I often felt a stronger connection to her than I did to my own family.

Could she be Lucy's real mother? I turned the photograph over, searching for a date, but found none. My dad appeared slightly younger than I remembered, though not by much. The real change was in his expression; he looked genuinely happy. I don't think I'd ever seen a picture of him with my mother where they both seemed so carefree. Most of our family photos were meticulously staged and pre-planned, complete with matching outfits. I had never come across a candid shot of them as a couple, but here was my dad, smiling broadly, radiating joy alongside Julia. They looked like a couple in love—despite the glaring age gap—awaiting their first child.

But if Lucy was my dad and Julia's daughter, then why did he need to 'loan' her from Derek Hall? The question gnawed at me, unravelling the thread of understanding I thought I had about my family.

A wave of dread washed over me, and I inhaled deeply, feeling my hands tremble as my breath quickened, becoming increasingly difficult to control. The realization struck me like a thunderclap: my father was involved in something sinister.

The last time I had seen Julia was on New Year's Eve, when she stood at our door, engaged in a hushed, urgent conversation with Lynne. I'd watched from the stairs, my heart racing as I sensed the tension between them.

"No! You can't do that to them, Julia!" Lynne's voice was frantic.

"Why not? They've done everything they can to hurt me!" Julia sobbed, her pain palpable.

"Lynne, have you seen Jake? He needs to get ready!" My mother called from somewhere downstairs, interrupting the conversation.

Julia left in a hurry, and Lynne closed the door with equal swiftness.

By this point, I had retreated, not wanting to be caught eavesdropping.

Why had Julia been so distressed that day? What had happened to her afterward? It felt like she had vanished from our lives entirely. When I asked Lynne about visiting her, she casually mentioned that Julia had moved away with her boyfriend and started a new job. I hadn't even known she had a boyfriend, which struck me as odd—Lynne usually shared everything about Julia. After Lucy disappeared, Julia's name rarely surfaced in conversation, and no one ever brought her up.

At the time, I had no reason to doubt Lynne's words and had simply let the memories fade. I had wanted to suppress all the painful experiences from my childhood, and somehow even the good moments had slipped away with them.

A fleeting shadow darted across my vision once again, accompanied by a chilling breeze. My mind tried to convince me it was just a bat, but my trembling hands betrayed a different reality. A heavy, foreboding presence settled on my shoulders, making my head feel as though it were filled with cement. Reluctantly, I glanced up, catching a glimpse of her reflection in the half-covered mirror. This time, Lucy looked angry. Only her face and shoulders were visible, the draped sheet obscuring the rest of her.

By now, I braced myself for what I knew to expect. Her piercing blue eyes seemed to bore into my very soul. Unlike before, she wasn't dirty; she resembled the way I remembered her—clean, with brown hair framing her small, round face.

"Lucy," I whispered, my voice quaking.

"Please don't be mad at me. I'm sorry," I pleaded, desperation creeping into my tone.

Her head tilted slightly as if she were weighing my words.

"Are you real? Are you dead?" I managed to ask, though I already knew the answer.

Slowly, she parted her lips, inhaling the cold, dusty air. Moving closer at the same deliberate pace as before, she seemed to be carefully considering her approach. I held my breath, captivated by her beauty, which shone through the pain she carried. It had been so long since I'd seen her like this. My little sister, stunning and delicate, like a perfectly preserved porcelain doll, suddenly crashed through the tall mirror, landing with a soft thud in front of me.

I screamed, scrambling backward, my hands pushing against the floor as I tried to escape her. When she had been in the mirror, I could convince myself it was all in my head, but now, with her so close, I could no longer deny the reality. Shards of glass rained down around us as the sheet fell away from the floor-length mirror, revealing both our reflections in the fractured glass. A coward stared back at me, tears streaming down my face, while my sister remained motionless. I didn't want to look at her, but my body betrayed me, forcing me to turn my head.

"I'm so sorry," I sobbed, my eyes drawn to her once-beautiful face, now transformed into something horrifying. Her eyes were black, piercing my very soul, while a dull ache throbbed in my head. Her skin was an unnatural pale, tinged with shades of blue and purple. Deep lines carved into her once-chubby cheeks, now long gone. The dirt under her fingernails returned as blood began to trickle from her forehead, splattering onto the floor with a sickening thud. It poured from her, thick and relentless, creating a pool of crimson that swirled across the floorboards like a predator stalking its prey. A metallic stench filled my nostrils, making me gag.

"Find me," she croaked, her voice hoarse and raspy. The sweet, light tones I remembered had aged decades in an instant.

"Where?!" I pleaded, desperation clawing at my throat.

She stared at me, cold and silent, her gaze holding me captive for what felt like an eternity. The blood ceased to flow, and terror gripped me; I couldn't tear my eyes away.

"Ahhhhhhhhhhhh!" she screamed, suddenly breaking her gaze. Her arm lifted as if to shield herself from an unseen threat.

"Please—Ahhhhhhh!" she cried out as her arm was yanked forward, the fear in her eyes palpable as she struggled to catch her breath.

"Help me, Jake!" she pleaded again, her innocent face reappearing, filled with a desperate longing for my aid.

I froze, paralyzed into silence.

In an instant, she was hurled into the air and slammed hard against the ground, the impact visibly distorting her fragile form. Her small body seemed to shrink even further, fingers twitching helplessly. Desperate breaths escaped her lips, her eyes searching for me. I crawled to her side, a cold realization dawning on me—she was dying. Her leg and neck were grotesquely twisted, and blood began to trickle slowly from her head, quickly escalating to a torrent. Her once bright blue eyes, filled with life, now stared blankly into the void.

"I'm so sorry," I whispered to her lifeless form, my tears burning as they streaked down my cheeks. My sister was gone, and I felt responsible for her demise. Deep down, I had always known the truth, but witnessing it was a new depth of anguish I had never imagined. I cradled her still body, weeping uncontrollably until the tears ran dry, leaving me hollow.

"Jake?" Jade's voice echoed from the other side of the attic. "Jake, are you in here?"

I lay on the floor, my head pounding and my eyes heavy with sleep. Jade's footsteps grew louder, inching closer. Gathering what little strength I had, I rolled onto my side, struggling to rise to my knees, groaning at the pain that radiated through me. I felt as if I'd been run over by a truck.

"I'm here!" I called out, my voice strained.

"Where?"

"By the—" I began, but my words faltered. The large mirror, once shattered and revealing the horrific scene, was now restored, save for one lingering crack. Lucy's body had vanished, along with the blood that had pooled around us. Had it all been a dream? Was I slipping further into madness, or was it simply the weight of stress? The box remained, along with the notebooks and the photograph of Julia and my dad, a stark reminder of the truth I had unearthed before Lucy's apparition had appeared.

"Babe, what are you doing?" Jade's voice broke through the haze as she found me on the floor.

I wasn't about to confess that I had just witnessed my sister and watched her seven-year-old self die in front of me, impossible as that seemed.

"I came to look through some of my dad's old notebooks to see if I could find anything and lost track of time," I replied, realizing that it was dark outside. I must have been up there for hours.

"Did you find anything?" She settled down next to me and picked up one of the notebooks.

"Yeah... I found something troubling. My dad and Julia—she's Lynne's niece—I think they were together. Look at this picture of them. She's pregnant, right?" I asked, my voice tinged with uncertainty.

"She is pregnant…and she looks really young, maybe eighteen or even younger. Your dad looks to be in his late thirties at best. Does your mum know about this?"

"I have no idea. I don't think so, but I can't be sure."

"You have to tell her. Or at least ask her about it. She might know something."

"I can't talk to my mum about it. She'll freak out if she doesn't already know. If this is Lucy's mum and dad, then… I don't know what that means." I felt the weight of the revelation pressing down on me.

"Well, where is Julia now? Is she local?"

"I have no idea. Lynne told me Julia moved away right after Lucy disappeared, and I never saw her again."

"What? Jake… That can't be a coincidence. What if Julia took Lucy? If Lucy is her kid, then why wouldn't she try to get her back?" Jade reasoned, her brows furrowing.

"No, Julia wouldn't do that. And if it's true, my dad wouldn't let Lucy go willingly with her. He was shattered after Lucy went missing; it drove him to madness. He would have searched for her. Julia lived with Lynne; she wouldn't have had the means to just disappear with Lucy."

"But what if she did? Maybe she was too young when she had Lucy, and one day she decided to come back for her. Perhaps it was an agreement at first, but then she regretted it and took action." Jade offered, her tone hopeful yet cautious.

"I suppose that makes sense… But Julia never really spent time with Lucy, did she?" I pondered, trying to recall, though now I wondered if I had missed something crucial.

"If Julia did leave with Lucy, and Lynne possibly helped her…then Lucy could still be out there." I felt a flicker of hope ignite within me. It was the first time in years I had entertained the thought that Lucy might still be alive.

"Look at this," I said, holding up the notebook and pointing to the page detailing Lucy's transaction. "My father was part of some society that was involved in buying and selling things in dubious ways."

"Who are all these people?" Jade asked, her brow furrowed as she scanned the names. "Jude Collins, Derek Hall, Ted Andrews, John Monroe, Thomas Price, Marcus Orton… Who are they?"

"They're my dad's friends, all influential in the town. Jude was the mayor when I was younger, and Derek used to be a police officer assigned to Lucy's case—he's the commissioner now. Mr Andrews is the principal at my old school, and John lives next door in the other estate. I think Thomas is our old reverend, but I can't be sure of his last name… I don't know any other Thomas'. Marcus is Dr Orton, the one who came to help you. I've known most of these guys my whole life, but I never saw them all together like this. I can't believe Reverend Thomas or Mr Andrews would be involved in something like this—or my dad, for that matter. It just doesn't make any sense!"

"How well did you know these men?" Jade probed.

"I mean, I was just a kid back then, so I didn't really know them well. But I trusted them at some point. They were always around for family parties and events. Derek is my godfather, and Dr Orton literally nursed me back to health a few times. As for Jude, I only knew him briefly; he never really interacted with me and Lucy. He was probably too busy. I do remember him being quite interested in Lucy during a midnight mass right before she disappeared. My mum acted strange about us talking to him, and there was even a fight between them that night. But if Derek is the one who 'sold' her, what role would Jude have played?"

"I don't know, Jake. Maybe you should take this to the police?"

"No way. Derek is the police commissioner now. I need more concrete evidence before bringing a twenty-year-old notebook and a photograph to them."

"Well, you need to start asking questions then. Lynne might be a good place to begin. Or what about Bill? He was around back then, right? He worked alongside Lynne, so he might know something or have seen something."

I hadn't considered that. Bill was our gardener and groundskeeper then, and he still was now. He didn't work daily like he used to; my mother could no longer afford that, but he came around often enough to keep the grounds in order. He would be showing up before the funeral, with the wake being held in our house.

"Yeah, I'll talk to him tomorrow – he's an odd character, you know he keeps a loaded shotgun in the shed? He let me try it out one time and my mum went nuts. I don't know how he didn't get fired." I half chuckled at the memory and half at Jade's shocked face.

"My mum must have some idea about all this—there's no way she hasn't looked for answers herself, being here alone all these years." I said changing the subject back on track.

"Why wouldn't she want to help find her own daughter?" Jade asked.

"I'm not sure. She seemed determined when Lucy first went missing, but that resolve faded, and we stopped discussing her. It felt like Lucy was always there with us, an elephant in the room we couldn't ignore, but eventually, we just stopped talking about her. I think that's what drove my dad mad. It drove me mad, too! I needed to talk about her, but it felt so forbidden, and I never got the chance to know how my parents really felt. For all this time, I thought it was just too painful for them, but now... I wonder if it was the shame of losing her, or maybe of how they lost her in the first place."

Everything was starting to click into place regarding how my family had crumbled after Lucy's disappearance. The grand parties that once filled our home had ceased, and my parents' friends had vanished from our lives. My dad had stopped working as much, leaning more on alcohol to cope, while family members distanced themselves. I had been pulled from school, left to languish alongside my parents in our hollow home.

"Jake, I'm so sorry you've had to carry this burden your whole life." Jade placed her hand over mine, gently stroking it.

"Let's grab something to eat and get some rest," I suggested, feeling the weight of the day pressing down on me.

Chapter 16

That night, we managed a few hours of restless sleep. It was, without question, the worst Christmas Day Jade had ever endured. For me, though, Christmas had long been a hollow tradition. After Lucy disappeared and my dad was taken away, the holiday had lost any magic it once held. My mum would go through the motions—piling gifts under the tree and insisting on a proper Christmas dinner—but it always felt forced, like a poorly rehearsed play we both dreaded performing. Once I turned eighteen and left for university, I avoided coming back during the holidays whenever I could. Jade and her family had become my escape, helping me create new, lighter memories. But even those couldn't dispel the shadow of unfinished business that had loomed over me for years.

Boxing Day arrived with a quiet intensity. Bill would be here soon to tidy the grounds for tomorrow's funeral, and Lynne was expected to clean the house. I knew I couldn't avoid the difficult conversations waiting for me. Jade still slept soundly in our bed, her breath steady as I slipped out of the room. In the kitchen, I tried to force down some breakfast, but the oats just sat there, untouched, as my thoughts churned. Through the window, I spotted Bill out by the fountain, tending to the frost-covered grass that led to the edge of the woodland.

It was time to confront the past, one conversation at a time.

As I approached Bill, I noticed him crouched by the fountain, tugging at weeds that had forced their way through the cracks in the concrete, curling and clawing at the edges like they were trying to reclaim the structure. He let out a groan as his back cracked audibly, a sound that made me wince. Bill shouldn't still be doing this; his body had long since earned the right to rest. I wondered why he hadn't retired—or why my mother hadn't insisted on it. He had to be well into his seventies by now, though he'd seemed old even when I was a child. His dark skin was deeply lined, his once-strong hands gnarled and weathered. His grey hair, cropped shorter than I remembered, had receded further, and I noticed the small curve of a hearing aid behind his ear.

"Jake!" Bill's face lit up as he saw me, his voice as warm and familiar as ever.

"Hi, Bill." I stepped forward and hugged him without hesitation, the gesture as natural as breathing. The earthy scent of leaves and damp moss clung to him, filling the air between us.

Being back here wasn't easy, but seeing Bill reminded me of the parts of my childhood that had been safe and kind. He'd always been there for me. When my father was too busy or too far gone, Bill stepped in. He had his own family, of course, but by the time I came along, his kids were grown with lives of their own. That left him plenty of time to kick a ball around with me or lend an ear when I needed it—especially after my dad ended up in Ashmoor.

"How are you, son?" Bill asked, his voice carrying the same warmth it always had, as if no time had passed at all.

"I'm okay...but I just—I don't know," I admitted, struggling to put my feelings into words.

"I know, Jake. I know." His face softened, and he sighed deeply. "I'm so sorry about your dad. He was like a son to me, you know. A good man, always. Even when he was in the hospital, he made sure I was taken care of—kept me on here, even though I didn't expect it." A faint smile tugged at his lips, though it didn't reach his eyes.

"I didn't know that..." I muttered, a few tears slipping down my cheeks as I thought about my dad.

"You know, you could always retire, Bill," I said gently, trying to shift the conversation. "I'm sure my mum could find someone else to keep things running. You don't owe us anything."

"No, Jake." He shook his head firmly. "I need the work. It keeps me moving, keeps my mind sharp. And these gardens... I've been tending them so long, they feel like a part of me. It'll be a sad day when I can't come out here anymore." His gaze fell to the ground, as though the thought pained him.

I hesitated, unsure how to approach what I really wanted to ask. "Bill, can I ask you something?"

"Anything, Jake." His tone turned serious, and he straightened up slightly.

I took a deep breath, steeling myself. "I was up in the attic yesterday...looking through some of my dad's old things. Just trying to find something to take back with me as a keepsake," I lied. "And I found a picture. Of my dad...and Julia. Lynne's niece. You remember her, don't you?"

At the mention of Julia, Bill shifted uneasily. The easy warmth in his expression was replaced with something heavier—hesitation, maybe even worry. "Yes," he said after a pause, his voice quieter now. "I remember her. What sort of photograph was it?"

I pulled the picture out of my back pocket, my hands trembling slightly—maybe from nerves, maybe from the lingering emptiness in my stomach. I held it out to him, watching closely for his reaction.

Bill's eyes flicked over the photo quickly, then darted away. He opened his mouth as though to speak but closed it just as fast, his lips pressing into a thin line. Something was on the tip of his tongue, but he held it back.

"Bill...were they together? Did my father have an affair?" I practically pleaded, my voice trembling under the weight of my own desperation.

"Well... I..." Bill hesitated, his words faltering as he glanced down at the photo again. "I wasn't sure... I've never seen that photograph before. But your parents...they weren't always happy, you know. I think your dad might have stepped out, and I'd heard whispers about him and Julia. People talk, Jake."

He was holding something back; I could feel it. The nervous shifting of his feet, the way his gaze darted around the garden but never landed on me for too long—it was obvious.

"Please, Bill," I urged, leaning closer. "Just tell me what you know. Is Lucy my dad and Julia's child? How long were they together? Does my mum know about them?" The questions poured out of me in a rush, my brow furrowed, my chest tightening.

Bill let out a deep, weary sigh, bowing his head as if the words he was about to say carried more weight than he was ready for. "I don't know what your mum knows, Jake," he began cautiously. "And I can't say for sure about Lucy. Maybe she was...maybe she wasn't. What I do know is that one day, she just appeared. Out of nowhere."

He straightened slightly, his voice growing quieter, as though sharing a secret he had kept buried for years. "Your parents acted like they'd been planning to adopt for ages, but that wasn't true. With you, there was all this excitement— fanfare, preparations, everything. But with Lucy..." He paused, shaking his head slowly. "It was sudden. Abrupt. She was just *there* one day. And I didn't question it. I didn't think it was my place."

His words hung heavy in the air, mingling with the earthy scent of the garden. My thoughts raced, colliding with one another in a blur of confusion and realization. Bill's hesitation only made the pieces fit together in a way I wasn't sure I was ready for.

"Bill, you didn't know about my dad and Julia?" I asked bluntly, pressing him for an answer. He hesitated. "I'd seen them together a few times, in the chapel... Julia was so young, I didn't realize who she was at first." He gestured towards the chapel where we'd held midnight mass. "They were...you know...involved. Your dad asked me not to say anything, but I didn't feel right about it, so I told Lynne. Julia meant the world to her, and I knew she wouldn't take it well. She didn't, and I thought that was the end of it. Your dad wasn't happy with me for a while after that, but I heard they kept going. I shouldn't be telling you this, Jake... You don't need to hear about your father's mistakes."

"No, Bill... I need to know who my dad was and what happened to Lucy. I know he got her in a strange way, but I think he might have been her real father. Please, I have to know." My voice was tight with urgency, and I could feel my desperation rising.

"Lucy's been gone almost twenty years, Jake... The police searched for her. I don't think you'll find anything more." Bill's voice faltered as he spoke. "Don't do this to yourself... Look what happened to your dad when he dug into it."

But I couldn't stop. "Bill... What aren't you telling me?"

He looked down, taking a deep breath. "You need to talk to Lynne... She was there, she knows more than I ever wanted to. But be careful, Jake... You might find answers you don't want, answers that could hurt more than you can imagine. Think about your mother, too, before you go digging any deeper."

He sighed, turning back to the weeds as if to end the conversation. His old back creaked as he got back to work, leaving me standing there, feeling the weight of his words. I watched him for a moment before walking away, my thoughts already moving to the next person I needed to confront: Lynne.

Lynne was busy tidying up the kitchen, wiping down surfaces and clearing away the remnants of my breakfast. The bowl of porridge I'd left behind had already been put away, and a wave of guilt washed over me. I suddenly felt like a child again, as if I was back in that time when Lynne had always been the one picking up after my messes.

"Hey, Jake!" She looked up from her work, her face lighting up as she made her way toward me. "Are you okay? I heard about Jade's accident from you mum. Also, congratulations sweetheart. You're going to be a great father." She gave me a warm, tight hug.

"Thanks, Lynne… It hasn't really sunk in yet, with everything going on." I sighed, feeling the weight of the situation pressing down.

"I can imagine. I'm just trying to get everything sorted for tomorrow. Normally, I wouldn't come in today, but of course I had to make an exception. I'll make Jade some lunch too. I checked in with her, and she's resting." She gave me a soft smile.

"You don't have to do that. I can make something for her… You know, Jade and I do everything ourselves—cooking, cleaning. I'm not the snob I used to be," I joked, trying to lighten the mood.

"You were never a snob, Jake." She shook her head gently. "I do it because I care about you, not because it's my job. It's not about duty—it's about love. I still see you as my boy, even though I don't get to see you much anymore."

Her words, though not meant to sting, hit me harder than I expected. It was as if she was reminding me of the distance that had grown between us, and I couldn't help but feel the weight of it.

"I'm sorry," I said, my voice catching. "I miss you, but…being here—it just hurts. I come back, and everything feels so broken." My eyes welled up, and I couldn't hold back anymore. The exhaustion of the last few days had finally caught up with me, and I was too tired to pretend.

"It's not your fault, Jake," Lynne said gently. "He'd been ill for so long. He had his demons… I know you're hurting, but honestly, it was going to happen. He was never going to be the same." Her eyes were filled with concern, but I wasn't sure if they were for me or for him.

"Lynne…" I hesitated, bracing myself for what I needed to ask. "I need to know…why did my dad feel so guilty? Why did he carry that weight?"

She didn't speak at first, just looking at me like she was waiting for more. I pressed on, the words slipping out before I could stop them. "Yesterday, I was in the attic, looking through some of his things. I found a photograph of my dad…with Julia." I let the silence hang between us, watching her face carefully, but she didn't react. She already knew, I realized. Bill had told me enough.

I took a deep breath before continuing, "In the picture, they were close… Julia's stomach—she was definitely pregnant. I'm sure of it. Was my dad… Was he in a relationship with her? Is Julia Lucy's real mother?"

I held out the photograph, the same one that had been burned into my mind. Lynne stared at it, her eyes blank, almost as if the image didn't register at all. Then, after what felt like a long time, she finally spoke.

Lynne slowly set the photograph down on the counter, her hands trembling slightly. She didn't meet my gaze, her eyes fixed on the picture, as though she could somehow disappear into it. For a long moment, she didn't speak, and I felt the weight of the silence press down on me.

"I never wanted you to know this, Jake," she finally murmured, her voice barely above a whisper. "But…yes, your father and Julia were involved. They were…more than just friends. I don't know how long it had been going on, but I know it wasn't just a fleeting thing. They were close." She paused, as if gathering the courage to continue. "And about Lucy… I don't know for sure if she's his child, but I wouldn't be surprised. Julia…she never made much sense of it either. She came to us with the child one day, and they acted like it had always been the plan. But it wasn't, not really."

I could feel my heart pounding in my chest, each beat like a heavy drum. "What do you mean it wasn't the plan? How could they just—"

"It was complicated, Jake. Your father and Julia…they had their own issues. And Lucy? I'm not sure she was ever meant to be a part of their lives, not in the way she ended up being. I think your dad tried to make things right, but there were too many secrets, too much guilt."

I could barely breathe, the air thick in my lungs. "So…what does that mean? Did my father—did he know she was his daughter?"

Lynne didn't answer right away. She seemed lost in thought, as if the words were stuck, unwilling to leave her lips. "He knew. He knew, but I think he buried it deep inside. It's why he was so…troubled. It's why he couldn't let go of the past. And why he couldn't look at you, Jake, without seeing the mistakes he made."

The words hit me like a punch to the gut. My father—my whole life, I'd wondered why he seemed so distant, so broken. And now I had the answer. But it only raised more questions.

"Lynne…" I swallowed hard. "If my father knew, then why didn't he do something? Why didn't he try to fix it?"

Her gaze softened. "Because he couldn't, Jake. Some things…they're just too far gone. Your father, he had his demons. And I think he thought that by keeping Lucy away, by not acknowledging what happened, he could protect you. Protect everyone. But in the end, it only made things worse."

I felt a cold, hollow ache inside me. The pieces were starting to fall into place, but it didn't make the puzzle any easier to solve. I was tangled in a web of lies and half-truths, and I didn't know if I was ready to face all of it.

"So where does that leave me now, Lynne? What am I supposed to do with all of this?"

Lynne looked at me, her eyes full of pity and something else—something I couldn't quite read. "I don't know, Jake. I really don't. But I think… I think you need to know the truth. Whether you're ready for it or not."

"Yes…" Lynne's voice trembled, her gaze distant as she spoke. "Your mum wasn't happy about it but she knew. I think it took her a while to realize it was Julia, but eventually, she did. I think she wanted to believe it wasn't happening, but she couldn't avoid the truth. After Lucy came here, they stopped seeing each other. Julia came back to me after that, but by then, she was a shell of the person she used to be. When I saw her with you over the years, I could tell she was still struggling. When she came to live with me, it was a different story. She was so broken. That's why I let you visit her – it brought her a little happiness. But she still struggled with abusing drugs no matter what." Lynne's voice cracked, and she wrapped her arms around herself, stifling a sob.

"I'm so sorry, Lynne. I didn't know Julia had been through…that," I murmured, my heart aching for her.

"With addiction?" she asked softly, her eyes clouded with old pain. "It was hell. Your dad tried to help her. Paid for rehab a couple of times, but your mum put a stop to it. Then, for a while, Julia seemed to be doing better…until everything came crashing down. It was just after Lucy went missing that Julia left. I think she was done with it all. She told me she wanted to leave, just take off. All she left behind was a note: 'Gone away. Not sure when I'll be back'. And that was it. I didn't hear from her again. I thought maybe your dad's situation would bring her back, but she could be anywhere now."

"You haven't heard from her in nearly twenty years? Isn't that strange?" I pressed, feeling the panic rise. "And she left around the same time as Lucy. You don't think…maybe she has Lucy with her?" My words tumbled out in a rush. "Do you have any idea where she might've gone?"

Lynne's face hardened. "No. Lucy was already gone by the time Julia left. Don't you dare try to suggest Julia had anything to do with it," she snapped, her voice rising. "She was a good girl, and your parents ruined her. I can't talk about this anymore."

Her words hung heavy in the air, and the tension in her voice left no room for argument. "Your mother's looking for you," Lynne said coldly. "You should go find her."

"Lynne-"

"Go and speak to your mother. I think it's something to do with the funeral." She dismissed me. I'd offended her now and I knew better than to carry on with her.

I found my mother in the living room, cradling a cup of tea. She and Pete had stayed up late last night, and I'd only caught a brief glimpse of her to exchange gifts before Jade and I retreated to bed. She'd seemed disappointed that I hadn't joined her for Christmas dinner, but understood Jade wasn't feeling well. The truth was, I hadn't had the energy to face my mum and Pete yesterday, not after what I'd discovered in the attic. I was afraid of pushing my mother for answers the way I had with my father. Despite her occasional harshness, I knew how fragile she could be. Guilt weighed heavily on me from my dad's death, and I didn't want to add to it.

"Morning, sweetheart," she greeted, offering me a small smile. "How's Jade?"

"She's alright. I think she'll be down later, but she needs some rest."

"Of course. I can't believe how much has changed since you both arrived. Usually, things are so quiet, but now it's all happening at once. Your dad, the baby…it's a lot to take in." I was surprised by how understanding she was. Not long ago, she had been so angry with me about my dad.

"I'm sorry about Dad. I never meant to upset him like that." I said, sitting in the armchair beside her.

"Oh, Jake." She sighed, reaching out and giving my hand a gentle squeeze. "Don't blame yourself for that. He's finally at peace. Yesterday, I went to the chapel to pray for him. It felt so strange, but there was this warmth…almost as if he was there. I've never felt that kind of presence before, that kind of love. It really comforted me. I was upset at first, but I shouldn't have been so hard on you. Your father…well, it's been a long time coming. But I believe he's finally forgiven himself, and now he's resting. And I forgive him too." She closed her eyes for a moment, as if gathering herself.

"I didn't know you still went to chapel. I don't think I've stepped foot in there since that last Midnight Mass we did."

She shifted, sitting up straighter and opening her eyes. "I didn't go for a long time either. But shame isn't a good reason to stay away. It's brought me some peace that I didn't know I needed. I feel closer to Lucy, to your dad, now. That's why we'll have the service in our family chapel. It's the right thing to do for him. He'll rest there, with the rest of the family."

A lot of our family had been buried or had their ashes scattered near the chapel, a tradition meant to keep us close, even in death. But things had changed when Lucy went missing. After that, nobody wanted to rest here. Even my great-uncle, who'd passed away a few years ago, had his ashes scattered at a local church instead.

"Oh… I thought the wake was here tomorrow," I said, feeling confused. "Are you sure about having him in the chapel?"

"Yes," my mother replied, her voice steady. "I know I pushed your dad away for a long time because of everything. He wasn't perfect, but maybe I should've forgiven him sooner. If I had…maybe he wouldn't have gotten so sick. Maybe he'd still be here."

Her face twisted with the effort to hold herself together, her emotions starting to crack.

"Mum, why were you so angry at Dad?" I asked, though I already knew some of the reasons. I needed to hear it from her.

She stared blankly for a moment, as if weighing her words. "He wasn't always easy to be around, Jake. You remember that, don't you? But even before all that, he was hurtful to me. I don't want to make you hate him, but it wasn't the fairytale I thought it would be when we got married. I thought things would get better once we had you, then Lucy, but it never did. He never changed. No matter what I did, he was never happy."

She let out a heavy sigh, as if the weight of the years had finally come to rest on her chest.

"What exactly did he do, Mum?" I pressed, needing clarity.

Her voice grew steady, almost detached. "He was unfaithful. Over and over, without remorse. Whenever I confronted him, he made me feel like I was overreacting. Everyone knew about it—our friends, our family. But I still had to put on the façade of being the perfect wife. It wasn't fair, Jake, and he let it go on for years. He didn't want a divorce, not because he cared, but because of how it would look. I went along with it for a while, but after Lucy, I wanted to leave…and he stopped me. He had all the power. If I left, I'd have nothing: no house, no money…no you. I never had a career of my own, and he knew how desperate I was. He kept me here. I was almost relieved when he got too ill to be of any use." She said it with a finality that hit me hard—her words laid bare a truth I'd never understood.

"I had no idea you felt that way, Mum." My throat tightened. "Did you know who he was having these affairs with?"

"No." Her answer was quick, too quick. "I didn't know them, Jake. Just…just women from clubs, I guess. It doesn't matter now." She dismissed it as if it was all part of the past. "We don't need to dwell on that. What matters now is moving forward. Your father's death…in a strange way, it might bring us together. I can't wait to be a grandmother, to spend more time with Jade. And we have so much room here—you can come and stay anytime. We'll rebuild, start fresh as a family."

I felt a wave of frustration building. "But, Mum, I need answers first. I need to know what happened to Lucy. Where did she come from? And where did she go? We can't just sweep her under the rug like we have for the last nineteen years. She deserves more than that." The pain in my chest grew heavier as I realized how easily my mother seemed ready to let go of the past, as if everything had already been forgotten.

Her eyes fluttered closed again, and she let out a heavy sigh. "Jake, we're never going to get those answers. There was no trace of her, and we don't know what happened. You need to understand that. This will haunt you forever if you don't let it go."

"Fine," I said, my words tight with frustration. "I'll just let go." I stood abruptly, the anger bubbling up inside me, and stormed out of the room. As much as I wanted to confront her about Julia, I knew the timing was wrong—right before my father's funeral. Maybe she didn't even know it was Julia in the picture, and I couldn't bear to think of what that would do to her. I wasn't ready to cause her more pain.

Chapter 17

I was up early, bracing myself for a day filled with relatives arriving for the funeral. Most of the guests would either be strangers to me or people I hadn't seen since I was a teenager. The thought of making small talk with those who hadn't been around when we needed them was the last thing I wanted, but I also knew there were a few who might have answers about Lucy—answers I desperately needed. I even asked Jade to subtly ask questions. Maybe people would open up more to her, an outsider in their eyes.

"Jake, your grandmother is here! Come down to see her!" my mum's sharp voice called from downstairs.

"You ready for this?" Jade asked softly.

"Yeah. It's just my grandma. She's…fine. A little cold, but fine," I replied, adjusting my shirt.

"Your dad's mum?" she clarified.

"Yeah. She's in her eighties now. Last time I saw her was at my graduation. She and my mum hate each other, though. Always have. When Dad was in the hospital, she was furious with us—thought it made him look weak. Said she was embarrassed." I shook my head at the memory.

"Jake! She's almost at the door!" Mum's voice grew more urgent, as though the Queen herself were arriving.

"Let's go before her head explodes," I said, rolling my eyes.

Jade smirked and leaned in, pressing a small, tender kiss to my lips. For the first time in what felt like days, the tension in my chest loosened, if only for a moment. I lifted my hand, gently cupping her face, letting the world outside the room fade. "Thank you for being here," I whispered.

"I'm always here for you. Through everything," she replied, her smile soft but resolute. It was all the strength I needed to face what lay ahead.

The door shut behind her with a heavy thud, and the weight of her presence seemed to fill the entire room. My grandmother, Constance, glanced around the house with a critical eye, as if cataloguing every speck of dust and flaw in the decor.

"Jake," she said briskly, patting my arm in what might have been her version of a hug. Her sharp blue eyes softened for a moment, but it didn't last. "You've grown into a fine man. I only wish it were under different circumstances that we'd see each other."

"Yeah, me too," I replied, stepping back and trying to ignore the chill her words left behind.

That's why I let you visit her – it brought her a little happiness Pete cleared his throat, clearly eager to move past the moment. "Can I get you something to drink, Constance? Tea, coffee?"

"No, thank you," she replied, her eyes narrowing slightly. "I came for the service, not for pleasantries." I could feel my mother bristling beside me, her lips pressed tightly together. "Well, it's good of you to come," she said stiffly, her tone betraying the tension simmering beneath the surface.

I stepped in quickly, not wanting this to spiral into another one of their legendary battles. "Grandma, why don't you sit down? It's been a long trip, and there's plenty of time before the service starts."

Constance hesitated for a moment before conceding, lowering herself into the armchair with an air of regal disdain. Jade and I exchanged a glance—her subtle smirk told me she'd already pegged my grandmother for who she was. As Pete disappeared into the kitchen, likely grateful for the escape, I sat down beside Constance. "How have you been, Grandma? It's been a while since we've seen each other."

"Yes, well," she began, smoothing her dress, "things have been…busy. It's not easy to lose a son, Jake, even if he was…complicated." Her voice faltered slightly, but her expression remained composed.

I couldn't help but wonder what exactly she meant by 'complicated'. It wasn't the time to ask, but the question lodged itself in the back of my mind like a thorn.

"I'm sorry about Dad," I said, catching the overpowering scent of her perfume as I leaned in.

"What are you sorry for?" she replied flatly. "You're not the reason he did what he did. Honestly, I'm surprised it didn't happen sooner." Her tone was cold, almost dismissive.

"This is my wife, Jade," I said quickly, steering the conversation away before it could spiral.

"Hello, Jade. I'm Constance King, Jim's mother." She extended her hand, a gesture far too formal for family. There was no way she'd accept a hug from someone outside the bloodline.

"It's so good to meet you," Jade said, taking her hand in both of hers. "I'm so sorry for your loss."

"Thank you, Jade. Losing my boy is awful. Especially since I lost him mentally years ago," my grandmother replied, her voice trembling faintly. "Seeing him in that…state was a different kind of grief."

I swallowed the sudden knot in my throat. I'd never considered how my father's decline must have affected her. But then again, she had chosen to leave us to deal with it alone.

"Have Lynne make me a tea, please," my grandmother said, waving a hand dismissively. "And Luther, take my bags to my room."

Luther, her driver and assistant for as long as I could remember, stepped forward with a quiet nod. In his sixties now, he had become more of a caretaker than an employee, though I couldn't imagine she treated him any kinder than she treated us.

Without waiting for anyone to respond, my grandmother rose and moved toward the adjoining sitting room. She made a beeline for her usual seat—a grand, ruby armchair that had once belonged to her father. She sank into it with an air of entitlement, as though this house still belonged to her. And, in her mind, it did. She'd given it to my parents as a 'wedding gift', but I knew better. It was hers, and we were simply its temporary custodians, no matter how long we lived here.

"Jade, come over here," my grandmother commanded, her tone leaving no room for discussion.

"Good luck," my mother muttered under her breath as she slipped into the kitchen.

Jade hesitated, her eyes flicking toward me for reassurance. I gave her a small nod, though I felt the same weight of Constance's unyielding presence. She could easily intimidate anyone unprepared for her sharp words or cold demeanour.

"So, come and tell me about your lives," Constance began, her gaze flicking dismissively between us. "I wasn't invited to your wedding, and I don't even know what you two are doing now."

"It was a very small wedding, Grandma," I explained, keeping my voice measured. "But I'm sorry for not telling you. It's just been such a long time since I'd seen anyone."

Constance waved my apology off as though it were an afterthought. "It's all right, Jake. Your mother should have been the one to make sure you were all right, and she didn't. She was never a natural mother or homemaker." Her words dripped with judgment, and I fought the instinct to defend my mum—though I knew it wouldn't make any difference.

Jade stepped in, likely sensing the tension. "I work at the university as a lecturer, and Jake is teaching at a school."

"Oh, a teacher..." Constance said, her lips tightening into something resembling a smile but lacking warmth. "How ordinary. I always thought you were destined for bigger things, Jake. I understand you have inheritance to fall back on, but you should at least aim to build your own wealth. Secure any future generations you may bring into the world."

I bit back my irritation. This was exactly why I'd distanced myself. If I'd stayed in touch, I wouldn't have been allowed to live my life on my terms. A teacher was unthinkable in her world. She would have steered me toward law, finance, or some other prestigious path. But I'd chosen freedom over her expectations, knowing full well she saw it as a betrayal.

Constance's sharp eyes lingered on me, filled with quiet disappointment. Once, our family had been the talk of the town—an esteemed name woven into the community through wealth, charity, and influence. But the weight of that legacy had dwindled. Constance, too old to maintain the grand façade, now rarely appeared at social events, and the name 'King' carried less reverence than it once had.

Even my uncle, Ethan, had abandoned the family mantle. He'd moved to America in his twenties and severed ties with my dad long before Lucy came into our lives. Growing up, I'd been too scared to ask why he didn't stay in touch. My mother had only ever told me he had a family of his own—a wife and two kids—and they never visited.

For Constance, I was the last hope of salvaging what remained of our family's legacy. But I'd walked away, and her eyes bore into me now, a reminder of her quiet disapproval.

"Is Uncle Ethan coming today?" I asked, hoping to steer the conversation in a different direction. The moment the words left my mouth, I could feel the shift in the room. It seemed to hang there, catching my grandmother off guard.

A heavy silence followed, stretching on longer than I expected.

"I don't know," she replied curtly. "Perhaps you should aim for a promotion and look into a position at a private school. I could speak to Ted Andrews, see if he can pull some strings for you at your old school." She barely acknowledged my question, clearly eager to change the subject.

"I'm happy where I am. I don't plan on moving anytime soon," I said, trying once more. "Has Uncle Ethan been in touch? I haven't heard from him."

I pressed the question again, but her response remained elusive.

She took a slow, deliberate breath before speaking. "Jake, I don't entertain nonsense. You know well that I have no intention of speaking to Ethan again until he decides to stop running from his problems and blaming everyone else. Your father understood what he was like. I had hoped your father would be different, but even he couldn't hold it together in the end. You, though, Jake—you're capable of more. I know you don't have the drive right now, but in time, all of this will be yours."

Her words caught me off guard. It was more than I expected to hear from her.

"You know, once you're ready for it, this house is yours. I'm not sure your mother has told you, but this place rightfully belongs to you now. You've started a family, so it's time for you to make it your own. Your mother needs to move on. It's time for you to bring some life back into King House. Don't you agree, Jade?" She asked, and I realized my mother must have already mentioned that we were expecting.

Moving back to my childhood home with Jade felt like a nightmare I never wanted to face. The thought of returning to this place, with its suffocating memories and haunting silence, filled me with dread. I would've preferred to leave it empty forever. Every inch of this house seemed to carry the weight of old pain, and I couldn't help but feel like it was slowly making me worse. No wonder my dad had deteriorated so quickly—this house had its own way of dragging people down.

"Oh, wow…that's such a generous offer. I didn't realize it was like that," Jade said, her voice full of surprise. "It's such a shame there aren't any children here now. I was telling Jake how lucky he was to grow up in a house like this.

My place was tiny, especially with all of us living there, and the garden was barely big enough for anything. This, though…it's incredible in comparison." Her tone was more upbeat, almost excited. It hadn't even crossed my mind that Jade might consider living here; I assumed she'd feel the same way I did.

"But we're really happy in our own home in Manchester," I added, squeezing her hand for reassurance. "It's close to work, and Jade's family."

"Right, it would be a big change since we're settled already," Jade agreed, nodding in understanding.

"Well, you shouldn't let work dictate where you live. You can work anywhere," she said, her voice tinged with a hint of finality. "But homes like this are rare. My grandfather had this place built in 1895. It's important to keep it in the family, to preserve it. He had many children, including my father, who fought off his siblings to claim it. He was my grandfather's favourite, just like I was his. Life was simpler then. We did what we were told. It's not like that anymore. Today, everyone wants something. I'm glad they were all gone before they could see what happened to this family."

Her words hung in the air, heavy and bitter. Her lips pressed together tightly, as if holding back more painful memories.

She was a shell of the woman she once was, all joy long gone. Her standards were so impossibly high that even if I gave in to her demands, it would never be enough. Guilt began to creep in as I watched her frail body shrink, her eyes downcast, avoiding ours. But then I caught myself, remembering what I'd learned in therapy over the years. She was the adult who had let me down, who had abandoned me when I was most vulnerable. When Lucy went missing, I was shattered, and all she offered was cold indifference, leaving us to struggle alone. Now, with my father gone and no one left to uphold the family image, she finally pretended to care. It wasn't love—it was duty. I was the last hope for this family, the one she could mold into what she wanted. If anyone else were around to carry the torch, she'd push me aside without hesitation. If she knew that I was seeing Lucy regularly again, I knew exactly how she would react—her 'love' would vanish in an instant.

"Why don't you try talking to Uncle Ethan? I know he and Dad had their issues, but what exactly happened? If he's your only son, don't you think he has a right to King House?"

Her expression hardened immediately. "Absolutely not, Jake. Ethan gave up any claim to this house the day he left. He knew what it meant when he walked away. He never understood the way your father and grandfather handled things—didn't have the stomach for it. If he ever came back, willing to accept his responsibilities and play by our rules, then yes, perhaps. But he doesn't get it, and he never will."

She sighed heavily, the air between us thick with the weight of her words.

Just then, the loud bang of the front door slamming shut echoed through the house, followed by a violent cough. Bill. He always let himself in, no matter what, and I felt a wave of relief. His presence would interrupt the tension.

"In here, Bill!" I called out.

His shuffling steps grew closer, and soon enough, Bill entered, with his wife Deb following behind. She didn't know the family as well as Bill, but he always spoke so fondly of her. She must have come along for moral support.

"Awful day," Bill muttered, settling into a chair beside Deb. "It's good to see you all, though. I just wish it were under better circumstances."

"It has been a while," Constance said, her gaze cold and distant as she ignored the gravity of the situation. "Do you still work here, Bill?"

I gave Bill a half-hearted smile, grateful for the change in conversation.

"Yes, ma'am. Only a couple of days a week now, but it's enough to keep me going. I really am sorry about Jimmy. I miss him." Bill's voice faltered, and he looked down, placing his hand over his mouth.

"Me too, Bill," Constance replied quietly, her expression hardening. "It's a shock, but…in a way, it was expected. That place didn't help him. All it did was keep him sedated. It was cruel, really, keeping him in there. But where else do you put someone like him?" Her voice softened, but the bitterness lingered.

The decision to place my dad in Ashmoor had been my mother's, though she had been persuaded by family and friends for months leading up to it.

My dad had been acting erratically for almost two years before we brought in a nurse, but even that wasn't enough to stop what was coming. At times, I couldn't tell whether his ramblings were from drinking or from another episode. The screams from his room became unbearable. He'd been moved to one of the guest rooms, and we tried to contain him as best we could. On the rare occasion when he was lucid, he'd talk about wanting to go back to work or see his friends, but it never lasted long. Eventually, when he started holding conversations with a wall in public, it was clear he needed to be kept inside. I hadn't reached that point yet, but I couldn't shake the fear that it might one day be my future.

A loud thud jolted me from my thoughts. Jade's lips curled into a faint smile, clearly trying not to laugh at my reaction. After all, it was my father's funeral, and there was no telling who else might have shown up.

"Who's that?" Constance asked sharply, her eyes narrowing toward the hallway.

"I have no idea," I replied, just as my mother rushed past the doorway to answer it. For a fleeting moment, I wondered if it could be Uncle Ethan, finally deciding to show up. After all, only close family was supposed to be meeting here first—Bill and Lynne included.

The creak of the front door opening broke the silence, followed by a pause so heavy it seemed to press down on the room. We all leaned in slightly, straining to catch a clue.

"Hi, Toni." The voice that followed sent a jolt through me. It was one I hadn't heard in years.

"Lisa? How did you know?" my mother asked, her tone more stunned than welcoming.

"Word gets around, Toni. I'm so sorry." The sound of an embrace followed as my aunt Lisa's voice softened.

Another unexpected guest. Death has a way of drawing out people you thought you'd lost forever.

Lisa had been a fixture in my childhood—my mother's sister and, for years, one of her closest friends. Then one day, she was just gone. No more visits, no calls, no explanations. Her absence had hurt more than I could admit, especially when I was young enough to still hope for stability. But now, here she was, arms around my mother as if no time had passed.

Jade nudged me gently, her expression asking who had arrived.

"My Aunt Lisa. On my mum's side," I whispered.

Before Jade could respond, my grandmother interjected, her tone sharp and impatient. "Jake, you should be helping your mother. This is your father's funeral. It's your duty to greet the mourners with her." She didn't even look at me as she spoke, as if my lack of action was yet another disappointment in her eyes.

Her words sent a jolt of anxiety through me. I stood up quickly, my steps hesitant as I made my way to the front door where my mother and Lisa stood. Their embrace lingered before they slowly pulled apart, and Lisa's gaze found mine.

Her face softened with guilt, her expression almost maternal as she studied me. Though I was thirty-one, I could tell she still saw the boy I once was. The boy she had known before everything fell apart.

"Jake," she said, her voice tender as she opened her arms to me. "I'm so sorry about your dad, sweetheart."

Without hesitation, she pulled me into a hug. It was warm and familiar, unlike the stiff, obligatory gestures I was used to from most of my family. Lisa had always been the exception—the only one who gave me genuine affection when I was younger, more than my parents ever did.

"It's okay, Lisa. It's good to see you…even under these circumstances," I replied, my voice quiet but sincere.

Before she could respond, my mother's voice broke through. "Oh, there's Reverend Thomas!" she said, her tone shifting as she peered out the window.

Lisa pulled back, her brow furrowing. "He's going to be here?" she asked, her voice tinged with surprise—or was it something else?

"Of course he is. Jim considered him one of his closest friends, and he conducted countless services in our chapel. That sort of bond doesn't just disappear," my mum said with a touch of finality.

I hadn't seen Reverend Thomas since that last Midnight Mass, just before Lucy disappeared. I remembered overhearing his voice once after that, speaking in hushed tones with my parents late at night when I was supposed to be in bed. But publicly, he'd distanced himself from our family for years. At the time, I hadn't thought much of it—my focus had been consumed by grief for Lucy and, later, by the chaos of my father's decline. But now, with the clarity of adulthood, I could see how many people had abandoned us. Adult after adult who should have been pillars of support had simply walked away.

My father's so-called friends vanished when his life began to fall apart. My mother's friends and family had done the same, leaving her to shoulder the wreckage of our family alone. Surely, we couldn't have been surrounded by so many unkind people. But the pattern was undeniable.

The sound of the door creaking open snapped me out of my thoughts. Reverend Thomas didn't knock or announce himself; he simply let himself in. His hair, still a deep, glossy black, gleamed unnaturally, defying his advancing years. Yet the lines carved into his pale face betrayed the passage of time.

"Antonia. Jake. My condolences for your loss. I pray you find solace in knowing Jim is now free from pain. He rests now with our Father and those who have gone before him," he said, his voice steady but detached.

His words were measured, his tone distant. For a man who had supposedly been one of my father's closest friends, he spoke as if delivering condolences for a stranger. This was my father—the man he had known for decades—and yet, he seemed utterly unburdened by any real emotion.

"Thank you for agreeing to help us during this time. It's what Jim would have wanted," my mother said.

"The last time I spoke with him, he mentioned my work. He said he admired it. Asked if I'd consider doing more in the chapel. I think he believed there were still regular services there," he replied, letting out a long sigh.

"You saw my dad? When was this? Did he say anything else?" I asked, suddenly intrigued. He might have shared something about Lucy. Talking to a priest, especially in his final days, would have seemed like the right moment to unburden himself.

"Oh, it was a few weeks ago. I'd visit your dad from time to time, offer some spiritual support. There was nothing unusual, Jake. Don't feel guilty. People make their own choices; no one is to blame for what happened," he said, his hand resting condescendingly on my shoulder.

I felt the weight of guilt press on me, but it wasn't about my father's death. If he had truly struggled with Lucy's disappearance, surely, he would have confided in someone like Reverend Thomas. Wouldn't that have been the moment to admit the truth?

"Right then, Antonia, let's go over the service one last time, shall we?" Reverend Thomas said, guiding my mother down the dimly lit hallway toward my father's old study. He moved through the house with a comfort that felt almost too familiar. My mother didn't seem bothered by it, but Pete's face tightened, his unease impossible to miss.

"Jake, could you make me a drink in the kitchen?" Lisa asked, her voice hesitant. We hadn't returned to the reception room, and I could tell she was avoiding my grandmother's icy stare. I glanced over at Jade, who gave me a quick nod and a small smile, silently signalling that she was fine on her own for now. At least she had Bill.

As I made my way to the back of the house, a chill crept over me. My hands began to feel numb, and my mind started to spin. Not today, I told myself. I couldn't afford to fall apart now. Today, I had to be present for my family—especially for Lucy. This might be my only chance to talk to people I might never be able to reach again.

I forced myself to take a slow, deep breath, focusing on five random things around me—a lamp, a chair, the floor, the ticking clock, and the kettle. Anything to ground myself in the moment.

"Jake, you look pale. Why don't you sit down? I'll make us some tea. I know how tough it can be to lose someone—when my father passed, we were young, but it still hit hard. It's never easy."

I sank into the chair at the small kitchen table, trying to steady my racing thoughts. "Why did you leave, Lisa? After Lucy disappeared. You vanished too. I think the last time I saw you, I was fourteen."

"No, you were sixteen," she corrected softly. "I stopped by on your birthday to drop off a gift…but you weren't well. You probably don't remember. I sent something for your eighteenth and twenty-first birthdays, but I never heard back. I moved away for a while. Your mother told me you'd left too, but I should've tried harder. The truth is, after Lucy…things just got too hard for me. I couldn't handle it anymore."

She paused, as if gathering herself, her voice faltering. "Your parents…they weren't the same. They became like vipers, always suspicious of everyone. And with everything that happened with your dad—well, it was too much for me. I couldn't stay in that environment. Your dad became violent, Jake. I tried to stop him, tried to get the police involved…but they wouldn't listen, and your mum just told me to stay out of it. So, I did. I'm sorry for that. I should've stayed."

I could see the weight of her words hanging in the air, the confession long overdue. It was clear she'd been carrying this burden for years, and I wasn't sure how to respond.

"I didn't know any of that." I leaned forward and gently took her hand. I needed my family, and Aunt Lisa had been a light in my life at various points, even though she'd always kept a bit of distance. My mother and Lisa had clashed often, and Lisa had always felt out of place in our grand, sprawling home. She had never married or had children, choosing instead to carve out her own path with independent projects, travel, and adventures, while my mother had settled into a more conventional life.

They hadn't come from a particularly wealthy background like my father's, but they were respectable. My mother had a knack for being in the right places at the right time.

She'd sought out my father, believing his life and wealth would offer something better than what she'd known. That belief had created one of the many rifts between the sisters. My father hadn't thought much of Lisa either. He used to say she asked too many questions, that she didn't contribute enough to society, and that she was an embarrassment when she came around. Once their mother passed when I was five, the distance between them only grew. There was no one left to force them together.

"I should've tried harder for you, Jake," Lisa's voice softened, and I could hear the regret in it. "It's not fair, the hand you were dealt. When I think about the life your mum and I had growing up…and then look at what happened to you, it breaks my heart. I begged Toni to leave after the garage incident. I was so scared for you. I offered to take you with me. But she wouldn't hear it. Everything was about appearances, always trying to keep up, ever since she met your dad. She wasn't like that before. It's like she lost herself in all of it."

The sorrow in her eyes was burning deep, and it left a heavy weight in the pit of my stomach. I hadn't realized just how much Lisa had cared, or how deeply she had suffered seeing what happened to me. To us.

I couldn't picture my mother living without caring what others thought, leading a life simply for herself. Even now, after being with Pete for ten years, she wouldn't let him be seen with us in front of anyone from her life with Dad. I wasn't sure Pete would even be allowed to sit at the front with us, especially not with Constance here.

"Jake, please know that I tried. I really did," Lisa said, her voice heavy with regret. "I was the one who called the police after the garage. Your mother wasn't thinking straight—she thought it would get better on its own. If this damn family didn't have all these connections, you would've been taken out of there, you know. It was wrong, all of it."

Her mention of the garage made me flinch. That was one of the memories I'd locked away, deep in my mind. It had been easier to pretend it hadn't happened, to push it aside because I'd been told to. I hadn't ever shared it with Jade or anyone. I thought it was just me and my mum who knew about it. And now, as Lisa spoke, the smell of the garage flooded my senses with brutal clarity. I didn't want to revisit that moment, but suddenly I was fourteen again, half-drunk, my face pressed against the leather seat of Dad's Mercedes as I lay there, feeling too tired to care about anything else.

Dad had suggested we move from drinking in his study to the car. I'd never been invited to drink with him before, so I'd known better than to question his decisions when he was drinking. We didn't talk about Lucy—her name was off-limits. Instead, he asked how I was adjusting to being homeschooled. I was on my fifth tutor in two years, I was never given an explanation for why the others had left. Three had simply stopped showing up one day. It wasn't like we couldn't afford it—my family paid well and gave great benefits. Lynne, Martha, and Bill had stayed around, as loyal as ever, but the tutors kept vanishing. It made no sense.

My seventh tutor, Dahlia, had stayed on until I finished school. She'd come after Dad was admitted to Ashmoor, and I think she stayed because she understood how lonely I was. She must have known what it was like, but I think it was also that she felt uncomfortable there—just like everyone else had.

"I don't want to go back to school, Dad," I mumbled, the thought of facing those boys again unbearable. The torment I'd suffered at their hands had made me dread returning. The isolation I felt—being kept away from others—only made it worse. I didn't want to be reminded that people thought my parents had Lucy killed for money, or worse, that they blamed me for her disappearance because I hated sharing my parents with her. None of it was true, but it was what they believed. And that gossip had lingered in the town long after the rest of the world moved on.

"Son, you have to go back to school. You need friends, or you'll end up like your mother," he said, his tone more sober than usual. "No friends, just depending on your husband for everything. You need people to help you, protect you."

His words didn't feel like the usual drunken rambling. I knew his ways too well by now. And though I was tipsy myself, something felt off.

"Nobody wants to be friends with the kid whose sister disappeared," I blurted out, my frustration spilling over. It felt like everyone—family, friends—had slowly pulled away. Even his own friends had stopped visiting.

"You're right about that," Dad muttered, his voice low. "Lucy was the worst thing that ever happened to us. I wish things had turned out differently... I do. But, I know your mother will never forgive me." He let out a long, weary sigh, staring straight ahead as the car engine roared to life. "I loved her, son. But sometimes…things just can't work out. I've tried not to blame myself and just move on, but this house, this family…it's cursed. Everyone's ashamed of me, and the damage is too much to fix. I know you don't understand all this yet, Jake, but you'll only inherit my sadness. All the happiness we once had…it's gone. It was never real. I was too much of a coward to give you or your mother what you really needed."

He rolled down the windows, but I couldn't muster a response. My mind felt too foggy to comprehend his words fully. I was too dizzy and exhausted, my body heavy, and sleep quickly took over.

"I always loved you, son," he murmured, but I was already slipping into unconsciousness.

I woke to find myself in my bed, Lynne's hand clasped in mine, her eyes wet with tears. My mother and Doctor Orton were standing in the doorway, their faces unreadable.

"He'll be fine, Antonia," Doctor Orton said, his voice steady. "You got to him quickly enough. Just keep an eye on him, and make sure he takes these every few hours." He handed her a blister pack of tablets. I ended up on them for a long while after that.

"Thank you, Marcus. Could you please keep this discreet? I'm happy to arrange a larger fee if necessary," my mother offered, her tone calm but strained.

"Of course. I'll be in touch." He nodded, then added, "I'd recommend keeping the boy away from Jim for now. It would also be wise to consider hiring a carer for his…mental health. It doesn't have to be documented if you prefer. I can arrange for someone from Ashmoor to make house calls. Jim's going to be difficult to manage with the new medication, so getting extra help now would be best."

"Yes, whatever you think is appropriate. Please send someone as soon as possible," my mother replied coldly, turning her face away from me as she spat the words. "I can't stand to look at him, let alone care for his miserable existence."

That was the beginning of the end for my father. He was moved into a separate section of the house, a room with its own bathroom and kitchen appliances so he wouldn't have to wander into the main house. The medication had him so fogged up that he could barely stand on his own. His mental state deteriorated rapidly, and his words became nothing more than incoherent rambling. Daniel, his nurse, eventually had to live with us full-time, caring for

136

him as his condition worsened. But even then, my mother insisted that Ashmoor was the only option. She said it was for the best, but deep down, I knew it wasn't about what was best for him. We had the means to take care of him, but I think my mother just wanted him gone.

I was kept away from my father as much as possible. I was only allowed to speak with him when my mother or Lynne were present. I didn't question it, not because I didn't want to, but because I understood why. My father had done terrible things to both of us. What he did to my mother was even worse. To leave her completely alone in that state seemed unbelievably cruel. They hadn't been in a good place for years, but why would he want to abandon her like that? I hadn't known that Lisa had called the police. Not that it had done any good. My father's so-called friends had most likely protected him, as they always did.

My thoughts drifted back to the kitchen where I gave Lisa a small, strained smile. My lips trembled as I fought to keep control.

"Hey, you two. We're heading to the chapel now," Jade called from the doorway.

My stomach twisted, heavy with the dread that had been growing for days. Laying my father to rest meant facing the truth of what had happened to him, and why. My mind told me it was his illness—he had been slipping away for years, and I had just been the final push. But deep down, my heart whispered that Lucy had a hand in it. She had been with him, guiding him toward his end.

The hospital couldn't explain how he'd gotten onto the roof. The CCTV footage had mysteriously been corrupted, a detail that still didn't sit right with me. I couldn't shake the feeling that it was a sign, a warning. Lucy was out there, and I was running out of time to find her.

I didn't want to end up like my father, lost to the same darkness. And I certainly didn't want to repeat his mistakes, becoming that kind of man for my own child.

Chapter 18

More than two hundred people filled the chapel, crammed together so tightly that some stood at the back or spilled out through the open doors. The air buzzed with hushed voices and shuffling feet, an almost oppressive reminder of how far our family's infamy had reached. I was stunned by the turnout. For years, we'd been pariahs—an isolated, broken family—and yet, here they all were.

Among the sea of faces, I recognized Ted Andrews, my old headmaster, standing stiffly near the aisle. Daniel, my father's nurse, sat a few rows behind him, his gaze firmly fixed on the floor. Jude Collins, the former mayor, was perched uncomfortably at the edge of a pew, and beside him, Doctor Orton and his wife exchanged sombre glances. Derek Hall, the police commissioner, nodded politely to someone across the room, while Dahlia, my former tutor, lingered near the middle, her hands clutching the strap of her bag tightly.

The crowd wasn't just old friends and acquaintances—there were also strangers, curious locals drawn in by the scandal that clung to our name like smoke. A few faces from my school days stood clustered in the corner, their eyes darting toward me. I spotted my uncle Ethan far at the back of the chapel, trying to stay hidden.

I sat in the front row, my eyes fixed on the polished oak casket that now held my father's lifeless body. As Reverend Thomas began to speak, my grandmother's frail hand gripped mine, her paper-thin skin scratching against my own. Her trembling was faint but steady, like the ticking of a distant clock. Beside her, my mother's breaths came in short, rapid bursts, a clear sign that the same dread crushing me was suffocating her too.

Above the congregation loomed a large photograph of my father and Lucy. He sat with her perched on his lap, a version of him I barely recognized now— vibrant, full of life, his dark hair slicked back and neatly combed, dressed in a sharp suit with his signature expensive watch glinting in the light. His face was lit with an effortless smile, the kind that once charmed everyone in the room.

Lucy mirrored his joy, her tiny arms looped around his neck, her laughter frozen in time.

I'd seen this picture before, tucked away in the shadows of his study, but blown up and placed here, it carried a different weight. Tragic. Haunting. It was as though this wasn't just my father's funeral—it was Lucy's too. Both of them gone, lost in different ways, but somehow, their absence felt eerily intertwined.

"God will now take Jim into His kingdom, where he shall find rest and be reunited with his beloved father and daughter," Reverend Thomas proclaimed, his voice steady and reverent.

The words pulled me sharply from my thoughts. I felt my mother stiffen beside me, her sharp intake of breath barely audible over the murmurs rippling through the crowd. My grandmother, silent until now, released my hand, her grip fading like the warmth of a dying flame.

The atmosphere in the chapel shifted palpably, the weight of Reverend Thomas's assumption pressing down on everyone present. Lucy. He had spoken as though her death was a certainty, a truth that had never been proven. Whispers rose from the back of the room, spreading like cracks in fragile glass.

To hear it said so boldly, in front of all these people, felt jarring—almost accusatory. Lucy's disappearance had always loomed like a shadow over us, unresolved and unspoken. To call her gone, here of all places, felt like another betrayal. My chest tightened as I glanced at the faces around me, scanning for their reactions. I couldn't tell whether they were grieving for my father, or for the ghost of a girl who might still be out there.

Thomas cleared his throat, his eyes quickly dropping to the floor as he pressed on. "Jim King was a pillar of this community for many years, as was his family. His work, his connections, all serve as his legacy. Jim had a rare gift— he could see the potential for friendships before they even began. I was honoured to call him both a friend and a partner in many ventures, as I know many of you would agree." His gaze shifted toward Ted, Derek, and Jude, each of them struggling to hold back tears. They had been close to my father once, but their absence during his later years, especially as his mental health unravelled after Lucy's disappearance, was a silent betrayal.

"Jim was a devout Christian who always put his faith first, using this beautiful building to host religious events and ceremonies to bring the community closer to God," Revered Thomas continued. It felt like a hollow lie. My father wasn't a Christian any more than he was a teetotaller. Officially, we were Church of England, but in every other sense, we weren't. The only reason we hosted these religious events was to maintain appearances, a way to show off to the community while my parents threw their parties afterwards, drinking and smoking, while Lucy and I were shut away upstairs.

What struck me more than the disingenuous words was the fact that only Revered Thomas was speaking—no one else had gotten up to say a word. A hymn chosen by my grandmother followed, and then a poem handpicked by my mother. Neither of them had any real connection to him. For someone who supposedly 'touched so many lives' and was so 'loved', there was nothing personal about this funeral.

As his only child, my grandmother had asked me to prepare a passage to read—a Bible verse. But it didn't feel right. It felt forced, like so many other things in this room.

"Now, I would like to invite Jake, Jim's only son, to read a passage from John 11:25 and 14:27," Revered Thomas announced, stepping aside to give me the space.

Jade met my eyes, offering a silent but comforting glance. My grandmother had insisted Jade sit next to her, positioning her as though to remind me of family ties, as if it would somehow make this moment easier. But all I felt was the weight of it.

I stood, my hands trembling so visibly that the paper crinkled in my grip. Each step toward the altar seemed to drag on longer than the last. I couldn't bring myself to look up. Not at the room, not at the people, and certainly not at the coffin that felt so out of place at the front of the chapel. I hadn't even dared to glance behind me since entering. Instead, I focused on breathing, steadying myself, as if talking to myself would make this all less real.

"I had planned to read some passages from the Bible, but it doesn't feel right. I think my dad would want me to speak about him, about who he truly was. When I was younger, we had a lot of good times together. He taught me how to fish, play football, and got me into westerns—something I still can't shake, unfortunately." I let out a small chuckle, and the sound gave me a little strength. I lifted my gaze just a bit, but I still couldn't bring myself to meet anyone's eyes.

"When it was just me and Dad, things were good. But then came Lucy, my sister, and I wish she could be here today. She made our family feel whole, and she brought out a gentler side of Dad. He truly loved her, and he never stopped feeling her loss. That's what it meant to be his child—he gave his love fully. I just wish he'd been able to face his pain sooner." My voice faltered, and a quiet sob slipped past my lips before I could stop it.

I glanced up at the crowd, feeling a wave of dizziness take hold. At the back of the chapel, I spotted something so familiar it made my blood run cold. There she was—Lucy. She stood perfectly still, vivid as ever, her crimson shoes cutting through the sea of black that surrounded her. Her face was gaunt, her expression twisted and unnatural. Slowly, her hand rose, and her finger pointed directly to the front of the chapel.

My eyes followed her gesture, landing on my mother and Aunt Lisa, sitting side by side—an unsettling sight, considering how distant they usually were. Lisa's eyes were brimming with tears, her shoulders trembling with quiet sobs, while my mother stared ahead, completely vacant, almost lifeless.

I quickly looked back to Lucy, but she was no longer at the back. She was closer—right in the middle of the aisle now, moving forward inch by inch.

Each step she took left behind muddy shoe prints, marking her path as she came nearer, until she stopped. And then, her eyes locked onto mine—her gaze so intense it felt like she was staring right through me. Time seemed to freeze. My heart pounded loudly in my ears, drowning out everything else. Sweat began to trickle down my forehead as I stood frozen, unable to move or tear my eyes away from her.

The room felt suffocating, the air thick with dread. My mind raced, trying to make sense of the impossible, but it was no use. Lucy's form remained before me, unblinking, her presence a suffocating weight. I couldn't breathe, couldn't think, just trapped in that moment where the past and present collided, and all I could do was stand there paralyzed.

"Find me!" Lucy's voice shrieked, the sound cutting through the air like a knife. I took a shaky step back, gasping for breath.

"Jake, it's okay. Come back to me now," Jade's voice was gentle, her hand reaching out to me. But I couldn't move. I had stopped speaking, my body frozen as the crowd around me stared with pity, thinking I had choked. They couldn't see her—the vision of Lucy, still standing there, pointing toward my mother and aunt.

The rest of the service became a haze, as if I were watching from far away. I couldn't make sense of the words being spoken about my father, the crowd's murmurs lost in a fog. One moment, the ground beneath my feet shifted and I found myself standing by the graveside, the oak casket being lowered into the earth.

The sound of sobs filled the heavy air. I saw my mother step forward, her hands trembling as she scattered the first few handfuls of dirt onto the casket. Then she let out a sound I had never heard from her before—an agonizing wail that seemed to reverberate through the very ground, all the way back to the house. I'd seen her cry before, heard her muffled sobs behind closed doors, but this…this was something different. A raw, unbearable grief that echoed in my bones.

The screams coming from her were raw and agonizing, like they were tearing through her from some deep, unspoken place. Pete moved toward her, trying to offer support, but she shoved him away, crumbling to her knees in despair. The whole scene felt painfully uncomfortable, a heartbreaking mix of grief and tension. I couldn't just stand there anymore.

"Mum, it's OK," I said softly, wrapping my arms around her, slowly pulling her into a comforting embrace. Gradually, her screams softened into quiet sobs. I whispered into her ear, "He's in a better place now. Maybe even with Lucy."

I didn't believe those words. I didn't believe he was with Lucy, and I certainly didn't believe he was in a better place. The truth was my father was probably in Hell—if there was any place like that. He'd never been given a chance to redeem himself, and neither I nor Mum had given him that chance. Perhaps that's why her reaction had been so violent, so unrestrained. It was too late for him now.

Later, at the house, everyone had returned for the wake. There hadn't been this many people here in years, but somehow, it felt like no time had passed. They moved through the house like it was still their home—familiar with the layout, knowing where the bathrooms were, where to find extra glasses, as if nothing had changed. Dad's old friends had even slipped into his study, which had been off limits for years. Derek and Ted were already pouring whiskey for their group when I walked in. Dr Orton, Reverend Thomas, Jude Collins, and John Monroe were sitting together, their voices low and heavy with sympathy.

"Jake! Son, I'm so sorry about your dad. He was a great man, a real loss. If only things had gone differently…" Ted said, his words trailing off.

I didn't know how to respond. "It's fine, Ted. Honestly, I feel like he was gone a long time ago," I said flatly, the weight of my own truth sinking in.

"Don't say that, Jake," Derek said, his voice soft but insistent. "He still cared about you so much…even after everything. He told me how sorry he was for that night, how badly he wished he could've been better. Some people just can't face their demons, and it comes out in the worst ways." He gave my shoulder a firm squeeze, as if to justify my father's actions—his attempt at murder-suicide that Derek had worked so hard to cover up.

Trying to shift the conversation, I asked, "What was the Sunlight Society?" The question hung in the air, abrupt and sharp. It wasn't the best time, especially in the middle of my father's wake, but I knew this moment would be fleeting. I'd never have all of them in one room again like this, and I was desperate for answers.

The temperature in the room seemed to drop. A heavy silence settled over the men, who had been laughing and exchanging stories just moments before. They all exchanged wary glances, as if silently deciding who would speak first.

Jude Collins, settling back in the armchair my father used to occupy, let out a forced chuckle. "Ah, that's just a name we used for our old group back in university days. Did your dad ever mention it to you?"

I hesitated, unsure whether to lie or confront them directly. "Yes, he mentioned something about you guys—the Black Bears—and some loan schemes. I didn't quite get it all, though. Something about a mouse, a tiger, and some other animals. Could you explain it? I think he said you gave him a mouse, Derek?"

Derek's whole body stiffened. His jaw clenched, and for a brief moment, his fist tightened as he inhaled sharply. "Not sure what he was talking about, bud. He…uh, he said some pretty crazy things toward the end. Maybe he was just confused. We're definitely not swapping animals." He let out a nervous laugh, and the others quickly joined in, forcing a chuckle that didn't quite reach their eyes.

Jude, sitting in my father's chair, chimed in with a feigned casualness. "Yeah, Jake, maybe cars here and there, but never animals. Did your dad even ever have a pet?"

It was clear they weren't going to make this easy. Why would they? This was a secret they'd kept buried for years. I was just another obstacle they didn't need right now.

"Maybe the animals were something else?" I ventured, hoping to get some reaction. The room went quiet.

Jude finally spoke, his voice oddly thoughtful. "Come to think of it, Jake… He always called Lucy his 'little mouse'. Maybe that's what he was referring to. Derek helped with the adoption, after all. That could've been it." He leaned back in the chair, trying to look casual, as if he owned the place. "Yeah, that's right," Ted added quickly, backing him up. "Your dad was so grateful to Derek back then. Your mum and dad wanted Lucy so badly. He was probably talking about that."

Their words felt rehearsed, too smooth, too quick to dismiss the idea. I didn't buy it, but they were good at this—good at pretending. Pretending nothing was wrong. Pretending the past was just a blur, something to be swept under the rug. But I could feel the tension, the way they all shifted slightly in their seats, trying to stay calm, hoping I wouldn't dig deeper. "Lucy was my sister," I said, my voice steady despite the turmoil in my chest. "She wasn't some pet or some…mouse. You're telling me that's all it was? A pet name?" I let the question hang in the air, watching as their faces faltered, just for a moment. Ted tried to recover quickly, clearing his throat. "Of course, Jake. It was just a nickname. Nothing more."

Derek gave a forced chuckle. "Yeah, your dad was always a bit odd with his terms. You know that." But I could see through it. The way their eyes darted around the room, the subtle exchange between them. They were hiding something—something I wasn't going to let go of, not now. "Maybe," I said quietly, letting the word linger. "But I still don't understand why my dad was so involved with you all. Or why the animals? What was really going on?"

The room went still. A few uncomfortable glances were exchanged, but no one answered. I had the feeling they were regretting the choice to let me in here, to let me ask questions they weren't prepared to answer.

"Did they really want Lucy that badly? I never heard them talk about wanting another child. It felt like one day, she just appeared," I asked, still trying to piece things together.

"Of course they did, Jake. You don't just adopt a child on a whim. It's a long process with a lot of paperwork. Maybe they didn't tell you because you were so young at the time. Once they were matched with Lucy, it all happened quickly, almost immediately," Derek replied, his voice steady. "You could always ask your mum about it, but maybe not today. She's still very upset," he added, resting his hand on my shoulder as if I were still a child.

"Yeah, maybe," I muttered, turning away and walking out of the room without another word. At least I had learned something new—Lucy had been the 'mouse' my father had spoken of, and Derek seemed to have played a role in her adoption.

I avoided the pitying glances of the mourners as I scanned the room for my mother, who had disappeared from view. Jade was talking quietly to Daniel, my father's nurse, so I made my way toward my mother's bedroom. I figured she might be hiding, likely retreating after her emotional breakdown at the service.

The hallway, dimly lit, felt heavy and oppressive as I drew closer to my parents' old room. I hadn't been in there since I was a child. There had always been an unspoken rule to stay out. But now, it belonged to my mother and Pete. The door, which once loomed like a boundary, now seemed less imposing.

I knocked three times, my heartbeat quickening as I waited for any response. Silence stretched out. I knocked again, more firmly this time. "Mum, are you in there?" I called quietly.

A flicker of movement caught my eye in the dim hallway, and without thinking, I pushed open the door to my mother's room, slamming it behind me. My heart raced as I stood in the room, grateful for the soft glow of the lamp that kept the shadows at bay. The room looked just as it always had—unchanged since my childhood. The same old furniture, the sage curtains that hung over the large windows, and the wooden floors that creaked underfoot. But my mother wasn't here.

I hesitated, not wanting to leave the safety of the room, even though I knew I should go back downstairs. As my eyes scanned the space, something caught my attention—a small brown teddy bear, tucked behind the mirror on my mother's dressing table. Just enough of it stuck out for me to recognize it instantly. That bear had been all over the news when Lucy disappeared, and it had vanished with her. I hadn't seen it again after that day. If my mother had found it after Lucy's disappearance, surely, she would have told the police—or at the very least, Dad and me. Why hadn't she said anything?

The soft cotton felt almost warm against my skin as I held the teddy, my fingers brushing over its worn fabric. It was surreal, holding something of hers after all this time. Once Lucy had disappeared, I was rarely allowed near her room, and though she had a collection of toys, this bear had been the only one that mattered to her. It had been her constant companion, the one thing she had always clung to. I'd always been comforted by the thought that she had taken it with her, wherever she went. At least she wouldn't be completely alone. But now, holding it in my hands, I realized she never had it. It didn't make sense. Why would my mother hide it? Why would she keep something so important to Lucy a secret? A cold shiver crawled up my spine, and my heart began to pound. Something was terribly wrong.

"Put it back," Lucy's voice echoed softly, a whisper that sent a jolt of fear through me.

I turned around fast. Nothing was there. My hand raced to my ear, her voice still lingering. A gross, rotting smell began to invade my nostrils. I placed teddy back where I found him.

"Put him back!" Lucy shouted this time into my other ear. "I have!" I yelled back, my heart beginning to pound.

The teddy bear shot through the air with a sudden force, slamming into the door with a sharp thud before it fell to the ground. A heavy silence took over the room, and I stood frozen, too paralyzed to move. The air felt thick, as if the entire house was holding its breath. I didn't dare make a sound, fearing that any movement would make everything collapse around me.

Then, the doorknob turned slowly, creaking open. I heard small, familiar footsteps padding down the hallway toward Lucy's room. I knew them without question. It was her.

Hesitantly, I bent down, grabbed the bear from the floor, and moved towards her room. The cold hallway seemed to warn me, but something pulled me forward anyway. My body seemed to move on its own, as if guided by an unseen force. I pushed open the door to her room and placed the teddy bear gently on her bed, where it belonged.

The room felt unnervingly warm compared to the chill of the rest of the house. The foul, decaying smell that once clung to it was gone. I took a moment to look around—this was her space, untouched by time or decay. For the first time in ages, everything felt...right. And though I knew something beyond understanding was happening, in that moment, it felt like it was meant to be.

Chapter 19

Jade

I felt out of place at a funeral for someone I barely knew. The heavy awareness that everyone in the room knew I was one of the last people to see Jim made it even worse. The looks they gave me—full of judgment and unspoken questions—spoke volumes. Me and Jake had visited him, and moments later, he was gone. What had we done to make him act so drastically?

Jake had headed straight for his father's study when we arrived, leaving me standing alone, awkwardly hoping no one would approach me with their condolences. The twisting knot in my stomach made it all worse. I couldn't tell if it was the unexpected pregnancy, the emotional whirlwind of the past week, or a mixture of both. I just wanted to go home. But Jake's mental state needed attention. Leaving now would mean carrying all this darkness with us. I couldn't let that happen. We needed to be different than his family had been—to break free and make it out of this cycle.

"It's Jade, right? I'm Daniel, I used to care for Jim. I'm sorry for your loss," he said, extending a shaky, limp hand.

"Yes, I'm Jake's wife. He's mentioned you before. I think you were one of the few people he could talk to when he was younger. It must be difficult for you too, after caring for him for so long," I replied.

Daniel gave a tired sigh, looking down. "It's hard being back here, honestly. This house...it's so grand, but it's cold, almost like it has its own mood. Quiet, unsettling. I always felt bad for Jake. He didn't have any real friends, just me and his tutor, but only the ones willing to brave this place would stick around." He paused, lost in thought. "I honestly thought this day would've come sooner. Once Jim went to the hospital, I figured it was only a matter of time. But he held on...for longer than anyone expected."

"How come?" I asked, genuinely curious.

Daniel hesitated, his eyes drifting to the floor before he answered. "Well... Jim was very sick. But there was always something about it, you know? I'm not sure how much of it was in his mind, and how much of it was...real. This house, it didn't help. But sometimes, I could get through to him. Late at night, I'd hear him wandering around, trying to get out. Once, he made it out and I found him by the woods, mumbling about playing with Lucy. He was so convinced she was still here. No amount of medication or therapy seemed to work. Antonia never spoke to him about her. I think it hurt too much for her to even think about. Once I was the one looking after him full-time, she stopped checking in, stopped even speaking to him. But Jake, he still tried, even though it meant facing his mother's anger. He was a good kid. He went through a lot growing up here. I'm glad he has you now."

He raised his glass toward me, a silent toast to both the past and the future.

"I don't think he ever truly left this place," I said, my voice betraying a mixture of frustration and fear. "I think he just learned how to pretend for a long time. But I'm worried about him. After everything that happened with his sister and now his father, he's not the man I married anymore." The words tumbled out before I could stop them. I hadn't realized how much I was holding in until it spilled over in front of a stranger.

Daniel's expression shifted from sympathy to genuine concern.

"Jade, listen to me," he said, his tone growing serious. "You need to take Jake and leave this house. If you're noticing any signs that he's acting like his father, you need to get out of here, and you need to do it tonight. I can't explain it all, but this house is...it's not right. When I lived here, strange things happened—things I still can't make sense of. I'm convinced that's why Jim ended up the way he did." His voice lowered to a near whisper.

"What kind of things?" I asked, my voice low with a mix of fear and curiosity. "Weird things have been happening to me, too, and to Jake, but he doesn't talk about it. I can tell he's going through it, though." I searched his eyes, hoping for some kind of reassurance. Finally, I had found someone who knew that something was wrong here.

Daniel hesitated, his gaze dropping for a moment before he spoke again, quieter this time. "It's hard to explain... Just strange, unexplainable occurrences. Things that never happened before or after my time with this family. Trust me, Jade. You need to get out. Take Jake and leave this house. Antonia's toxic, and she's trying to drag you both down just like it's done to her. There's a reason no one in their family wants to be around them. Whatever's happened here…it's bigger than you think. Lucy's disappearance wasn't an accident, and no matter what you or Jake do, it won't change anything. Just get yourselves out of here, before it's too late."

His voice was earnest, desperate even, and I couldn't help but feel the weight of his words.

"I don't think Jake will go anywhere now. He wants to find out what happened." A part of me wanted to find out for Jake too.

"I hope that works out for you. I really do." He said knowingly.

Chapter 20

Jade

After a sleepless night, I told Jake we needed to go to the police. The notebook implicating his dad and his friends, paired with the teddy bear he'd found yesterday, might not amount to much, but it was enough to suggest something bigger was at play. Jake hadn't argued, but we'd prepared for the day in heavy silence. Now, we sat across from each other, eating breakfast in the same muted stillness, the weight of the decision pressing down on us.

I hadn't expected company, so when Lisa strolled into the kitchen, I nearly dropped my coffee. I hadn't realized she'd stayed the night; everything after my conversation with Daniel had become a fog.

"Morning, you two," she greeted, sliding into the chair across from us with an easy familiarity. "Well done getting through yesterday. That was…rough."

Her presence, while warm, felt jarring. It was like the tension between Jake and me was suddenly exposed under her bright demeanour. I nodded stiffly, glancing at Jake, who kept his eyes fixed on his plate.

"Thanks, Aunt Lisa. How long are you staying for?" Jake asked, his voice unusually soft, almost hesitant.

"Only today, sweetheart," Lisa replied with a weary smile. "I have work to get back to, and other things, you know. I didn't sleep a wink last night either." The dark circles under her eyes spoke volumes, and I couldn't help but wonder if something had kept her up—something more than grief.

"Yes," Jake muttered, stirring his coffee aimlessly. "This house has a way of doing that."

I glanced at Lisa, debating whether to share what Daniel had told me yesterday. "I spoke with Daniel," I began cautiously. "He mentioned that Jim found this place…difficult. Daniel said he could barely stand being here himself."

Lisa's hand paused mid-air as she reached for a cup. Her smile returned, but it didn't quite reach her eyes. "Oh, well," she said lightly, "it is an old house, after all. Drafty halls, creaky floors… It's easy for the mind to play tricks on you, especially when you're feeling vulnerable." She poured tea from the pot with steady hands, though her tone hinted at something deeper. "I know all about that."

I exchanged a glance with Jake. Vulnerable. Tricks. It felt like Lisa was brushing off something she didn't want to talk about—something she wasn't ready to face.

There was a pause. Lisa's face shifted, her brows knitting together in a way that betrayed her struggle. She took a deep, shaky breath but stopped short of speaking.

"Lisa, are you okay?" I asked, breaking the silence.

"I just…" she began, her voice trembling. "I feel like I can't leave today without telling you something." Her gaze lifted to Jake, her eyes glistening with unshed tears.

"I haven't been honest with you, Jake," she admitted, her voice heavy with regret. "Not for a very long time. And I don't know if you'll ever understand why—sometimes, I don't even understand it myself."

She inhaled sharply, pausing to gather her composure, but her emotions betrayed her. Tears were beginning to well in her eyes, their shine reflecting the weight of whatever secret she was holding back.

"So, twenty-seven years ago, I found myself in a lot of trouble. I was completely off the rails—Jake, you've probably heard some of the stories. I was young, reckless, and desperate. I needed money, not just to get by but to feed my habits. Drugs, parties, bad decisions—I lived in that world for far too long. I'm not proud of the things I did to survive back then."

Lisa hesitated, wringing her hands as though trying to squeeze the shame from her skin. "One of the ways I got by was…being with people for money. I'd go to parties, meet men—sometimes for cash, sometimes for something to get me through the night. It wasn't my whole life, but it was enough to pull me into a very dark place."

Jake's expression froze, his fork lingering mid-air. Lisa's voice cracked, her vulnerability cutting through the room's tense atmosphere.

"During that time, I met Julia. She and I…we ran in the same circles. We got into all kinds of trouble together. At first, we were just two lost souls helping each other survive. But then I got pregnant." Lisa's voice grew smaller, but her words hung heavy in the room.

"I was only nineteen. It was terrifying. I had no support, no stability, and no way to bring a child into that kind of life. I couldn't face telling anyone—not Julia, not your mother, and definitely not our father. He would have been furious, especially since…well, the baby's father was a married man. The shame of it all would've crushed me, so I kept the pregnancy hidden from everyone."

Lisa wiped at her eyes, but the tears kept coming. "When she was born, I made the hardest decision of my life. I gave her away. I had no choice… I couldn't give her the life she deserved. I told myself it was the right thing to do, but even now…even now, I feel the weight of it every single day."

"Only her father knew," Lisa continued, her voice trembling as the weight of her confession hung in the air. "I thought he would take care of her, but instead, he abused her from the moment she was born—used her like a pawn in his twisted games. She didn't grow up with love or family, Jake. She was raised in an orphanage by nannies he handpicked so he could keep tabs on her from a distance. Even as a baby, she wasn't free from his control."

Lisa's hands trembled as she clasped them tightly, her knuckles white. "It was unbearable knowing the life she was destined for once she got older. So, after a while, I couldn't stay silent anymore. I went to your parents, Jake. I told them what I'd done, what I'd allowed to happen. I begged your father—begged him to use his connections to get her out of that life. Jude… Jude was the key to making it all happen. I knew they could pull strings to take her in under the guise of adoption."

Her voice faltered, and she looked down at her lap, tears brimming in her eyes. "You probably don't want to hear this, Jake, but your father and his friends…they were dangerous men. They did things—things so vile I can't even say them out loud. Your mum didn't know at first, but when she found out the truth, it destroyed everything she thought she knew about him."

Lisa's face contorted with anguish as she wiped at her eyes. "When Lucy finally came here, I thought it meant she'd be safe. Antonia…she was overjoyed to have a daughter. She gave Lucy all the love and care I couldn't. For the first time, I felt some hope—like maybe, just maybe, she could have a normal life with a real family."

"I honestly thought it would work out," Lisa whispered, her voice trembling. "I'm not exactly sure what happened that night, but I know it was somehow tied to Jude Collins and your dad. They wouldn't tell me anything after Lucy disappeared. They shut me out completely. I'm so sorry, Jake."

She broke down, the burden she'd carried for so long finally breaking free, her tears soaking into her hands.

Jake's expression was unreadable as he asked, "Lisa, why didn't you tell the police any of this?"

"I couldn't," she said, her words heavy with regret. "Not without tearing apart everything, without destroying the family. Your parents…they would've gone to jail. So would Jude. I thought if I kept quiet, maybe, just maybe, if Lucy was still alive, one day your dad would tell me. But then… I believed it was just a fight, a misunderstanding. That Lucy was somewhere, stuck in limbo." She took a shaky breath. "That's what your dad made it sound like. But now…now I'm not so sure. I think he knew. I think he knew she was dead."

Her voice faded, leaving behind the echo of her confession, as the weight of the truth seemed to hang in the air.

"Jude Collins is Lucy's real father?" I asked, my voice barely a whisper, disbelief washing over me.

Lisa's gaze faltered as she nodded, her eyes clouded with guilt. "Yes. He's listed on the birth certificate. Your dad kept a copy of it in his study. I'm sorry I didn't tell you sooner, but…you're an adult now, Jake. You deserve to know the truth." Her voice cracked as she added, "I'll be leaving soon, after I say goodbye to your mum. But I think it's best if you speak to her. I'll tell her I've told you everything."

Jake's brows furrowed. "So, Julia wasn't Lucy's mother?"

He was referencing the photo he'd found—the one that made him think his father had fathered Lucy with Julia. His question hung in the air, thick with tension.

Lisa almost choked on her tea. "What? No… Why would you think that?" She wiped her mouth, her face flushed with surprise and frustration. "Julia wasn't Lucy's mother. It was me."

"Just something I found…a picture of Julia in some of my dad's things." Jake said, partially telling the truth.

"Well… I don't know anything about your father and Julia, she never mentioned anything about that to me and we were close for a time. Then she went off the radar and I never heard from her. It was around the same time as Lucy. It wouldn't surprise me if your dad was seeing her though."

We'd thought that Lucy was Julia's baby, so what did this mean now?

She left without finishing her tea, her departure leaving an uneasy silence behind. Jake, seething, rose abruptly and stormed toward his father's office. I followed his frantic movements, trying to help him tear the room apart. Drawers flew open, papers scattered across the floor, furniture was shoved aside. "Where would he have hidden it?" Jake muttered to himself, his eyes darting around the room.

"Does he have a safe?" I asked, unsure of what we were looking for.

"No, no safe," he replied quickly, his voice tight with frustration. "But he did have a locked box."

He moved toward the fireplace with purpose, his hands reaching behind a family portrait—one of those unsettling photos where the eyes seemed to follow you—where he retrieved a small, tin box.

"How old were you here?" I asked, studying the photo of the four of them, frozen in time.

Jake glanced at it briefly, a flash of distaste crossing his face. "I was ten. We had to sit there for hours. It was torture. Lucy was too young to stay still, kept running off and making it even worse. I didn't get one break. Not one."

He placed the box on the desk and began frantically searching for the key.

Clang! Clang! Clang! I jumped, the sound echoing through the silence.

The metal bent open just wide enough for Jake to pry into it.

Inside, several papers were neatly folded, each one carefully tucked away despite the box's modest size. I watched as Jake sifted through the papers, his eyes scanning each one with increasing urgency. Finally, he found what he was looking for.

"Here it is. Lucy's birth certificate. Mother – Lisa Reynolds. Father – Jude Collins. Date of birth: 17th April 1997." Jake's voice wavered slightly, the magnitude of the revelation settling over him. "This is it... Lucy's parents. She was my cousin."

He paused, taking a deep breath, as the reality of the situation slowly sunk in.

I placed a hand on his arm, my heart heavy with the weight of it all. "Jude Collins should be ashamed of himself. He could've given Lisa and Lucy a better life. Even if he didn't want anyone to know about her—he's wealthy enough to make it happen."

"If he did have something to do with her disappearance...if he sold her...or any of that sick shit. I will end him." Jake said with a malice in his eyes.

****

The police station still held traces of Christmas—tinsel draped across the walls and small tabletop trees dotted around the room. It all felt distant, like a separate world from the one we had just left. We had asked to speak with a detective who handled cold cases, hoping to avoid running into Derek Hall. After what felt like an eternity of waiting, we were finally ushered into a private room.

The detective who greeted us seemed far too young for the weight of the case she was about to hear. She introduced herself with a firm, professional tone.

"Hi, I'm Detective Slone. I apologize for the wait; it's always a madhouse here after the holidays. I understand you have information about the Lucy King case?"

She took a seat across from us, her dark hair pulled tightly into a bun, making her sharp features look even more drawn. Her eyes were shadowed by heavy circles, giving her an air of exhaustion.

"Yes, we've uncovered some information that I believe has been kept from you, along with some evidence," Jake said, sliding Lucy's birth certificate and his father's notebook across the table. He'd decided against showing her the photo of Julia, pregnant with Jim, smiling like a family. It didn't make sense that it was Lucy – maybe Julia had taken her baby and left after everything went wrong. If that were the case, Jake might have another sibling out there, and Julia could hold the answers.

"The birth certificate was in my father's office," Jake continued. "It shows that Lucy's parents are actually my Aunt Lisa and Jude Collins."

"Jude Collins? As in *Jude Collins* the mayor?" Detective Slone's eyes widened in disbelief.

"Yes, that Jude Collins," Jake replied. "He and my father were close, but in the notebook, it looks like they were involved in some kind of secret society. They traded things, but it's written in a code. Derek Hall is mentioned by name in it. From what I can tell, it seems these men were involved in trafficking, dealing with objects and people...and some of those people were children."

Detective Slone glanced over the notebook, her expression hardening. "So, you believe there's a human trafficking ring operating in this town involving your father, the mayor, the police commissioner, and other key figures? Is that correct?"

Jake nodded, his jaw tight. "Yes. And they're connected to Lucy's disappearance. If you look at the dates, the 'mouse'—a code word, it seems—was only on loan when we got Lucy, and it expired right before she went missing. It all adds up."

Detective Slone's gaze sharpened as she leaned forward, scrutinizing him. "How did you come across this information?"

Jake hesitated for a moment before answering. "I've been staying at my parents' house over Christmas. Found these in the attic and in my father's study."

She raised an eyebrow, her voice cool and sceptical. "They've been there all this time? Your house was searched multiple times after your sister disappeared. How are you just now finding these documents?"

Her tone turned accusatory, her eyes narrowing as she awaited Jake's response.

"I'm not sure if they were moved, but that's where I found them. The house was searched, but I'm not sure how thorough it was. It never felt like the police stayed long, and my dad had a lot of pull," Jake explained, his voice tinged with frustration.

Detective Slone nodded, scribbling something down. "Alright, Mr King, thank you for sharing this with us. I'll begin looking into it with my colleagues. This could be the most significant lead we've had in a long time."

A faint smile appeared on her face—small but genuine—for the first time since we'd met her.

"Thank you, Detective," I said quietly, relieved that someone was finally taking us seriously.

A heavy weight had been lifted from us. With the police now involved, there was hope that something might finally be done, even if it meant facing the uncomfortable truth about the police commissioner's involvement. We couldn't carry this burden alone anymore, and maybe, just maybe, this could give Jake the closure he needed. The drive back to his childhood home was silent, each of us lost in our thoughts. I dreaded the potential confrontation with his mother, wondering if Lisa had already spoken to her. How much did Antonia know about Jim's involvement with his friends? And how much did she blame herself for what happened to Lucy?

Chapter 21

Jake

My mind was spinning. Everything I thought I knew about my life had been a lie. Lucy wasn't my sister—she was my cousin. Her entire life had been dictated by the cruel and reckless adults around her. I couldn't help but feel a surge of rage. If my father were still alive, I'd make him answer for everything. How could he have been involved in something so monstrous and not protected her?

Jade had retreated to take a nap after we returned from the police station, and I felt the need to escape the house. It was suffocating. I needed to clear my head, so I stepped into the garden, hoping the fresh air would settle my thoughts. Inside, the silence felt unbearable. There was no sign of Mum, Pete, Lynne, Bill, or Lisa, but my uncle Ethan's and grandmother's cars were parked outside. They must be somewhere in the house.

A cold breeze sliced through me as I walked, the crunch of frosted grass beneath my feet echoing in the quiet. The sharpness of the Baltic air burned my lungs, but it still felt easier to face than the suffocating chill of the house. Despite the number of people inside, it felt empty—lifeless. The windows were dark, the curtains drawn tight, and an oppressive silence hung over everything. It had never been a warm home, but now it felt more like a tomb, standing without purpose, drained of life.

"Jake! What are you doing out here? It's freezing! We need to talk," my mother called from the kitchen door, Uncle Ethan right behind her.

"Is it about Lisa?" I asked, cutting straight to the heart of the matter.

"Yes, she told me what she said to you," my mother said, her voice tight with frustration. "I don't know why she chose now, of all times, to bring this up. We're all still grieving your father. Lisa has a way of making everything harder than it needs to be."

I stood there, my thoughts spinning.

"This is a hard truth to face, I know," Ethan added with a weary sigh, his brown eyes pleading. "But at least you know the truth now, son. It ate at your dad for years. I wasn't ever his biggest fan, but I know he never forgave himself. Maybe it's time for this family to move on from the past."

His words hung in the air, thick with tension. His resemblance to my father was unsettling, from the strong build to the familiar tone of his voice. I couldn't help but wonder if it was as unbearable for my mother to speak to him as it was for me.

"Ethan, with all due respect, I'm not your son," I said, my voice trembling with frustration. "I haven't seen you or most of the people who showed up yesterday in years. After Lucy disappeared, I was left to deal with everything on my own. And even more so when Dad went into the hospital. None of you were there, and now I know why. Because you were all lying to me. How many of you knew about Lucy? How she came into our lives? How we got her? I can't trust any of you anymore." I let out a bitter laugh, unable to comprehend what they expected me to say to them.

"Jake, what could I have said to you at twelve?" My mother's voice wavered, but there was no hiding the guilt behind her words. "Lisa didn't want anyone to know about Lucy being her daughter, and it would've been dangerous for you to learn about Jude. I thought I was protecting you, keeping you safe from all that darkness. I never wanted you to grow up to be like your father. It wasn't my place to tell you. I thought it was better for you to stay in the dark." She looked at me then, her eyes softer than I'd ever seen them, as if I were seeing a side of her I hadn't known existed. Her words, though meant to explain, only made me feel more disconnected. I had always felt so distant from her growing up, especially after Lucy came into the picture, and now it felt like her attempt to protect me was almost too little, too late.

"Your mum got caught up in all of this. She never asked your dad to do any of the things he did, Jake. I may not have always been around, and I'm sorry for that, but I couldn't stay and support your dad, especially with your grandmother always expecting me to just go along with everything he did. I know this is a lot to process, but you can't let it drag you down. You and Jade are starting your own family now. You need to let this go—it won't end well if you don't." Ethan continued, his tone insistent.

"Why does everyone want me to move on so badly?" I snapped. "Why can't I still care about Lucy and want to know what really happened to her? It feels like I'm the only one still fighting for her, the only one who hasn't just forgotten about her."

"Jake, I don't want you to destroy yourself the way your father did. After all these years, it's unlikely we'll ever know what really happened. It's tragic, but it's the truth. You can't keep living in the past. For years, you seemed fine, like you'd moved on. I just want you to go home and let this go—if that means letting me go too, then so be it." My mother crossed her arms, her face hardening.

"I never forgot about Lucy," I shot back, my voice rising. "I never forgot about you or Dad. It's been eating at me, haunting me slowly, until it all came crashing down. I'm not running from it anymore. Jade and I went to the police today. We gave them everything we know. They said they're going to follow up on the new leads, investigate it all. So, you should probably be ready for them to show up." I met her gaze, unflinching.

The colour drained from my mother's face. Her lips trembled, and she quickly glanced toward where the treehouse once stood, her eyes flickering between it and me as if expecting something to appear. I turned to follow her gaze, but there was nothing there.

"Jake, the police are useless. Have you forgotten what a mess they made twenty years ago? Nothing's changed. Even though your dad's gone, Jude Collins is still around, and he won't let this go any further. If I were you, I'd take Jade and leave before they find out you've gone to the police—or before your grandmother catches wind of it," Ethan added, his face creased with concern.

"There are different people in the force now," I replied, my voice steady despite the rising tension. "It's better they know. They've got the evidence. I won't fail Lucy like every other adult in my life has. I don't know how the two of you can sleep at night."

"I don't sleep, Jake! You've made a huge mistake going to the police. You think your dad was the worst of it, but he was nothing compared to the people still in power around here. You've put a target on all of us now. Please, listen to your uncle. Stop this before it gets worse. If the police find anything, they'll let you know. I'm sorry I didn't tell you when you were old enough, but your father would have killed me if I did. I was terrified, and he could be so violent at times. You must understand, I didn't want you to know any of this…not the bad stuff." Her eyes welled with tears.

"Do you know what happened to her mother? Is there anything you're still hiding from me? What about Dad and Julia? Did you know about them?"

Her sharp intake of breath confirmed everything I needed to know. I had caught her off guard, and it hit her hard.

"Julia was a fool, and your father's biggest mistake. He would've admitted it if he were here. I don't know what Lynne's been filling your head with, but she should know better if she wants to keep her job and her place in this house," my mother spat, her tone dripping with venom.

"I didn't hear it from Lynne. I found a picture in the attic—of Dad and Julia. She was pregnant. At first, I thought maybe she was Lucy's mother, but now it's clear Dad had another child. Isn't that right?"

She went silent, avoiding my eyes.

"Okay, I think we all need a moment to process. Let's head inside and get some tea," Ethan suggested, his voice trying to calm the tension.

"No…no, I need to go to bed," my mother muttered, turning and walking away. She either didn't know how to handle the truth or was avoiding facing me altogether.

"Do you know about my dad's secret child?" I asked, my voice steady but carrying the weight of my frustration.

"I knew about Julia," Ethan admitted, his gaze dropping. "But you should talk to Lynne about the rest—she's in the kitchen cleaning up. I've always kept my distance from all of this. I didn't support it then, and I still don't. I'd better check on your grandmother before I leave." His eyes were full of unspoken truths, but it was clear he wasn't going to be the one to reveal them.

Chapter 22

Jake

Walking back into the house, I found Lynne scrubbing the oven while Jade sat nearby, nursing a cup of tea.

"I couldn't sleep, so Lynne made me a tea," Jade said, her lips curling into a faint smile that didn't quite reach her eyes. The exhaustion was written all over her face. This entire situation was draining her as much as it was me—maybe even more. I should be focusing on her, on us, especially with everything going on, but instead, it was all about my family and their mess. The sooner this nightmare was over, the better.

I sat down beside her, gently rubbing her back.

"I remember what it's like being in your first trimester, honey," Lynne said without turning from the oven, her tone casual but warm. "It's hard and lonely, never mind all the other symptoms that'll come with it later. If you need anything while you're here, you just let me know." She straightened up and glanced over her shoulder. "Do you think you'll be sticking around much longer, or are you planning to head back home soon?"

"Thanks, Lynne. I'll need to head home soon once I start having appointments. Doctor Orton was great, but I'd like to see a midwife. It doesn't feel real yet, so I don't think we'll be staying much longer," Jade said softly, her hand resting on her stomach.

"No, it didn't feel real for me either until my first scan. That's when it all starts to sink in," Lynne replied, rising from the oven to toss the coal wipes into the bin. Her tone was warm but distracted, as if she knew the conversation was heading elsewhere.

"Lynne...can I talk to you about something?" I asked, my voice hesitant. Speaking to someone who genuinely cared for me made it harder; I didn't want to put her in an uncomfortable position. Especially not when it involved her niece.

"I've already spoken to Lisa. I know what she's told you…there isn't much more I can add to that," Lynne said, her voice heavy with regret. "All I can say is that I'm sorry this past week has been so overwhelming, Jake. I still see you as that small boy sometimes. I just want to shield you from all of this." Slowly, she moved closer to the table and sat down across from me.

"It's not just about what Lisa told me," I said carefully.

She let out a weary sigh. "I thought as much." Her shoulders sagged, and she pressed a hand to her mouth, as if trying to stop herself from saying too much. "Go on, Jake. Ask me what you need to."

"Lynne, you believed Lucy was Julia's baby…but if what Lisa says is true, then what does the picture of the two of them together mean? Was there another baby?" I pressed, my voice tight with unease.

Lynne let out a heavy sigh, her hand trembling slightly as she reached for her cup of tea. "I wasn't entirely honest with you the last time we spoke, Jake. I knew Lucy wasn't Julia's baby. Lisa and Julia were close when Lisa had Lucy, and Julia gave her so much support—too much, in hindsight. I wish with everything in me that I had kept Julia far away from this family. Maybe then her life wouldn't have been destroyed. Maybe she'd have a little family of her own now. But I let her down, Jake. Even when I began to piece together what was happening, I didn't do enough to stop it."

Her voice cracked, but she continued. "Julia was only seventeen when she got pregnant by your dad. She wouldn't tell me at first who the father was—I thought it must have been some boy from school. I even confided in your mother, trying to get advice. But after a fight with your father about you, Julia finally admitted the truth. She told me she was in love with Jim King, that he made her feel seen and wanted in ways no one else had. But he didn't love her back, Jake. Not in the way she wanted."

"She told me she was pregnant with his child, but Jim had already decided the baby would be raised as his and Antonia's. He wanted to pass the boy off as a legitimate heir to the King name. Antonia had struggled to conceive for years, and your grandmother was pressuring them for grandchildren. Jim saw this as the perfect solution. As the biological father, he believed it was his right to take the child. And Antonia…well, I don't think she had much of a choice. Once your grandmother got involved, there was no stopping it."

Lynne's words hung in the air, heavy and suffocating. Her face was etched with guilt, and for the first time, I saw the full weight of her regret.

"Julia is my mother. You knew all this time. Why? Why did she agree to let my parents take me? Why did you? How could you lie to me, telling me she was Lucy's mother?" My voice cracked, rising in anger. This wasn't just a betrayal—it was the unravelling of everything I thought I knew. The people I had trusted, who I believed were kind and honest, turned out to be as tangled in this mess as anyone else. Jade tightened her grip on my hand.

"Julia loved you," she said softly, her voice thick with regret. "But she was young. She loved your dad too, and he promised her things—said she could still be part of your life. He told her Antonia and he would eventually get a divorce. He made her believe they'd marry, that things would be different. But he made it clear she had to keep doing things for his friends, too. She didn't want to, but she was completely drawn to him, to his promises."

I could see the pain in Jade's eyes. She hesitated for a moment, then continued. "At first, I thought it was the best option—Julia would finish school, maybe even go to college, and she could still see you. I thought she'd have the life she deserved, and that maybe, over time, things would get better."

"I didn't know the full extent of what your dad and his friends were involved in—not until Julia was already in too deep. By then, they had leverage over her—things they could use to blackmail her, debts they used to control her. They destroyed her life and made it clear they could do the same to me if I didn't play along. As long as you were being loved and cared for, I tried to justify it, tried to tell myself it was worth it." She paused, her face hardening with the memory.

"When you were a baby, Antonia adored you. You were perfect to her, the ideal child. But over time, I think seeing Julia still trying to hold on to some connection to you—seeing her still try to be involved—became too much for Antonia. Lucy was different. She was perfect too, but for different reasons. She was technically her niece, with that blood tie, and her parents didn't want her. Julia loved you with everything she had, but she couldn't bear for you to know her—she was too ashamed of letting you go."

Jade took a deep breath, wiping away a tear that slipped down her cheek. "When you keep a secret for so long, it becomes part of you, becomes the truth you tell yourself. I let you believe that Julia was Lucy's mum because I thought it would give you peace, some kind of closure—thinking they'd run off together, that maybe you wouldn't have to wonder. And, if I'm honest, a part of me was still protecting Julia."

She looked down, tears slowly soaking into the wooden table.

A heavy silence hung in the room, stretching on for what felt like hours, each moment thick with unspoken words.

"I don't think your mum ever wanted you to know the truth," Jade said gently, her voice quiet but steady. "She probably thought you wouldn't want anything to do with her if you did. I know she can be difficult—she's made mistakes, but she's also been through a lot. Your dad put her through hell. She gave everything to him, and he never gave her the same in return. I know it's hard, but maybe you should try to go easier on her. You're all she has left now."

Her words, though soft, cut through the tension in the room. Jade and my mum hadn't exactly been close, but there was a deep empathy in her voice, a kind of understanding I hadn't expected.

"There's just so much lying, from everyone," I whispered, my voice trembling. "I don't think I can take it anymore. Tomorrow, I'll probably find out something else, and nothing ever brings me any closer to finding Lucy." My voice cracked, and I felt my strength slip away.

"The police know what they need to, Jake. You can leave it with them now. At least you've done everything you could. You haven't let anyone down," Jade said, her voice steady, offering me a quiet reassurance.

Lynne shifted, her tension palpable.

"She's right," Lynne added, her tone softer but still firm. "You haven't done anything wrong. You deserve the truth, and I'm sorry it's taken this long for you to get it. But at least now you know. Maybe tomorrow, you two should just leave for a while, get away together."

She stood, pushing her chair back with a scrape that broke the stillness.

"I also have something for you," Lynne continued. "It's a letter from your mum—Julia. I found it years ago when I was cleaning out her old room. It was hidden in a drawer. I don't know when she wrote it, or if she ever meant to give it to you, but I've kept it all this time. Since you came back, I felt like…maybe I knew something like this would happen. I don't know. But here."

She handed me the yellowed envelope, her hands trembling slightly before she turned and walked to the next room, resuming her cleaning as if everything were normal.

To my Jacob,

I think about you every single day. It's almost obsessive. I thought maybe I just needed a bit of time to adjust and then I would be okay but I'm not. It's as if

164

a part of me died the day you were taken. I see it now for what it was, you were taken from me. I haven't got anything to offer you now. I wish I hadn't been so blind. I worry for you and even for your sister, neither of you deserve to be locked away in that horrible house. I'm trying my hardest to save up some money so I can take you away. I know you'll want to come because you hate it there. But I don't think you'll want to leave Lucy behind, and I just can't take her with me too. I won't do to your mother what she so willingly did to me. I can't wait for us to be together again. I'm sick of being controlled by your dad and his friends. We can start a new life – just you and me! I won't be able to give you the life you've become accustomed to, but I know you. You aren't like them. You are my beautiful boy, and I know I'll get you back one day. I'm hoping that it will be soon. I'm not sure how to tell you about me or if it's the right thing to do but I can't do this for much longer. I can't live my life knowing you are so close to me but out of reach. Your father lied to me and its clear he'll never let me be part of your life no matter what it takes. I was a fool to ever fall for him.

I am coming to save you though my darling boy. It's taken over a decade, but I am almost there. I just need a little more cash for a safety blanket and then I'll take us away. I'm working on some leverage to keep your father off our case once we've made our escape. I so hope you come along and don't want to stay. The reason I've stayed so long was for you and only you. I'm so frightened of what our future holds, but as long as we are together, we'll be okay. I've never loved anything more than you.

All my love,

Mum

Tears spilled uncontrollably as I collapsed into Jade, my sobs wracking my body. The emotions I had buried for so long surged to the surface, overwhelming me. The truth hit harder than I expected—I would never know Julia as my mother. In the end, she had run away without me. Maybe, after Lucy, she had become too scared or convinced herself I was better off without her. But there had been a time when she was so dedicated to getting me back, so desperate to have me in her life.

I wondered how I would have reacted at twelve if she had told me the truth. I probably would have thought she was lying, because my mum never liked her. I couldn't imagine her getting away with kidnapping me—not with my mum's influence. She must have known that too and decided to leave.

A part of me wondered if I could find her now, if she was out there somewhere, living a life where she was loved. Maybe she had a family of her own, a child she was allowed to raise. She would have been only two years younger than I am now when she left, just a young woman with so many dreams and regrets, just like me.

I couldn't bring myself to talk to anyone else that day—the police, Lisa, Lynne, or even my mother. Instead, I retreated into my bed, curling up like a child, hiding from the world until it was time to sleep. The house felt louder than usual, the bustle of people finally leaving after yesterday's chaos. I was grateful none of them sought me out. They probably all knew I had learned the truth about Julia and didn't have the courage to face me. As the darkness crept in, I allowed myself to surrender to sleep, the quiet of the night pulling me into a deep, exhausting rest.

Pitch-black darkness enveloped me, suffocating my senses. The hairs on my arms stood rigid, every muscle tensed in response to an unseen presence. A cold chill crept slowly up my spine, and a deep sense of dread began to seep into my bones. I lay on my back, acutely aware of Jade beside me. As my eyes adjusted to the darkness, the feeling of terror crystallized into something more tangible.

I inhaled sharply, trying to scream, but my body refused to move. Frozen in place, I could feel it—the weight of my father's corpse, bloody and broken, hovering above me. The rancid stench of decay filled the air, pressing into my nostrils with a nauseating force. A wave of sickened heat surged in my throat, and I gagged violently, the acid taste threatening to choke me. My tear-filled eyes blurred the grotesque vision, but it didn't matter—his image was burned into my mind forever. His face was barely recognizable, squashed and distorted beyond recognition. One eye remained intact, but it was bloodied, staring at me in silent horror.

I tried to force my limbs to move, to break free from the invisible weight pinning me to the bed, but my body remained unresponsive. My chest tightened as panic set in, my breaths shallow and frantic. The corpse leaned closer, its rancid breath brushing my face. Its remaining eye seemed to bore into me, filled with a grotesque mix of rage and sorrow.

"Why didn't you stop it?" a voice rasped, low and guttural. The words slithered into my ears, sending a fresh wave of terror coursing through me. It wasn't just the voice of a dead man—it was my father's voice.

My vision blurred further, my body trembling as the figure's mangled hand reached out, inches from my face. The gory, broken fingers twitched unnaturally, and the metallic tang of blood filled the air. My stomach churned violently. I wanted to scream, to cry out for Jade, but I remained trapped, suffocated by fear and paralysis.

Suddenly, the figure began to shift, its form rippling like a disturbed reflection in water. The battered face melted away, replaced by another— smaller, softer, but no less horrifying. Lucy's lifeless eyes stared back at me now, her face streaked with mud and decay. Her mouth opened, and bugs poured out, skittering over my chest and neck. I gagged, choking on my own breath.

"You let me go," she whispered, her voice echoing unnaturally in the room. "You didn't come for me."

The weight pressing on my chest vanished, and my body lurched forward as if released from invisible bonds. I gasped for air, clutching at my throat, the phantom sensation of insects still crawling over my skin. The room was empty now, dark and silent, except for the sound of my ragged breathing. I turned to look at Jade, but she was still asleep, her face serene and unaware of the nightmare that had consumed me. I wanted to wake her, to tell her what I'd seen, but the words wouldn't come. My throat felt raw, my mind splintered.

All I could do was sit there, trembling in the darkness, as a single thought consumed me: I had to find Lucy. Whatever it took, whatever truths it uncovered, I couldn't let her memory haunt me like this anymore.

Chapter 23

The pub felt quieter than usual, the hum of low conversations barely registering as I stared into my drink. Jade sat across from me, her hand resting lightly on the table, a subtle anchor for both of us. We needed this, a brief escape from the house and the chaos that had swallowed our lives. But even here, the weight of unanswered questions hung over us.

The door creaked open, and a cold draft swept through the room. I glanced up, and my stomach tightened. Ted Andrews and Derek Hall stepped inside, their eyes scanning the room like wolves searching for prey. They spotted us immediately.

"Don't turn around," I muttered to Jade, my voice low.

"What?" Her brow furrowed as she glanced over her shoulder. The moment she saw them, her face hardened. "What are they doing here?"

Before I could answer, Ted and Derek were already making their way over, their heavy footsteps punctuating the silence. Ted reached our table first, looming over us like a storm cloud. Derek hung back, his wiry frame taut, his eyes darting around the pub as if making sure we were alone.

"You've been busy," Ted said, his voice low and even, but the threat beneath it was unmistakable.

I leaned back in my chair, meeting his gaze. "We're looking for answers. Last I checked, that's not illegal."

Derek let out a short, bitter laugh, the sound grating against my nerves. "Answers," he repeated, shaking his head. "You think stirring up old ghosts is going to help anyone? Some things are better left buried, Jake."

Ted leaned closer, his massive hands pressing against the table. His voice dropped, barely above a whisper, but it hit like a hammer. "You don't know what you're messing with. There are people involved in this who don't take kindly to questions. You keep pushing, and you're going to get yourself—and her—hurt."

My fists clenched under the table. I wanted to tell him to back off, to let him know I wasn't afraid of him or whoever he was working for. But before I could speak, Jade's hand covered mine.

Her voice was steady, but I could hear the tension underneath. "Are you threatening us?" she asked, her eyes fixed on Ted. "Because if you think you can scare us, you're wasting your time."

Ted straightened, a smirk tugging at the corner of his mouth. "Call it a friendly warning. Walk away now, and we can all forget this conversation ever happened. But if you don't…"

Derek stepped forward, his voice cold and sharp. "You'll wish you had."

For a moment, none of us moved. Ted's gaze lingered on me, daring me to respond, but I stayed silent, my teeth clenched so hard my jaw ached. Finally, they turned and walked out, leaving the door swinging in their wake.

The cold air seemed to linger, wrapping around me like a vice.

"They're scared," Jade said quietly, her hand still on mine.

"They should be," I replied, my voice tight. "Because I'm not stopping."

After Ted and Derek left, the tension in the room stayed behind like an unwelcome guest. I tried to steady my breathing, but my hands were still trembling, a mix of anger and unease coursing through me. Jade didn't let go of my hand, her grip firm, grounding me in the moment.

"We should go," she said softly, her eyes scanning the room. She wasn't just suggesting it—we both knew staying here made us too easy to find.

I nodded and stood, throwing a few notes onto the table for our untouched drinks. As we stepped outside, the cold night air hit me, sharper and more biting than before. I looked around instinctively, half-expecting to see Ted or Derek lurking in the shadows, but the street was empty.

We walked in silence for a while, the crunch of gravel under our feet the only sound. The adrenaline was wearing off, leaving behind the familiar ache of frustration and exhaustion.

"They're hiding something big," I said finally, breaking the quiet. My voice sounded raw, even to me. "Why else would they go out of their way to warn us off? They're scared we're getting too close."

"Maybe," Jade replied, her tone cautious. "Or maybe they're just trying to intimidate us for someone else. Whoever's pulling their strings."

I glanced at her, the faint glow of a streetlamp illuminating her face. Despite everything, she looked calm, her expression steady. It was one of the things I admired most about her—how she could keep her composure even when everything was falling apart.

"What if they're right?" she added after a moment, her voice quieter now. "What if this doesn't lead anywhere? What if it just puts us in danger?"

I stopped walking and turned to face her. "We're already in danger, Jade. Ever since Lucy disappeared, danger has been part of my life. Ted and Derek showing up doesn't change that—it just proves we're onto something."

Her gaze softened, but there was still hesitation in her eyes. "And if they come after us? If they try to—"

"They won't," I interrupted, though I wasn't entirely sure of it myself. "I won't let them. They think they can scare me into stopping, but they don't know me. I've spent my whole life being haunted by this. I can't stop now—not when we're this close."

Jade sighed, rubbing her temples. "I just want to make sure it's worth it, Jake. I don't want to lose you in this."

"You won't," I said, though my voice wavered slightly. "I promise."

We started walking again, but the weight of her words hung between us. For the first time, doubt crept in, whispering questions I wasn't ready to answer. Was I putting her in danger? Was I putting myself in danger? And what if, after all of this, we still didn't find Lucy—or worse, we found something we couldn't live with?

I pushed the thoughts away as best I could, focusing instead on the path ahead. One step at a time, I told myself. One step closer to the truth.

My phone buzzed in my pocket, the screen lighting up with 'Mum' in bold letters.

I stared at it, my stomach twisting. She rarely called, and when she did, it was never good. She also must know we'd be back home soon so it must be something that couldn't wait.

"It's my mum," I said to Jade, picking up the phone.

"What is it?" I asked, my voice sharper than I intended.

There was a pause on the other end, and for a moment, I thought she might hang up. Then her voice came through, low and unsteady. "Jake…it's about Jude Collins."

I sat up straighter, the tension in her voice pulling me taut. "What about him?" Why would my mother be calling me about the mayor. Especially, when we had just had a run-in with his two buddies at the pub. I would have half expected him to also be there threatening us.

"He's dead." She said coldly.

Her words hit me like a physical blow, the air rushing out of my lungs. "What? How?"

"The police found him earlier today," she said, her voice wavering. "After his interview. They're saying he…that he took his own life."

I started pacing. "No. That doesn't make sense. He wouldn't—"

"I don't know, Jake," she interrupted, her tone defensive. "I'm just telling you what they told me. He was found in his car, in some deserted area outside the city. A hose pipe…carbon monoxide poisoning."

I stopped pacing. My mind raced, trying to process her words. Jude Collins, dead, in an eerily similar fashion my father had once tried to end our lives. After being interviewed by the police. The police that had been sent by mine and Jades small accusation, to his door. A pang of guilt filtered through me. But surely an innocent man wouldn't do something like that if he wasn't afraid of what truths would be uncovered.

"They think it was guilt," she continued, her voice softening. "Maybe he couldn't live with what he'd done."

"No," I said firmly. "Jude might have had his demons, but he wasn't the type to just give up. He was scared, sure, but he was a survivor." It made no sense. It couldn't be a coincidence that Ted and Derek had just showed up to tell us to stop looking into Lucy's disappearance right after Jude Collins was found?

There was a heavy silence on the other end of the line, and then she said, "Sometimes people surprise you, Jake. Sometimes…they do things you never see coming."

I didn't respond. My thoughts were racing too fast, piecing together fragments of conversations, flashes of memory. Was Jude the weak link in their sick group.

"Jake," my mum said, her voice pulling me back. "Listen to me. Whatever you're doing—whatever you're looking for—you need to stop. Jude's death proves it. This…this is dangerous. It's not worth it."

My grip tightened on the phone. "I'm not stopping."

"Jake—"

"No, Mum. Whoever's behind this wanted Jude silenced. And now he's gone, just like Lucy. I'm not stopping until I find out the truth."

She sighed, the sound heavy with resignation. "I can't stop you, can I?"

"No," I said simply.

"Just...be careful, Jake. Please. Your father and his friends are not the biggest fish in this pond by a mile."

The line went dead, and I lowered the phone slowly.

"What happened?" Jade asked, although I'm sure she heard most of it.

"Jude Collins is dead," I said, my voice hollow. "They're saying it was suicide."

Her eyes widened, her fingers starting to tremble. "Do you think...?"

"I think," I said, my voice hardening, "that someone made sure he wouldn't talk."

This was a danger I hadn't fully realized until now. Jude's death wasn't just a warning—it was proof. Proof that we were getting too close, that someone out there was willing to do whatever it took to keep their secrets buried.

I glanced at Jade as she sat beside me, her face pale and drawn. I couldn't keep her here much longer. It was too dangerous. But at the same time, Jude's death felt like a sign. I was on the verge of something. I couldn't give up now.

"Jake," Jade said, her voice trembling, but still firm. "We have to tell the police about Ted and Derek. If they look into them, maybe they'll start connecting the dots. This is dangerous now, Jake. If I wasn't convinced before, I sure as hell am now. We need to leave before it's too late."

I saw the fear in her eyes, the raw desperation, and I knew I should comfort her, reassure her. She was my future, standing right in front of me. The only stable, good thing in my life. I should just say yes—pack up the car, drive away, start over somewhere far from here.

But I couldn't.

Lucy wouldn't let me. She had been haunting the edges of my mind for nineteen years, and now I was so close to finding the truth, I could feel it in my bones. If I ran now, she'd follow me—always there, crawling toward me in my dreams, pulling me back into the darkness. And now, it wasn't just Lucy. It was my father's bloodied, broken face in the mirror. It was Jude's lifeless body in his car.

This had to end.

"Jade," I began, my voice breaking slightly, "you can leave. Go back home. I'll understand. But I can't. Not yet. Not until I know what happened to Lucy.

I'm so close. I can't keep living with this pain of never knowing. If I don't finish this, I'll end up like my father. Or my mother. And I don't know which is worse."

Jade closed her eyes and exhaled slowly, as if she were willing herself to stay calm. When she opened them again, her expression was resolute.

"Jake," she said softly, but with a firmness that cut through the air like a knife, "I'm giving you two more days. Talk to your mum, talk to whoever you need to, but after that… I'm leaving. If you don't come with me, don't expect to be a part of our lives. We need you, Jake. I need you. You need help. Let the police do their jobs. You're going to get us killed chasing after this, because these people—Ted, Derek, whoever's behind this—they're dangerous. First your dad, now Jude? They were both tied to whatever this is, but we're not. We don't have to be."

"Please," she pleaded, her voice cracking with emotion. "Come home with me. Let it go."

Her words cut deep. The desperation, the sadness—it was all there, laid bare in her voice. This wasn't the Christmas either of us had imagined. I could feel her regret. Regret for coming here, for marrying into my mess of a family, for loving someone so broken.

I wanted to let go, I really did. But she didn't understand. She wasn't the one living with this torment.

"I'll stay with my mum," I said finally, the words coming out slower than I intended, like I was still trying to convince myself. "Until I have to go back to work in January. But I will come home. I just… I can't leave my mum this soon. She needs me right now."

Jade stared at me, her eyes searching mine for some hint of truth. I hoped my answer would ease her, buy me the time I needed.

"Okay," she said at last, though her voice was heavy with doubt. "If you need time to support her, I get it. But Jake, don't push anyone else. Not Lynne, not anyone. You don't know who they're talking to. You don't know how deep this goes."

"I won't," I lied, nodding to keep the peace.

The drive back to the house was suffocating in its silence. Jade stared out the window, her profile lit by the cold glow of passing streetlights. I kept my eyes on the road, my knuckles white against the steering wheel.

Two more days. That's all I had left to find answers before I lost Jade for good.

And I wasn't sure which terrified me more—the thought of losing her, or the thought of finding out what really happened to Lucy.

Chapter 24

When we got back to the house, Jade immediately headed upstairs. She didn't say much beyond a soft 'goodnight', her voice weary and hollow. I could tell she was still upset, her earlier plea to leave still hanging in the air between us.

"I'll come up soon," I called after her, though I wasn't sure if she heard me.

The house was quiet again, an oppressive kind of silence that settled into the walls and seeped into my bones. The kind of silence where even your own breathing felt too loud. My mother and Pete must have gotten an early night too.

I wandered into the living room, unsure of what to do with myself. A bottle of whiskey sat half-empty on the coffee table, and for a moment, I considered pouring myself a glass. But something about the night—the tension, the unease—made me feel like I needed to stay sharp.

As I stood there, the temperature in the room seemed to drop. A chill crept over me, raising goosebumps on my skin. At first, I thought maybe the drafty old windows were to blame, but then I felt it: the shift. The unmistakable feeling of being watched.

I turned slowly, my breath catching in my throat.

In the far corner of the room, hunched over like a shadow folded in on itself, was the ghost of my father.

His body was crumpled, his shoulders shaking with silent sobs. He looked less like the proud, angry man I'd grown up with and more like a broken version of himself. Blood streaked down the side of his face, the same injuries I'd seen in my nightmares. His suit was torn and dirtied, the fabric clinging to his gaunt frame.

"Dad?" I whispered, my voice barely audible.

He didn't respond. Didn't even lift his head. His hands were clasped over his face, and the soundless weeping continued, shaking his whole body.

I took a hesitant step forward, and that's when I saw her.

Lucy.

She was standing in the doorway, her small figure illuminated by a faint, ghostly light that didn't seem to come from anywhere. Her hair was tangled, and her dress hung loose on her tiny frame, mud streaking the hem. But her face—her face was calm, almost serene, her dark eyes meeting mine with an expression that felt both familiar and otherworldly.

"Lucy?" My voice cracked.

She tilted her head slightly, as if beckoning me, and then turned. Without a sound, she began to walk away, her bare feet making no noise against the floorboards.

"Wait!" I called out, my voice trembling.

I glanced back at my father, but he hadn't moved. His sobbing continued, quieter now, as if fading into the background. Whatever he was mourning, I couldn't help him—not yet.

I followed Lucy.

She led me through the house, her figure flickering like a candle flame in a breeze. She didn't stop, didn't look back, but I knew she wanted me to follow. My heart pounded as we moved through the dark, empty halls, past the kitchen, and out the back door.

The cold night air hit me like a slap, but I barely noticed. My eyes were fixed on her as she floated ahead of me, her glow just enough to light the path. She was leading me toward the woods behind the house—the same woods where we used to play as kids, where we'd built our little sanctuary.

The treehouse. The place she'd already tried to get me to come to. But it wasn't here anymore. It was torn down according to Lynne.

Lucy and I spent countless afternoons there, our secret hideaway from the world. It had been her favourite place, the only spot where we felt truly safe.

As we reached the edge of the woods, I hesitated. The trees loomed tall and dark, their skeletal branches clawing at the sky. Lucy paused, turning back to me for the first time. Her eyes locked with mine, and she raised a small hand, pointing ahead.

I swallowed hard and stepped into the woods.

The path was overgrown, the once-clear trail now tangled with roots and thorns. But I followed her light, my feet crunching over fallen leaves and twigs. She moved steadily, her glow guiding me deeper and deeper into the forest.

Finally, we arrived.

The old treehouse was still there. The wood was rotted and warped, the ladder long gone. The tree itself had grown taller and thicker, its gnarled roots twisting into the earth like the fingers of a giant. But it was there. I wasn't sure how but it was.

Lucy stood beneath it, her small hand brushing the bark. Then she turned to me, her expression unreadable, and pointed down.

The message was clear.

"Here?" I asked, my voice trembling.

She didn't respond, but the intensity in her gaze told me everything I needed to know. She wanted me to dig.

I dropped to my knees, running my hands over the cold, damp earth. My mind raced with possibilities, each one more horrifying than the last. What did she want me to find? What was buried here?

When I looked up again, she was gone.

I was alone in the woods, the ghostly light replaced by the dim glow of the moon filtering through the branches. The air felt heavier now, thick with anticipation and dread.

I didn't know what I was about to uncover, but I knew one thing for certain: Lucy was leading me toward the truth, and there was no turning back.

The silence of the woods pressed down on me, broken only by the sound of my own shallow breaths. I knelt there for a moment longer, my hands hovering over the damp, leaf-strewn ground. The cold seeped through the knees of my jeans, but I barely noticed. My mind was racing, my heart pounding against my ribs.

I didn't have a shovel—didn't even think to grab one. All I had were my hands and a growing sense of dread. Whatever Lucy wanted me to find, it had been buried here for years. And it would be here, waiting for me, whether I was ready or not.

I began to dig.

The earth was softer than I expected, damp from the winter rain, and the smell of wet dirt rose sharply into the cold air. My fingers clawed through the soil, pulling out clumps of mud and tossing them aside. I worked quickly, almost desperately, my hands growing numb from the cold.

As I dug deeper, my movements slowed. The weight of what I was doing began to settle in. My breaths grew heavier, each one clouding in the icy air. My mind kept racing ahead to the possibilities: bones, an old possession, a clue to what happened all those years ago. I didn't know which thought terrified me more.

After what felt like hours but was probably only minutes, my fingers hit something solid. I froze.

The object was rough, hard beneath my touch. I brushed away more dirt, my hands trembling now. As I cleared the soil away, I realized it was wood—old and splintered, its surface cracked with age.

A box.

It was small, barely larger than a shoebox, and its surface was weathered and warped from years underground. I hesitated, staring at it. My chest felt tight, the weight of Lucy's presence still heavy in the air around me. This was it. Whatever she wanted me to find, it was inside.

I reached for the box, my fingers gripping its edges. It was stuck, the damp earth clinging to it like a vice. I yanked harder, and with a sickening crack, it came free. The sudden motion sent me sprawling backward, the box clutched tightly in my hands.

I sat there for a moment, staring at it. My breath came in short gasps, my pulse roaring in my ears. The box was heavier than I'd expected, and the air around me felt colder now, almost suffocating.

I didn't want to open it.

But I had to.

With trembling hands, I pried open the lid.

Inside, wrapped in layers of filthy cloth, were the remnants of a child's possessions. A small, faded stuffed animal—a rabbit, its fur matted and its button eyes missing. A plastic bracelet, the kind we used to make with beads spelling out our names. Lucy's name was on this one, the letters cracked and faded but unmistakable.

And beneath those…

A small leather-bound book.

My fingers hovered over it, hesitant to touch it. It was smaller than a diary, more like a notebook, the cover warped from years in the ground. Slowly, I picked it up, the leather cold and damp beneath my fingers.

As I opened it, the pages stuck together in places, water stains blurring the ink. But I could still make out the handwriting—Lucy's handwriting. Childish and uneven, but hers.

The first page was a drawing. A crayon sketch of the treehouse, with two figures standing in front of it. One labelled 'Me', the other 'Jake'. Beneath it, in big, scrawled letters, were the words: **"Safe Place."**

My throat tightened.

I flipped the page.

More drawings. Notes. Little bits of a child's world. But as I went further, the pages began to change. The drawings became darker, messier. The notes stopped making sense. There were scribbles, frantic and chaotic, as if her little hands had been shaking.

Then, near the middle of the book, I found words that froze me in place:

"Bad man."

The letters were jagged, pressed into the page so hard that the paper had torn in places.

Below it was another drawing. A figure, towering and dark, with long arms and no face. He loomed over two smaller figures—Lucy and me.

The next page had more words:

"He watches us. He hurts us. Don't tell."

I felt like the air had been sucked out of my lungs. My hands shook as I turned the page again.

The final drawing was the most haunting. It showed the treehouse, but this time it was burning. Flames covered it, and the two figures—Lucy and me— were standing far away, watching. Above the flames was the dark figure again, looming, his arms stretched out as if reaching for us.

At the bottom of the page, written in shaky letters, was a single word:

"Run."

The notebook slipped from my hands, landing with a dull thud on the ground. My chest felt tight, my breath coming in shallow gasps.

Lucy's voice echoed in my mind. The way she had pointed, the urgency in her gaze. She had led me here for a reason.

I looked down at the box again, at the remnants of her childhood, and I knew this was only the beginning.

The truth was here, buried in the past, waiting to be uncovered.

And I wasn't going to run.

I stared at the notebook, my hands still trembling. The weight of what I'd found pressed down on me, thick and suffocating. The cold air bit at my face, but I barely felt it. My mind was racing, replaying Lucy's drawings, her frantic words etched into the pages.

"Run."

I didn't even hear her approach until her voice broke through the silence.

"Jake?"

I whipped my head around, startled, and saw my mum standing a few feet away. She was wrapped in her thick winter coat, her face pale and lined with exhaustion. Her eyes darted from me to the open box at my feet.

"What are you doing out here?" she asked, her voice trembling.

Her gaze fell to the notebook on the ground, and her expression shifted—shock, then fear. She took a cautious step closer, her hands trembling as they clutched the edges of her coat.

"Jake," she whispered, her voice breaking, "where…where did you find that?"

I picked up the notebook, holding it tightly in my hands. "Lucy led me here," I said flatly, my voice cold. "She showed me this place. And now I know why."

Her face crumpled, and for a moment, I thought she might fall to her knees. She pressed a hand to her mouth, stifling a sob.

"You shouldn't have found this," she said, shaking her head. "You weren't supposed to…"

"Weren't supposed to what?!" I snapped, my voice rising. "Find out the truth? About what Dad—about what all of you—were hiding?"

She flinched at the venom in my words, tears spilling down her cheeks. "Jake, please," she begged, her voice cracking. "Let's go inside. We can talk about this. I'll tell you everything. Just…not out here."

I stood my ground, clutching the notebook like a lifeline. "Why not out here? What are you so afraid of? Afraid Lucy might hear you?"

Her face twisted in pain, and she took another step closer. "Jake, please," she said again, her voice desperate now. "You don't understand. This isn't safe. None of this is safe. We need to go inside, where we can talk properly."

I hesitated, the anger and grief warring inside me. Part of me wanted to keep pushing, to demand answers here and now. But another part of me—the part that was still a scared little boy, lost and desperate—wanted to listen to her.

I looked down at the box in my hands, the weight of it unbearable. "If I come inside," I said slowly, my voice low and firm, "you'd better tell me everything. No more lies. No more excuses. I want the truth, Mum. All of it."

She nodded quickly, wiping her tears. "I promise," she said, her voice barely above a whisper. "I'll tell you everything, Jake. Just…come inside."

Reluctantly, I followed her back toward the house, the box clutched tightly against my chest. The woods seemed darker now, the shadows deeper and more oppressive. The weight of Lucy's presence lingered, a constant reminder that the answers I was seeking might not bring me peace—but I couldn't stop now.

As we stepped back into the house, the warmth hit me like a wave, but it did nothing to ease the chill that had settled in my bones. Jade must have already gone to bed; the lights upstairs were off, and the living room was eerily quiet.

Mum gestured for me to sit at the kitchen table, her hands trembling as she poured herself a glass of water. She didn't offer me one, and I didn't ask.

I placed the box on the table, watching her reaction closely. Her eyes darted to it, then away, as if she couldn't bear to look at it for too long.

"This was Lucy's," I said, breaking the silence. "Wasn't it?"

She nodded, her hands gripping the edge of the counter. "Yes," she whispered. "It was hers."

I opened the box, pulling out the notebook and the small bracelet. I held up the bracelet, the cracked plastic beads spelling out Lucy's name. "Why was this buried out there? Why did she want me to find it?"

Mum sank into the chair opposite me, her shoulders slumping as if the weight of the years had finally caught up to her. She looked at me, her eyes red and raw, and for the first time, I saw real fear in them.

"Because," she said, her voice trembling, "she wanted you to know the truth about what happened. About your father. About…everything."

I leaned forward, gripping the edges of the table. "Then tell me," I demanded. "No more stalling. No more cryptic answers. Just tell me the truth, Mum."

She took a deep, shuddering breath, her hands shaking as she reached for the bracelet. She turned it over in her fingers, staring at it as if it held the answers she needed.

"Your father," she began, her voice barely above a whisper, "he wasn't the man you thought he was. And Lucy…she knew. She saw things she wasn't supposed to see. Things he was desperate to keep hidden."

Her voice broke, and she covered her face with her hands. "He was so angry, Jake. So angry that she…that she wouldn't keep quiet. And when she disappeared, I… I thought…"

Her words trailed off, and she looked at me, her eyes filled with anguish. "I thought it was my fault," she whispered. "I thought I hadn't done enough to protect her."

My stomach twisted, the weight of her words sinking in. "What are you saying?" I asked, my voice barely steady.

She swallowed hard, tears streaming down her face. "I'm saying," she said, her voice trembling, "that your father had secrets. Terrible secrets. And Lucy… Lucy was caught in the middle of them."

The room seemed to close in around me, the air heavy with the weight of her confession. My hands tightened into fists, the anger and grief bubbling to the surface.

"What did he do to her?" I demanded, my voice shaking. "What did he do, Mum?"

She didn't answer, her sobs breaking the silence. But in her silence, I found my answer.

I leaned back in my chair, the truth crashing over me like a tidal wave. Lucy hadn't just disappeared. She had been taken. By my father. By the man I had once idolized.

And now, finally, I was beginning to understand why she had led me here.

Chapter 25

The kitchen was heavy with silence. The only sound was the low hum of the refrigerator, a mundane reminder of normalcy in a space that felt anything but. Jade and Pete still sleeping soundly upstairs away from their tortured partners.

Mum sat across from me, her hands trembling as they gripped the mug of tea she hadn't touched after taking a pause to make it. I felt it was because she was actually just buying herself more time. Her face was pale, lined with exhaustion, and her eyes were swollen from the tears she'd shed outside. She didn't look at me, instead focusing on a spot on the table as though the wood grain held the answers she needed.

I broke the silence first. "Start from the beginning," I said, my voice low and steady, though inside I felt like I was splintering. "Tell me everything."

She took a shaky breath, her fingers tightening around the mug as if it might anchor her. "It started with Julia," she said finally, her voice so soft I had to lean forward to hear her. "When she came back into your father's life, everything changed."

I frowned, confusion and anger swirling in my chest. "Julia," I repeated. "My real mum. What does she have to do with Lucy? With all of this?"

Mum hesitated, her gaze finally lifting to meet mine. "She…she was struggling, Jake. You were too young to remember, but Julia had always been troubled. She got involved with the wrong people, made bad decisions. And when she came back here, it wasn't to see you. It was because she needed money."

I clenched my jaw, the bitterness rising in my throat. "Money for what?"

Her hands shook as she placed the mug down, clasping them together as if in prayer. "Drugs," she said simply. "Heroin. Your father…he had been giving her money for years. Supporting her habit. But it wasn't out of kindness."

The implication hung in the air, and it hit me like a punch to the gut. "They were having an affair," I said flatly.

Mum nodded, her face crumpling with shame. "It wasn't just an affair, Jake. It was something darker. He kept her dependent on him, knowing she'd always come back if he gave her what she needed. And Jude Collins…he was the one who supplied her. He and your father were in it together."

My head spun, my breath coming in shallow bursts. "And Lucy?" I managed to say. "Where does she fit into all of this?"

Mum's expression darkened, and she looked away, as though she couldn't bear to say the words. "Lucy found out," she whispered. "She overheard a fight between your father and Julia. She saw things she shouldn't have seen. Jude Collins had her in the chapel one evening when I wasn't here. He um… He hurt Lucy. He had been for some time. He was a sick man, Jake. I didn't realise it was still happening when she lived with us. I thought when me and your father adopted her that she was safe from them. Julia was close to Jude, and I don't know how she knew he was there with her, but she did, and Julia went there high as a kite, ranting and raving. Saying Lucy was going to tell me about her and your dad. I knew already but she didn't know that. She wasn't herself. She was angry, paranoid. She thought Lucy was going to tell someone. And in that moment…"

Her voice broke, and she covered her face with her hands, her shoulders shaking.

I stared at her, the room spinning around me. "She killed her," I said, the words foreign and jagged in my mouth.

Mum nodded, her sobs muffled by her hands. "She didn't mean to," she said, her voice trembling. "She said it was an accident. That Lucy was screaming, and she just wanted her to stop. So she pushed her and she hit her head too hard on the alter. But it doesn't matter, does it? She killed her. And then she panicked. She didn't know what to do, so she called your father."

My stomach churned, bile rising in my throat. "And he helped her cover it up," I said, the weight of it settling on my chest like a stone.

She nodded again, tears streaming down her face. "He called Lynne," she said, her voice barely audible. "She came to the house, and the three of them…they buried Lucy. Out in the woods. Your father said it was the only way to protect Julia, to protect you. He made Lynne swear she'd never tell anyone. And she didn't. Not until now. You see we would have gotten in a lot of trouble with some bad people if they thought Lucy had been killed under your father's watch. Lucy was ours to keep, but not really ours. Your father thought over time he'd be able to pay his way into keeping her permanently. Derek helped to cover it up as he didn't want his involvement to become known."

I sat back in my chair, my head in my hands. The image of Lucy's little body being buried in the cold, dark earth was too much to bear. "And Julia?" I asked, my voice hollow. "What happened to her?"

Mum took a deep, shuddering breath, wiping at her tears. "She was devastated," she said. "She couldn't live with what she'd done. After Lucy…after the burial, she went to see Jude. She needed to get high, to forget. But Jude was furious. He blamed her for dragging him into this mess. And when she left his house, she…she was out of her mind, Jake. She got in her car and…"

Her voice broke again, and she covered her mouth, her eyes wide with horror.

"She crashed," I said, finishing her sentence. "She drove into a tree." Mum clarified.

Her hands trembled. "She died instantly," she said. "Your father said it was a blessing. That at least she didn't have to live with the guilt. But he wasn't sad, Jake. He was relieved. Because now there was no one left to tell the truth."

The room was silent again, the weight of her confession pressing down on both of us. I stared at the table, my mind racing.

"He told Jude to help him cover it up," I said finally. "Because if anyone found out, it would all come crashing down. The affair. The drugs. The lies. The abuse of children?"

Mum nodded, her face pale. "Jude was scared," she said. "But your father had leverage over him. He kept him quiet. Until now. They aren't the biggest fish in the human trafficking pond Jake. There are a lot of people above them who would've had them killed for gaining any kind of attention."

I clenched my fists, anger boiling inside me. "And now Jude's dead," I said bitterly. "Convenient, isn't it? Everyone who knows the truth is either dead or terrified to talk. So you and dad got Lucy from traffickers?"

Mum reached across the table, placing a hand over mine. "Jake," she said softly, her voice pleading. "I'm telling you this because you deserve to know. But you can't keep digging. It's dangerous. Your father…his friends…they're not the kind of people who let secrets like this come out. You need to let it go. It doesn't matter where we got her from. None of it matters now."

I pulled my hand away, standing abruptly. "Let it go?" I said, my voice rising. "You're telling me my father and his friends had a part in killing Lucy, and you want me to let it go? How am I supposed to do that?"

Tears streamed down her face as she stood, her hands clasped in front of her. "Because I don't want to lose you too," she said, her voice breaking. "Please, Jake. You've uncovered enough. Let the police handle the rest."

I turned away, the anger and grief swirling inside me. I didn't know what to believe anymore, but one thing was certain: I couldn't let this go. Not now. Not ever.

Chapter 26

The kitchen felt colder now, as if the truth had drained all the warmth from the room. Mum sat slumped in her chair, her tear-streaked face pale and lined with exhaustion. I stood by the sink, staring at the moonlit garden through the window. Somewhere out there, beneath the soil and trees, Lucy lay in an unmarked grave, her voice silenced, her story buried along with her.

"I can't leave her there," I said finally, my voice low but resolute.

Mum looked up, her face a mix of shock and fear. "What are you talking about?"

I turned to face her, my jaw clenched. "Lucy. I'm going to dig her up. She deserves more than this…this lie. She deserves to be laid to rest properly, with dignity. And the police need to know."

Her eyes widened, and she shook her head vehemently. "No, Jake. No. You can't."

"I have to," I said firmly. "This isn't just about Lucy anymore. It's about all of it—Dad, Julia, Jude, the abuse, the lies. They don't get to keep hiding behind their secrets. Lucy doesn't get to stay a victim forever."

Mum stood abruptly, her chair scraping against the floor. "You don't understand, Jake. You'll ruin everything. You'll ruin yourself."

I let out a bitter laugh. "Ruin myself? Look at me, Mum. Do I look like someone who's holding it together? Lucy's death has haunted me my whole life. You think I can just walk away now, knowing where she is? Knowing what happened to her?"

She stepped closer, her voice rising. "If you go to the police, they'll dig into everything—your father, Jude, the others. Do you know what kind of people they were? What kind of people they worked with? They'll come after you, Jake. After Jade. Is that what you want?"

I flinched at the mention of Jade, but I held my ground. "I'll deal with it. Whatever happens, happens. But Lucy deserves justice."

Mum's face twisted in anguish, and she grabbed my arm. "I'm begging you, Jake. Let her rest. Let it stay buried. Please."

I yanked my arm free, the anger bubbling to the surface. "Rest? How can she rest knowing what they did to her? How can *you* rest knowing you helped cover it up?"

Her face turned pale, her lips trembling. "I did what I had to do to protect this family."

I shook my head, disgusted. "Protecting this family? You mean protecting *him*. Dad. The man who destroyed everything he touched. You chose him over Lucy. Over me."

Her voice broke as she screamed, "I didn't have a choice!"

"Yes, you did!" I roared back, my voice echoing off the kitchen walls. "And now I'm making mine. I'm going to the woods. Tonight."

She grabbed my wrist again, tighter this time, her nails digging into my skin. "No, Jake. I can't let you do this."

I stared at her, a mix of anger and disbelief. "You *can't let me*?" I wrenched my arm free and took a step back. "You don't get to control me anymore, Mum. You don't get to decide who deserves justice."

Her breathing was ragged, her eyes wild with desperation. "If you go out there…if you dig her up…you'll destroy us all."

"I don't care," I snapped, turning toward the door.

Before I could take another step, she lunged at me, her hands grabbing at my arm, my shirt, anything she could reach. I stumbled, trying to shake her off, but she was relentless, her fear giving her strength. "You're not going to ruin this family, Jake!" she shouted, her voice shrill and panicked.

I spun around, trying to pry her off me, but her grip was unyielding. "Let go, Mum!" I shouted, but she clawed at me, her nails scraping against my skin.

"You can't do this!" she screamed, her face contorted with rage. "I won't let you!"

In a blur of motion, I pushed her away, harder than I intended. She stumbled backward, her feet catching on the edge of the rug. Time seemed to slow as she fell, her head hitting the edge of the countertop with a sickening thud before she crumpled to the floor.

"Mum!" I dropped to my knees beside her, panic flooding my chest. Her eyes were closed, her body limp. For a moment, I thought I'd killed her, but then I saw the faint rise and fall of her chest. She was breathing.

I sat back on my heels, my hands trembling. "I didn't mean to…" I whispered, my voice cracking. "I didn't mean to hurt you."

But there was no time for guilt, no time for second-guessing. I stood, my mind racing. I needed to move fast. She'd come after me as soon as she woke up, and I couldn't let her stop me again.

I grabbed my coat and the box containing Lucy's belongings, shoving it under my arm. My heart pounded as I stepped over Mum's unconscious form, pausing only to glance back at her one last time.

"I'm sorry," I whispered, though I wasn't sure who I was apologizing to— her, Lucy, or myself.

Then I opened the door and stepped out into the night, the cold air hitting me like a slap. The woods loomed in the distance, dark and foreboding, but I didn't hesitate. With every step, my resolve hardened.

I was going to find Lucy. And I was going to make things right, no matter the cost.

The woods swallowed me whole as I moved through the dense underbrush, the faint light of the moon guiding my way. The air was cold and heavy, carrying the scent of damp earth and decaying leaves. Each step felt weighted, the box clutched tightly under my arm as though it was the only thing tethering me to reality.

Lucy's treehouse came into view, its skeletal frame a shadow of what it once was. The ground beneath it beckoned me, the truth buried just a few feet below the surface. I was so focused on my goal that I didn't see the figure until I was nearly on top of him.

The beam of my flashlight caught movement—someone crouched near the base of the treehouse, a shovel in their hands. My breath caught in my throat. For a moment, I thought it might be the ghost of my father, but as I drew closer, the figure straightened.

Derek Hall.

His face twisted in surprise as the light hit him, but he quickly masked it with a sneer. "Jake," he said, his voice dripping with mockery. "Didn't think you'd be out here tonight."

I froze, gripping the flashlight so tightly my knuckles ached. Behind him, the shadowy outline of Lucy appeared, her figure translucent and faintly glowing. She was screaming—her mouth wide open in anguish—but no sound escaped her. It was as though the woods themselves were swallowing her cries.

"What the hell are you doing here?" I demanded, my voice shaking as much from the sight of Lucy as from the anger bubbling inside me.

Derek leaned on the shovel, his expression cold and calculating. "Funny, I was about to ask you the same thing."

"I asked first," I snapped, stepping closer. "Why are you here?"

Derek smirked, but there was something uneasy in his eyes. "Your mum called me," he said simply.

My stomach twisted. "What?"

"She wanted me to move Lucy," he continued, his tone matter-of-fact. "Said she'd keep you busy while I took care of things out here."

"No," I whispered, shaking my head. "She wouldn't…"

"Oh, she would," Derek said with a low chuckle. "Antonia's not exactly the saint you think she is, Jake. She's spent her whole life cleaning up after your dad. What's one more mess to cover up?"

I felt like the ground was shifting beneath me, my world crumbling with every word. "You're lying," I said, though even as I spoke, I knew he wasn't.

Derek's smirk faded, his expression turning serious. "I don't have time to lie to you, Jake. Not tonight." He gestured to the disturbed earth at his feet. "I've got a job to do, and you're in my way."

"Why now?" I asked, my voice rising. "Why dig her up now, after all these years?"

Derek sighed, leaning on the shovel again. "Because the walls are closing in. Jude's dead. Jim's dead. And now you're poking around in things that should've stayed buried. Your mum knows it's only a matter of time before the truth comes out. She figured moving Lucy's body would buy her some time."

"And you're just her errand boy?" I spat. "What's in it for you?"

He looked at me, his eyes dark and unreadable. "It's not just about Antonia," he said quietly. "I've got my own reasons for being here. Reasons you deserve to know."

I stared at him, my heart pounding. "What are you talking about?"

He hesitated, his gaze shifting to the ground as though he were trying to summon the courage to speak. Finally, he looked up, his expression grim.

"You think Lucy was just some random kid your parents adopted, don't you?" he said. "Some poor girl they took in out of the goodness of their hearts."

My throat tightened. "What are you saying?"

"I'm saying Lucy wasn't just your adopted sister, Jake," he said. "She was your *half*-sister."

The words hit me like a blow, knocking the air from my lungs. "No," I said, shaking my head. "That's not possible."

"Oh, it's possible," Derek said bitterly. "Lisa – your aunt, your mum's own *sister*—was Lucy's real mother. Jim got her pregnant. Another one of his little affairs. But this one was too close to home. Too messy."

I stared at him, my mind reeling. "'My dad"... I whispered, a sense of dread creeping in. "Lisa was Lucy's mum and..." I couldn't say it.

Derek nodded, his expression grim. "And your dad was her dad. That's why Antonia and Lisa hate each other now. Antonia couldn't stand the sight of her. Every time she looked at Lucy, the kid she thought she saved, she saw your dad's betrayal. His affair with her own sister."

I staggered back, the box slipping from my hands and hitting the ground with a dull thud. "No," I said again, my voice cracking. "That can't be true."

"It's true," Derek said flatly. "Lisa gave birth to Lucy and couldn't cope. She was an addict like your mother and sold herself just to get her next high. She even told Jude he was the father to get money from the poor bastard. He was thrilled to get a little girl though. Sick fuck. We aren't saints but Jude was on another level. After it was clear Lisa wasn't able to care for Lucy, Jude took her in, but his wife wasn't thrilled. As Lucy got older and was talking, she told Jude to get rid of her, so he let your parents to raise her. For a price of course and only under the circumstance that Jude was to have visits with her when he wanted too. He was a little...obsessed with her." Derek stared off for a moment before gathering his thoughts.

"Why would Lisa stay quiet about that? Didn't she want to be with her daughter?" I asked, my voice becoming hoarse.

Derek barked a laugh. "She was a mess just like Julia and your grandmother paid her off handsomely I heard. Lisa needed the money to get out of here, otherwise she would probably be dead in a ditch somewhere by now. Julia and Lisa worked together at a gentlemen's club and that's all their lives would have ever been...well it was all your mother's life was." He rubbed his stubble before setting the shovel back into the earth.

Fury flooded my veins.

"Lisa thought it would be easier this way. Lucy would have a decent home with good parents, she didn't know about what Jude was doing until after Lucy died. But Antonia…she never forgave her. Except the funny thing is… Your mum didn't know about the affair until Lucy was already adopted and Julia of all people let it slip to her one night. I think that truly made your mum mad. She thought she finally had this little girl that she was always asking Jim for. She thought they both were her adoptive parents, and they were on the same level but when she found out… Your dad really paid for that lie." He shook his head in such a casual way it was hard to believe what he was admitting to.

The ghost of Lucy moved closer, her translucent figure flickering like a flame in the wind. Her screams were silent, but I could feel the weight of her anguish, the pain radiating from her like heat.

"She didn't deserve this," I said, my voice barely above a whisper. "She didn't deserve any of this."

"No, she didn't," Derek said quietly. "But that didn't stop them, did it?"

I looked at him, my hands trembling. "Why are you telling me this? Why now?"

"Because you deserve to know the truth," he said simply. "And because someone has to clean up this mess before it destroys us all."

I shook my head, tears streaming down my face. "It's too late for that," I said. "The damage is already done."

Derek sighed, picking up the shovel again. "Maybe. But at least now you know who Lucy really was. And who your parents really were. Now you know the truth, that your real mum killed her maybe you can put this to bed. You don't want to ruin her name anymore, do you?"

I watched as he turned back to the grave, the sound of the shovel biting into the earth echoing in the stillness. Lucy's ghost stood behind him, her screams silent but deafening in my mind.

I didn't know what to do, what to think. My world had been shattered, the truth more horrific than I could have imagined. But one thing was clear: I couldn't let this end here. Lucy deserved better than this.

And I would make sure she got it.

Chapter 27

Rage boiled inside me, hotter and fiercer than I'd ever felt before. Derek Hall—this smug, self-serving bastard—was standing over Lucy's grave like it was some trivial chore to him. His words rang in my ears, twisted truths about my family that I could barely begin to process. Lisa. My dad. Lucy. None of it felt real, and yet the evidence was right there in the ground beneath us.

"You think you can just walk away from this?" I hissed, my voice low and trembling with fury.

Derek barely glanced over his shoulder, his hands steady on the shovel as he drove it into the earth. "I'm not walking away," he said, his tone infuriatingly calm. "I'm finishing what your mum asked me to do. Go home, Jake. This isn't your fight anymore."

"She's my sister!" I shouted, my voice cracking as it echoed through the woods. "You have no right to be here. None of you did!"

He sighed, wiping the sweat from his brow. "It's not about rights, Jake. It's about cleaning up the mess your family made."

That was it. The last thread of control snapped. I lunged at him, adrenaline surging through me as I tackled him to the ground. The shovel clattered to the side as we hit the dirt, my fists flying before I could even think.

Derek cursed, struggling beneath me, but I was stronger, faster, fuelled by years of suppressed anger and grief. I managed to grab the shovel, my hands gripping it tightly as he tried to wrestle it back from me.

"Let it go, Jake!" he barked, his face twisted with frustration.

"No!" I roared, yanking it free with a burst of strength I didn't know I had. I staggered back, the weight of the shovel almost foreign in my hands. Derek scrambled to his feet, but before he could make another move, I swung.

The blunt edge caught him across the temple, and he crumpled to the ground like a marionette with its strings cut. For a moment, I stood there, panting, the shovel trembling in my hands. My heart pounded in my chest as I stared at his motionless form, the moonlight catching the streak of blood trailing down his face.

I didn't have time to think about what I'd done. There was only one thing that mattered now.

I dropped the shovel at the edge of the grave and fell to my knees, my hands clawing at the disturbed earth. My fingers scraped against roots and rocks as I dug, the soil cold and damp beneath my nails. Time felt meaningless. There was only the sound of my breathing, the rhythm of my hands tearing through the dirt, and Lucy's silent ghost watching me from the edge of the clearing.

Finally, my fingers hit something hard. My chest tightened as I pushed more earth aside, revealing the edge of a small, weathered box. I dragged it up from the ground, the weight of it heavier than anything I'd ever held.

The wood was rotting, the nails rusted, but I knew what was inside before I even opened it. My hands trembled as I pried it open, revealing the small, fragile remains of my sister. Her bones were wrapped in what looked like the remnants of a blanket, faded and stained.

I didn't think. I didn't hesitate. I reached down and lifted her, cradling her remains against my chest as if she were still seven years old and needed me to carry her home.

And then I broke.

The tears came hard and fast, my body wracked with sobs as I held her close. "I'm sorry, Lucy," I whispered, my voice choked. "I'm so sorry. I should've protected you. I should've been there."

The wind shifted, and I felt her before I saw her. The ghost of Lucy stepped forward, her translucent form shimmering in the moonlight. But she wasn't the shadowy, screaming figure I'd seen before.

She was clean now, her face bright and unburdened, her mousy hair shining like it had when we were kids. She wore her favourite dress—the one with the daisies she'd insisted on wearing everywhere with a spotless white pair of shoes. Her smile was soft, her eyes filled with love.

"Jake," she said, her voice clear and sweet, just as I remembered.

I froze, my breath catching in my throat. "Lucy?"

She nodded, stepping closer until she was kneeling beside me. Her small hand reached out, and though it passed through mine, I swore I could feel the warmth of her touch.

"Thank you," she said, her voice steady despite the tears in her eyes. "Thank you for not giving up on me."

I shook my head, tears streaming down my face. "I'm so sorry, Luce," I whispered. "I—I couldn't save you. I wasn't there. I should've—"

She cut me off, leaning forward to wrap her arms around me. I couldn't feel the weight of her, but the gesture alone was enough to make my chest ache.

"You were the best big brother I could've asked for," she said, her voice breaking. "I miss you so much, Jake. I miss you every day."

"I miss you too," I choked out, my grip tightening on her remains. "Every day, Lucy. Every single day."

She pulled back, her smile bittersweet. "It's okay now," she said softly. "I can rest. You can let me go."

I shook my head, fresh tears spilling down my cheeks. "I don't know if I can."

"You can," she said firmly, her voice filled with a strength that belied her small frame. "You've already done so much for me. Now it's time to take care of yourself."

Her form began to flicker, the edges of her figure blurring as the wind picked up.

"No," I whispered, panic rising in my chest. "Don't go. Please, Lucy. Don't leave me again."

She smiled one last time, her form fading into the night. "Don't trust mum," she said, her voice a whisper carried on the breeze. "I love you."

And then she was gone.

I sat there in the dirt, clutching her remains and staring at the empty space where she had been. The woods were silent again, save for the sound of my ragged breathing.

I didn't know how long I stayed there, but when I finally looked up, the first rays of dawn were breaking through the trees. Lucy was gone, but for the first time in years, I felt a strange sense of peace.

She was free.

Chapter 28

The first light of dawn painted the woods in muted shades of grey and gold as I sat in the dirt, Lucy's fragile remains cradled in my arms. My body ached, my heart heavier than it had ever been, but something inside me felt clearer, sharper. Lucy was gone, but for the first time in years, the weight of her absence didn't feel like it would crush me.

A rustling sound broke the silence, and I turned to see Antonia stumbling through the undergrowth. Her face was pale, blood dried at her temple where she must have hit the floor when I knocked her out. Her eyes widened as they took in the scene: Derek's unconscious body sprawled by the grave, the disturbed earth, and me holding what was left of Lucy.

"Jake..." she whispered, her voice trembling. She stepped forward, her hands shaking as she raised them to her mouth. "Oh God. What have you done?"

I stood slowly, cradling Lucy as if she were still alive and fragile in my arms. "What I had to," I said, my voice steady despite the storm in my chest.

Antonia sank to her knees, tears streaming down her face. "Please," she begged, her hands clasped in front of her. "Please, Jake. I know what you're thinking, but we can't go back. We have to move on. Let her rest."

"Move on?" I snapped, my voice rising. "You've been telling me to move on my whole life, and now I know why. You've been lying to me. All of you. Lucy deserves the truth, and so do I."

She shook her head, sobbing. "You don't understand. You don't know what it's like to carry this…this guilt. I've been trying to protect you—"

"Protect me?" I barked, my voice raw. "You weren't protecting me. You were protecting yourself. And Dad. And Lynne. And whoever the hell else was involved in this nightmare. But not me. Not Lucy."

Antonia's sobs grew louder, her hands gripping the hem of her sweater. "Please, Jake. I'm begging you. Let this go. Let her go. I can't lose you too."

I stepped closer, lowering Lucy's remains gently to the ground before standing over her. "You already lost me," I said coldly. "You lost me the day you let this happen. The only way you get me back is if you tell me the truth. All of it. Right now."

My mum looked up at me, her face crumpling. She hesitated, and for a moment, I thought she might refuse. But then she nodded, her shoulders sagging as though the weight of her secrets was finally too much to bear.

"It was an accident," she began, her voice barely a whisper. "All of it. None of this was supposed to happen."

I folded my arms, glaring down at her. "Start at the beginning," I demanded. "Tell me everything. I know that dad was Lucy's biological father so just tell me."

"Oh, fuck Derek." Mum wiped her face, realising her accomplice had sold her out, her hands trembling as she spoke. "It started with Jude," she said, her voice hollow. "He...he was hurting Lucy. I didn't know at first. I swear I didn't. But when I found out, I tried to stop it. I thought I could protect her."

"Protect her?" I repeated, my voice dripping with anger. "You let her have contact with him."

"I didn't know how to stop him! Your dad told me it wasn't happening, and he wasn't hurting her just speaking to her." she cried, her voice breaking. "I was scared, Jake. Scared of what he'd do if I tried to interfere. And then Julia..."

She took a shuddering breath, her eyes flickering toward Lucy's remains. "Julia came back here that night. She was high, out of her mind, but she knew something was wrong. She found Lucy with Jude in the chapel and went mad. She started screaming at him, saying she was going to take Lucy away, give her to another family to keep her safe. But she wasn't thinking clearly. She didn't have a plan. She just wanted to get Lucy out of there. Lisa had been worried about Lucy and asked her to go because Jude had told her that he was seeing Lucy at the chapel that night. Lisa thought that maybe Julia would be able to frighten him or something. It was so reckless of them." She sniffled.

"And where were you?" I asked, my voice sharp.

"I noticed Lucy was gone, that's how it always happened, your father would distract me, or wait for me to be out and he would come and get her." Antonia said, her voice trembling. "I knew Jude would have taken her to the chapel. So, I went after them. But when I got there, Julia was already there, ranting and raving about how Lucy needed to be saved. And then..."

She hesitated, her hands clenching into fists.

"Then what?" I demanded.

Antonia's voice dropped to a whisper. "Julia told me the truth. About Lisa. About your father. She said Lucy was their daughter. That she'd known all along but didn't say anything because she thought it would destroy the family. Like she ever cared about that the home wrecking whore. I had raised her boy all those years for her. Gave you a proper home, an education, kept her aunt in employment! I had loved you for all those years and that is how she repaid me? By making a fool of me again? They all had! They all knew! Everyone except me! My own sister had asked me how the adoption was when she *knew*! Oh, how your dad and Lisa must have laughed at me. He thought Julia and Lisa loved him, they just wanted his money and drugs. That was it. They all thought I was nothing and none of them were ever afraid of little old Toni."

My breath caught in my throat, my mind reeling.

Antonia nodded, tears streaming down her face. "So when I heard Julia say it out loud, what had been staring me in the face, I just… I lost control. I tried to attack her. I was so angry, so hurt. I pushed her, but Lucy… Lucy got in the way."

Her voice broke, and she covered her face with her hands. "She fell, Jake. She hit her head on the corner of the altar. I didn't mean to hurt her. I swear I didn't. But she was so small, so fragile. And when I looked down and saw her lying there…"

She sobbed, her entire body shaking.

"Julia saw what happened," she continued after a moment. "She was hysterical, screaming that it was her fault, that she shouldn't have brought Lucy there. And I… I let her believe it. I told her it was her fault. She was high, Jake. Out of her mind. She didn't know what was real. She thought she pushed her, and Jude was more than happy for her to get the blame after what she caught him doing. I would have blamed it on Jude had he not been the sober witness to my crime."

My stomach churned, bile rising in my throat. "So you let her take the blame?"

Mum nodded, her face pale. "She ran out of the chapel, got in her car, and…she didn't make it far. She hit a tree at the edge of the property. The snow, the ice…she couldn't control the car. She died instantly."

"And then you called Dad," I said, my voice hollow. I already knew that part.

She nodded again. "I told him what 'Julia' had done. That she'd killed Lucy in a fit of madness. He…he didn't even flinch. He called Lynne, and the three of us buried Lucy in the woods. We thought it was the only way to protect Julia's memory. To protect the family. To protect you. Lynne didn't want anybody to know what her daughter did and your dad knew Julia was a loose end that had needed tying up."

I stared at her, my mind spinning with everything she'd just confessed. The weight of it was suffocating, the air in the clearing thick with the echoes of the past.

"You didn't protect me," I said finally, my voice shaking. "You destroyed me. You destroyed Lucy. And for what? To save yourselves?"

She reached for me, her hands trembling. "Please, Jake," she whispered. "I'm sorry. I'm so sorry. But it's over now. You don't have to carry this anymore."

I stepped back, shaking my head. "It's not over," I said, my voice firm. "Not until the truth comes out. All of it."

Antonia's face crumpled, but I didn't wait for her response. I picked up Lucy's remains, cradling her gently, and turned toward the car.

It was time to finish this.

The clearing fell silent except for the distant rustling of wind through the trees. My grip on Lucy's remains tightened as I turned toward the car. Every instinct told me to run, to keep her safe, but the crackle of leaves behind me made my body tense.

"Jake," my mother – no – Antonia's voice came, hoarse but urgent. I turned to see her standing, her face streaked with tears and panic. "Please, don't take her. Just let me—"

"No," I snapped, my voice cutting through the air. "She's coming with me. The truth is coming with me. You've hidden her long enough."

Antonia's expression twisted into something desperate, something feral. "You don't understand," she said, her voice trembling as she stepped closer. "I can't let this happen. Not after everything I've done to protect you. To protect this family."

"This family?" I spat. "You mean yourself. You mean Dad and Lynne. You never cared about Lucy, and you sure as hell didn't care about me."

Her eyes flared with anger, but she quickly masked it with a pleading look. "Jake, please. You're not thinking clearly. You're letting your emotions control you. Just…just give her to me."

I shook my head, backing away. "You don't get to make that decision anymore. You've lost the right."

That was when the groan came—a low, pained sound that sent a chill through my body. I turned sharply to see Derek Hall stirring, his body shifting against the dirt. His hand pressed to the side of his head where I'd struck him with the shovel. His eyes fluttered open, and when they landed on me, holding Lucy, they darkened.

"Antonia," he croaked, pushing himself to his knees. "What the hell is happening?"

Antonia shot a panicked glance at him, then back at me. "Derek," she said quickly, her voice shaking. "We need to stop him. He's going to ruin everything."

Derek's eyes flicked to the disturbed grave, then to me, and finally to the remains in my arms. A grimace crossed his face, but his body shifted, gathering strength.

"Jake," he said, his voice low and dangerous, "you don't know what you're getting yourself into. Hand her over. Now."

I stepped back again, holding Lucy tighter. "Stay the hell away from me," I growled. "This is over. Both of you need to stop pretending you're the victims here."

But Derek didn't stop. He pushed himself to his feet, his balance unsteady but his intent clear. Antonia moved beside him, her face pale but determined.

"This isn't about you," Derek said, his voice steadying as he took a step forward. "This is bigger than you, Jake. It always has been. You don't understand the damage you'll cause if this gets out."

"Damage?" I barked. "What about the damage you've already done? Lucy's dead because of you—because of all of you—and you have the audacity to talk about damage?"

Derek lunged, his hands reaching for me. I sidestepped, my shoulder colliding with his as I twisted away. But the movement threw me off balance, and before I could recover, Antonia was in front of me, her hands clawing at Lucy's remains.

"Let go!" she screamed, her voice raw with desperation.

"No!" I shouted, trying to push her away without letting go of Lucy.

But Derek was behind me now, his arms wrapping around my torso and dragging me backward. I thrashed against him, my breath coming in ragged gasps as I fought to keep my grip on Lucy.

"Stop fighting!" Derek growled, his voice in my ear. "Just let go, Jake. It's over."

I managed to elbow him in the ribs, and his grip loosened just enough for me to break free. But as I turned, Antonia's hand caught Lucy's remains, pulling them toward her.

"Don't you dare!" I shouted, reaching for her, but Derek grabbed my arm, twisting me around and sending me sprawling to the ground.

The impact knocked the wind out of me, my body slamming into the cold, hard earth. Pain shot through my back and shoulders as I struggled to push myself up, but Derek was already on me, pinning me down with his weight.

"Stay down, Jake," he hissed, his voice venomous. "You're going to ruin everything."

I looked up just in time to see Antonia cradling Lucy's remains in her arms. Her face was a mask of anguish, her tears falling freely as she clutched what was left of my sister.

"I'm sorry, Jake," she said, her voice breaking. "I'm so sorry. But you don't understand. You never did. I did this for you. For all of us."

"You did this for yourself," I spat, my voice shaking with fury and grief. "You're a coward, Antonia. All of you are cowards."

But she didn't respond. She turned, holding Lucy tightly, and began walking back toward the house.

"No!" I shouted, my voice raw as I struggled against Derek's hold. "Don't you dare take her! Don't you dare!"

Antonia didn't look back.

Derek leaned closer, his breath hot against my ear. "It's over, Jake," he whispered. "You lost."

I watched what was my mother, start to disappear into the trees.

Chapter 29

The chaos around me was a blur of noise, pain, and rage. Derek's weight crushed me to the ground as I strained against him, my vision tunnelling on the figure of Antonia retreating into the trees with Lucy's remains.

"Get off me!" I roared, but Derek's grip was unyielding, his knee pressed into my back.

A sharp, deafening blast split the air, making my ears ring. The pressure on my back disappeared instantly as Derek collapsed to the ground with a guttural scream. I rolled onto my side, gasping for breath, and saw him clutching his leg, blood pooling around his fingers.

"What the—" Derek's voice broke into a pained howl as he tried to crawl away, dragging his injured leg behind him.

I turned toward the source of the shot and saw Jade standing a few feet away, Bill's shotgun in her trembling hands. She must have checked the shed for it. Her face was pale, her chest heaving as she kept the barrel trained on Derek.

"Jade?" I croaked, my voice barely audible.

Her eyes darted to me, filled with a mixture of fear and determination. "Stay down, Jake," she said, her voice steady despite the tremor in her hands. "I've called the police. They'll be here any minute."

Derek groaned, his body inching toward the edge of the clearing. "You're making a mistake," he spat through gritted teeth. "You don't know what you're dealing with."

Jade took a step closer, the shotgun unwavering. "The only mistake would be letting you get away with this," she said coldly.

I pushed myself to my feet, my body aching, and staggered over to Jade. "How did you know?" I asked, my voice still shaky.

She glanced at me, her eyes softening for a moment. "Lucy," she said simply. "She was in my dream, Jake. She told me to come out here. To help you."

Her words sent a chill down my spine, but I didn't have time to process them. Derek was still crawling, his breath ragged as he tried to drag himself into the shadows.

"Let him go," Jade said sharply, nudging me when I took a step toward him. "The police will deal with him."

I hesitated, my fists clenching, but I nodded. For now, Derek wasn't the priority.

I turned toward the woods where Antonia had disappeared, my heart pounding. "She's got Lucy," I said, starting to move.

Jade grabbed my arm. "I'm coming with you."

I wanted to tell her to stay, to be safe, but I knew better than to argue. Together, we plunged into the dark trees, the cold air biting at our skin.

We ran in silence, the crunch of snow and brittle leaves beneath our feet the only sounds as we chased after Antonia. My mind raced, desperate to catch her before she disappeared completely.

After what felt like an eternity, we spotted her. Antonia was slumped on the ground near the base of an old, gnarled tree. Lucy's remains lay beside her, still wrapped in the cloth I'd held so tightly.

"Antonia!" I shouted, rushing to her side.

Her head lifted weakly, her face pale and glistening with sweat. She looked up at me, her eyes glassy and unfocused.

"Jake," she murmured, her voice barely a whisper.

I knelt beside her, my hands shaking as I reached out but didn't quite touch her. "What happened?" I asked, my voice breaking. "What did you do?"

She let out a weak, breathless laugh that turned into a cough. "My heart," she said, her words slurring. "It hurts here." She clutched at her chest.

Jade knelt beside me, her hand on my shoulder. "Antonia, the police are coming. They can help you. Just hang on."

Antonia shook her head slowly, her gaze shifting to Lucy's remains. "No," she said, her voice soft but firm. "It's too late for me."

Her eyes met mine, and for the first time, I saw something in them that I hadn't before—regret. "I'm sorry, Jake," she said, tears spilling down her cheeks. "I'm sorry I wasn't a better mother. I tried. I really tried. But I… I failed you. I failed Lucy."

Her words stabbed through me, and I struggled to breathe past the lump in my throat. "You didn't have to lie," I said, my voice shaking. "You didn't have to hide her."

"I thought I was protecting you," she whispered, her head tilting to the side as her strength ebbed away. "I thought…if you never knew…you could move on. Be happy. I was selfish. I did love you."

I shook my head, tears blurring my vision. "You were wrong," I said, my voice cracking. "All you did was make it worse."

Her gaze drifted past me, her lips parting in a soft, breathless gasp. "Lucy," she whispered, her face softening.

I turned instinctively, but there was nothing there—only the dark expanse of trees. When I looked back at Antonia, her chest had stilled, her eyes vacant.

"Antonia?" Jade said, her voice breaking the silence.

She was gone.

The forest felt impossibly quiet, the weight of her death settling over me like a shroud. My eyes shifted to Lucy's remains, still lying beside her, and I felt my chest tighten.

Jade squeezed my shoulder, grounding me. "Jake," she said softly, "it's over. You've done what you needed to do."

I nodded numbly, but as I looked at Antonia's still form, I couldn't help but feel the emptiness that came with her final words.

Her last breath had been for Lucy.

And maybe, in some way, she'd found peace too.

Chapter 30

The house was finally empty. The furniture had been sold, the rooms cleared, and the ghosts that had haunted its walls were left behind in the memories of those who had lived there. The silence felt different now—not heavy with secrets, but hollow, as if the house itself was relieved to see the end of its long, dark history.

I stood at the edge of the garden, looking back at the place that had been my home, my prison, and the keeper of truths I wished I'd never uncovered. Antonia's house—it would never feel like mine—was no longer a monument to grief and deception. Soon it would belong to someone else, someone who'd fill it with a new kind of life.

I had sold it to a developer who planned to knock it down much to Pete and my grandmother's dismay. Pete had a rude awakening the morning the police had showed up, he could no longer freeload and had had to move out. I didn't care what would rise in its place. All I knew was that I wanted no trace of it left behind.

"Are you sure you don't need to do anything else?" Jade asked, stroking her swollen stomach.

"Nope. We can leave." I breathed a sigh of relief finally.

The police had been relentless once I'd told them everything. Derek Hall, Ted Andrews, Reverend Thomas and others whose names I hadn't even heard until the investigation unfolded were all arrested. Their ring of human trafficking and exploitation, hidden beneath a veneer of respectability, had unravelled like a thread pulled from a tapestry. Derek had struck a deal, giving up the location of Julia's remains in exchange for a lesser sentence.

Julia's body had been buried in a shallow grave in a wooded area just outside the estate. When the police unearthed her remains, I didn't feel the closure I thought I would. Only more sadness. For her, for Lucy, for everyone who had been failed by the people who were supposed to love them. I gave my biological mother a new grave where she could rest peacefully and hoped it was good enough for her, in the end she had been the only person willing to help Lucy.

Lynne had been arrested too. Her role in Lucy's disappearance, her lies, her complicity—they were crimes I couldn't forgive, no matter how much she begged. She wrote to me from prison, letters full of apologies and explanations that I didn't bother to read after the first one. I couldn't bring myself to see her, couldn't stomach the thought of looking into the eyes of someone who had helped bury the truth along with my sister.

My grandmother had tried to stop me from selling the house. She'd called me countless times, leaving voicemails asking me to reconsider, claiming that the house was part of our family legacy. But what kind of legacy was it? A monument to abuse, betrayal, and loss? I'd blocked her number after the last message, and when the house finally sold, I didn't even tell her.

Ethan, my uncle, was different. He had left this family behind long ago, and now I understood why. He called me once, offering his condolences and telling me he supported my decision to sell. But his voice was distant, guarded. We were both escaping the same past, but we weren't escaping it together. I'd never really know how much of it he knew about.

Lisa, my aunt and Lucy's real mother was the last to reach out. She came to see me after a few months, her eyes hollow and her voice trembling with remorse. She begged for forgiveness, not just for what had happened to Lucy but for all the lies and betrayals that had followed.

At first, I couldn't bring myself to forgive her. She had been part of it all, hadn't she? But as she spoke, I saw the cracks in her armour. Lisa hadn't just been a perpetrator—she had been a victim too. Of Antonia, of Jim, of the same system of control and fear that had destroyed so many lives.

Over time, I softened. Holding onto that anger would only tie me to the past, and I didn't want to live there anymore. I forgave Lisa, not for her sake but for mine. She wept when I told her, and though we'd never be close, I knew it was the right thing to do. She kept in touch and looked out for me which was more than I had expected from her considering I wasn't her blood – not really.

Lucy's burial was quiet, private. I'd chosen a spot far from the estate, in a peaceful cemetery surrounded by trees that swayed gently in the wind. Jade stood beside me, holding my hand as I watched the small casket lower into the ground.

Lisa and Bill were in attendance.

This time, there were no lies, no cover-ups. Her grave was marked with a headstone that bore her name, *Lucy King. Beloved Sister. Forever Loved, Never Forgotten.*

As the small ceremony ended, I felt a warmth on my shoulder. I turned, half-expecting to see her ghost standing there, but there was nothing. Just the sun breaking through the clouds, casting light on the place where she finally rested.

Jade squeezed my hand, her eyes red but full of determination. "She's at peace now," she said softly.

I nodded, though part of me still wondered. The autopsy had said Antonia died of heart failure, but in my heart, I couldn't shake the feeling that Lucy had something to do with it. Her presence had always been strong, her will unyielding. Maybe she had found a way to claim justice in her own way.

Sometimes, in the quiet moments, I still felt her. A flicker of warmth, a fleeting shadow at the edge of my vision. I wasn't afraid anymore. I knew now that I wasn't going crazy all those times I saw her after she disappeared. It had been real. She had been real.

Jade and I moved to a bigger than average house on the edge of Manchester thanks to the house sale. It was still modest, quiet, and free from the weight of the past. We started over, rebuilding a life that was ours.

One night, as I sat by the window, looking out at the stars, I felt a strange sense of calm. Lucy was gone, but she wasn't. I could still hear her laughter sometimes, feel her small arms around me in my dreams.

"Thank you," she had said to me, her ghost shimmering in the moonlight. "I miss you, Jake. I miss my big brother so much."

I missed her too, but now, finally, I could let her go.

Jade walked up behind me, resting a hand on my shoulder. "You okay?" she asked.

I turned to her, smiling softly. "Yeah," I said. "I am."

We were about to welcome our first child, and I felt ready. I wanted to be a father, to do it right this time, to give my children the love and stability I never had.

I would forever mourn the loss of my sister and my own child's aunt. She should be here with me now, excited for the arrival of her new niece or nephew. But we'd never get to experience that now because she was taken away and hidden by the people closest to me.

Lucy's story was over, but mine wasn't. I would keep living for Lucy and what she should have been.

Epilogue

Jade

The late summer air drifts through the open windows, warm and carrying the scent of freshly cut grass. Laughter rings out from the garden, mingling with the soft hum of conversation. I stand on the patio, watching as Jake holds our daughter in his arms, twirling her gently. She squeals in delight, her tiny hands reaching for his face, and he presses a kiss to her forehead.

Our girl, Lucinda Elsie King is one year old today.

I take in the scene before me, the remnants of cake smeared across plates, the string of pastel balloons swaying in the breeze, the handful of friends gathered here to celebrate. There was a time when I wasn't sure Jake and I would ever make it to a moment like this. A moment free from the weight of the past, where we could just exist, just breathe, just be happy. But here we are.

Jake glances up and catches my eye. His smile is soft, filled with something deep and unspoken, and he mouths *I love you* across the garden. I mouth it back to him, smiling like an idiot.

As the sun begins to dip below the horizon, casting the sky in shades of gold and pink, I walk toward them. Jake shifts Lucy in his arms so there's space for me, wrapping an arm around my waist and pulling me close. Lucy rests her head against his shoulder, her small body warm and safe between us, her eyes growing heavy with sleep.

I press a kiss to her soft curls, then to Jake's temple, whispering, "Happy birthday, Lucy."

Jake lets out a quiet breath, holding me a little tighter, and in that moment, I know—we made it.

We're finally home.